Dangerous Exposure

Harvest of Faith Series, Book 1

By
Dianna Shuford

Copyright © 2020 by Dianna Shuford
Published by Forget Me Not Romances, an imprint of Winged Publications

Editor: Cynthia Hickey
Book Design by Forget Me Not Romances

All rights reserved. No part of this publication may be reproduced, stored in a retrieval system, or transmitted in any form or by any means—electronic, mechanical, photocopying, recording, or otherwise—without the prior written permission of the publisher. The only exception is brief quotations in printed reviews. Piracy is illegal. Thank you for respecting the hard work of this author.

This book is a work of fiction. Names, characters, Places, incidents, and dialogues are either products of the author's imagination or used fictitiously. Any resemblance to actual persons, living or dead, or events is coincidental. Scripture quotations from The Authorized (King James) Version.

Fiction and Literature: Inspirational
Christian Romantic Suspense

ISBN: 978-1-952661-16-7

Julie,
I hope you enjoy Addy's and Joe's story. Thanks for being a reader.
Dianna Shuford

Dedication:

To Rodney, my better half,
thank you for supporting me and helping me reach for
my dreams.

To Mom,
thank you for always believing in me.

Do not be overcome by evil, but overcome evil with good.
Romans 12:21 NKJV

Chapter One

Some days death struck with wicked precision, and today proved no different.

Addison Parker sighed when she met the empty gaze of the woman in the backseat. Glassy, vacant brown eyes that would never know the joys of life again. Sable hair that would never be styled or fussed over again. A daughter, sister, friend who would never be there for her loved ones again. The young woman identified as Lacy Dalton, abandoned inside the rust-colored Chevy Equinox, had been death's most recent victim.

The black expanse of the abandoned Union Station Mall's asphalt parking lot undulated in Atlanta's summer heat as Addison tossed her rope of braided hair back and stood beside the hearse-like crossover SUV. Her gut burned as death's odor filled her nose. "Hey, McBride, you find anything back there?"

Her partner, RJ McBride, stepped away from the rear of the vehicle, sweat rolling down his deep bronze cheeks.

"Nothing other than a spare tire and roadside emergency kit. Probably belonged to the victim, but processing the items will tell us for sure." He shook his head. "No blood stains, no loose fibers, and no identifying articles except those belonging to the victim we found in the front of the vehicle."

"Yeah, but let's process it anyway, just in case." She flexed her gloved fingers and raised her eyes toward the burn of the sun's rays. "Likely drug overdose?" Although she knew his answer, she needed it confirmed.

"Yep, and her hands were bound." He pointed to the ligature marks around the victim's wrists. "Looks like rope or twine was used based on the marks."

"Forced overdose?" The words slid through tight lips.

McBride grimaced. "Speculation at this point, but, yeah, I think that would be a good guess."

She swiped an arm across her heated forehead. "The murder could've happened elsewhere, and the body dumped here."

"If we're lucky, the crime lab will find something we've missed when they process the car." McBride stepped back as the medical examiner and a technician prepared the body for transport.

Addison took a deep breath as every team member followed strict procedures on scene. Maintaining objectivity was a must. Crime scenes left no room for luxuries such as sympathy. Still, she would pray for the Dalton family tonight, and do everything possible to solve this case, to bring them answers, to fight for the victim.

God willing, she would bring Lacy's killer to justice.

She swallowed hard and forced herself to focus on the vehicle once it was empty. She knelt by the passenger door and ran her hands over the carpeted floor, opened the console, and checked the seat edges. Her hands fisted. Nothing.

McBride nudged her foot with his own. "Parker, I think we've found everything."

"Just one more check." Lacy deserved a search that could lead to her killer.

"We've been thorough."

"Once more to double check. For the victim. I have a feeling we're missing something." They'd come up empty already, but a third search could yield evidence they needed. She massaged the driver's side carpet with her fingers, pushing under the seat, along the seat's hardware.

Her hand slapped against a hard object. As she leaned further in, she squinted as the sunlight speared through the side windows cutting into her retinas. A small cell phone with a feather caught in the casing. She pulled a bag from her pocket and slid it inside with steady, gloved hands. She sealed and labeled the single piece of evidence.

McBride grunted as she handed the bag to him.

She stepped away from the vehicle and breathed in the fresh honeysuckle that lay beyond the parking lot. The unnatural quiet surrounding the abandoned mall seemed to mourn death. Even the I-85 traffic beyond the sentinel of tall, gangly pines emitted hushed rubber voices on the road's pavement.

Over an hour on scene, and their sweep of the interior had produced little evidence, except a disposable phone with possible identifying numbers and information in it. Enough to provide hope. "That's it. We've found everything we're going to find."

"After three years of partnering, I can't figure out how you always know when to keep pushing." He shook his head. "Never saw that phone."

"Gut feeling." Addison shrugged. "It was stuffed into a depression near the seat railings. Like someone wanted us to almost miss it."

Her partner scanned the open trunk. "Everything's clean. Too clean." He stepped back and removed his gloves.

"The phone isn't much, but at least it's something." Each finger slid free of the gloves with a tug before she flipped her shades onto the bridge of her nose. "We've got to figure out how the perpetrator got the vehicle to this location without leaving any trace of discernible evidence. Let's check the grounds' video surveillance. With luck, the equipment will be in working order."

"Maybe, if the owner wanted to protect the property. It's worth checking out." He rubbed his finger across his chin. "You know, this crime is similar to the Hewitt case we investigated. No conclusive evidence, possible drug overdose, death occurring the same day of the week. Do the victims have anything in common?"

"It's worth checking out. We should look for similarities between the two crime scenes and analyze for a profile on the perpetrator if there are enough commonalities. This crime feels like it's personal to the killer because of the methods and binding used. Looking at both files together could give us a better picture of what we're dealing with." She cocked her head, gaze steady, facts scrolling through her mind like a Rolodex flipping card after card.

"Yeah." He released a long, slow exhale. "If we're right, two murders, same methods used, could mean there's a serial killer striking Atlanta's Southside."

She inhaled slowly with that thought. "If that's the case, then we need to make sure we stop it before another woman dies."

One more fact to fuel her need for justice.

~

Joe Vaughn rolled down his car windows in response to the southern heat since his car's A/C stopped working. Two printed articles from the Atlanta-Journal Constitution lie on the passenger seat of his car. Rhonda Hewitt and Meredith Banks smiled up at him from the accompanying black and white photos next to the write-up announcing their deaths. One week before each murder, the same pictures had graced his column in *The South Fulton Chronicle*, proclaiming each woman an asset to her community.

Should his suspicions prove true, he could be linked to each murder. Could his articles be the catalyst for the women's deaths or was it a coincidence?

He'd been trying to convince himself that his articles had nothing to do with the murders since stumbling across the AJC news articles last night. His third article on women serving their community appeared four days ago in Sunday's edition. Would his latest article spotlight become a killer's next victim?

When the scanner in his car shouted code ten-two this morning, Unit Henry, homicide, at the old Union Station Mall, he'd headed south of Hartsfield-Jackson airport without hesitation. The location reported, halfway between Lacy Dalton's workplace and her home, caused a cold knot to cramp his stomach. He'd never been good at ignoring his gut instinct, and now, he had one more reason to learn the victim's identity. Once he had all the facts puzzled together, he'd take the information to the investigators with a possible link to solve the case.

He slammed his car door and took in the activity

surrounding the abandoned vehicle. The bright yellow tape separated the many faces gawking at the police processing the scene. The movements inside the crime's perimeter continued as he sauntered toward the activity, surveying the scene for every detail. His gaze stopped on a familiar car. The cold knot in his stomach tightened.

A police officer blocked his path. "I'm sorry, sir, you can't proceed any further."

He surveyed the officer from behind the dark lenses of his sunglasses as he resisted the urge to resettle his sports coat with a shrug. The garment had gained ten pounds in June's excessive heat, which even at nine a.m. softened the black pavement underneath his feet. "Any news of what's going on here?" Shocks of hair brushed his temple as a hot breeze tugged at the strands, keeping it from sticking to his sweat-dampened face.

"Not right now. A public statement will be given soon." The police visor blocked all but the straight slash of the man's lips from view.

"Surely, a few details can be spared? Can I talk to the investigator in charge?" Joe offered his best you-can-trust-me smile, and pulled out his press ID. He had to get the details of this crime scene and find out the victim's identity.

As if on cue, his cell phone vibrated against his hipbone. Probably his editor wanting to know why the Community Fair piece wasn't finished.

"Everyone is busy. You can find out the latest information when the public does." The uniformed officer folded thick arms across a burly chest.

"Not even a few small details?" He stuck his hands into the pockets of his pressed chinos to hide his balled fists.

"Just a moment." The officer headed toward the activity

surrounding the vehicle.

Let the authorities find the guilty. Let the police do their job. Pray for justice. His stomach twisted and roiled as if he sat on a speeding roller coaster, but he ignored the faint voice he'd buried with his mother a year ago.

The authorities didn't always find justice. Hadn't found it for his family seventeen years ago. The prayers he'd voiced as a twelve-year-old hadn't been answered when his father's murderer was never found either. The community's innocent deserved to have someone looking out for them.

Details, impressions, descriptions. Watching the investigators and the medical examiner team, he noticed spiky brown hair and a pale hand belonging to the victim. Not enough to know if it was Lacy. Flashing red and blue lights warned onlookers away and 'do not cross' tape kept the curious public at bay. Kept those who sought the confidential information at a distance.

Those yellow streamers wouldn't stop him from uncovering the truth. A truth he intended to share if his suspicions were verified.

Mall security stood on the far side of the scene, speaking to a second uniformed officer. A police photographer and two plain-clothed investigators worked the area with single-minded intensity. The burly, uniformed officer delivering the request stopped beside the woman searching the car's passenger side interior.

Her meticulous movements and attention to detail probably had every city district attorney clapping in glee when her processed crime scenes stood firm against cross-examination of defense attorneys. His shoulders contracted at the thought of another family paying the price for sloppy investigative work.

The brunette glanced in Joe's direction and arrested his attention. Her petite frame drew his eye first, but the long hair secured in a braid that ended midway down her back kept him looking. He ran a hand across his damp forehead.

With a quick shake of his head, he refocused on his objective at hand. He pulled out his vibrating cell phone and glanced at the caller ID. Yup, it was Chuckie. He pressed the silent button and slid the phone back into his pocket.

Later. He'd deal with the boss later. Right now, he had to prove Lacy Dalton remained alive.

~

Addison shifted and nodded at Darrin Gray, the department's part-time photographer, moving around the cordoned off area with an expensive Nikon camera and the jaunty stride that defined the college student. "Hey, Darrin. Almost finished?"

"Yeah. A few more shots should do it." Darrin's blue-black hair sported a choreographed mussed-look. His wrinkled cargo shorts, T-shirt, and sockless Sperry footwear completed the photographer's trendy twenty-something appearance.

"Good. Let's get this crime documented and wrapped up." She turned at the tap on her shoulder. "Yes, Officer—," she glanced at the uniformed officer's badge, "Strickland?"

"Man on the left asked to speak with someone in charge. Showed a press ID." The brawny man crossed his arms over his chest and waited.

Addison raised a brow. "Did he give you a reason he needed to speak to someone?"

He shook his head. "Nope. Just keeps insisting there should be details that can be given out, and if I couldn't do that, maybe whoever was in charge could."

She glanced over the officer's shoulder at the man in question and gritted her teeth. White male, sandy brown hair, about six feet, early thirties. She knew the type, and she had learned the hard way not to trust them. *A Golden-boy wannabe.* One more interference keeping her and McBride from getting this scene wrapped up. Nope. They had a job to do, and nothing would keep them from completing their task.

She moved in the stranger's direction as the sun reflected a silver starburst sliding into the man's pocket. Interesting. Scanning for a visible weapon and noting the press identification he wore, Addison stopped before him. "Can I help you?"

Golden-boy flashed a bright, white smile before jerking his head in acknowledgment. "Officer. Or should I say detective?"

"Detective."

The corners of his mouth dropped at her curt tone. "Excuse me. Detective." He inclined his head, and then waved an arm in the direction of the activity surrounding the vehicle. "This is a murder investigation, is it not?"

"I'm sorry. Until the official press release the information gathered is confidential, Mister—"

His grin returned as if the flash of pearly whites were his Pied Piper instrument of choice. "Joe Vaughn, reporter for *The South Fulton Chronicle.*"

She crossed her arms when he held out his hand. Just what their investigation did not need. A reporter hindering their initial investigation. Her gaze raked over his too-loose jacket covering a lanky frame and button-down shirt tucked into pressed pants. He appeared honest with his pretty-boy face and hair brushed back to curl against his collar. Innocent, yet behind that façade lurked an aura that proclaimed him a man that had seen too much of life's harshness.

"Um-hm." Addison rubbed a trickle of sweat from her neck. "Did you have information pertinent to this investigation, Mr. Vaughn?"

He glanced across the empty parking lot toward the vehicle, and then returned his gaze to her. Dark lenses met dark lenses in the morning blaze of sunlight. "I didn't say that."

She pushed her hands on her hips, flipping her A. P. D. vest aside so her badge was visible. "Why *exactly* are you asking to speak with me?"

"That should be obvious detective. I report on events for the community's awareness. Making sure others know how to protect themselves, how we as a community can protect them, is part of my job." Golden-boy shrugged. "They need to know the details of this crime so they can take the steps necessary to protect themselves."

She glanced at her watch. Less than ninety minutes on site. Allowing confidential details of this scene to become public could jeopardize their case and cost additional innocent lives. That wouldn't happen at her crime scene.

This situation called for a tactful response. Diplomacy, a necessary tool she hated.

"I'm sorry. I can't help you, Mr. Vaughn." Okay. So she wasn't that good at it, but she got her point across.

"You don't sound sorry." His grin widened.

Was he flirting with her? *Unoriginal, Golden-boy.* She compressed her lips. "Officer Strickland," she called without looking away from the fork-tongued serpent before her.

Strickland lumbered over. "Yes, Detective."

"See that the crime scene borders are not violated and

arrest anyone who crosses the established perimeter." She tilted her glasses down, letting her gaze speak for her. "Good day, Mr. Vaughn."

She strode back toward the quarantined vehicle and pulled out her note pad.

Joe Vaughn. Reporter. Checking crime scene. Questionable. Further investigation needed?

She rocked her pen between her fingers. What was he *really* doing here? There were other reporters wandering outside the crime scene area so why was he interrupting their progress on the investigation for details that would be given out during their official press release? She watched him melt into the crowd. When he looked back at her, she narrowed her gaze on him.

Did he know more than he was disclosing, or was he more involved than they realized?

~

Joe parked street side in the new subdivision and double-checked the address scribbled on a scrap of paper against the mailbox. Five-Nineteen Rosewood Court.

He'd tried all morning to reach Lacy Dalton. To warn her to be careful. To tell her not to trust anyone she didn't already know. When he arrived at the crime scene this morning, he could tell the car's make, model, and color had matched Lacy's, but the dirt-smudged license plate couldn't be read. That didn't fit her fastidious personality. Perhaps Mike Griffith, Lacy's fiancé, could provide more information.

Joe pushed himself toward the white and blue house. He needed an answer to questions whether he wanted to hear them or not. The truth needed to be discovered, and he could have stumbled into a puzzle where only he could fit the correct pieces together.

His steps faltered when the two detectives exited through the front door. He froze as they glanced at him and frowned in unison. *Oh, boy.* If they were speaking with Mr. Griffith, his worst suspicions could be true. His heart stuttered with the thought. What could he tell the police? What facts did he know? Speculation and supposition weren't cold, hard facts. They approached him as if he were a new species of animal they wanted to study—intent and alert.

"Well, our reporter's back. I wonder what brings him across our path a second time today." The detective that had shut him down that morning spoke to her partner, but kept a steady gaze on Joe. The detective's direct approach was an admirable attribute, although inconvenient at the moment.

Even in the summer heat, her professional attire, a turquoise shirt tucked into belted black pants and black loafers, stayed fresh and neat after spending the morning in the sun. Her chestnut hair still trailed down her back in a thick braid, leaving her face unframed. While the partner stalked beside her in faded jeans paired with a collared polo shirt and ancient sneakers, his laid-back appearance made the woman even more appealing.

He gave them his easy-going smile and waited for them to reach him. "Hello, detectives. Perhaps we should introduce ourselves since we keep running into each other."

"I do think we need *your* name." The woman reached for her notepad.

The detective beside her studied Joe as if memorizing every detail. "I'm Detective McBride, and this is Detective Parker. And you would be?"

"Joe Vaughn. Reporter for *The South Fulton Chronicle*." He stuck his hand out toward Detective Parker, swung his hand toward Detective McBride, then let it drop when his invitation was ignored. "You wouldn't be following me, would you?"

"Is there a reason we should be following you?" Detective McBride inched further left, boxing Joe between the two.

Any war fought on two fronts never ended well for the middleman. *I'm not losing this battle.* "Nope. Just doing my job." He angled himself to see both detectives. McBride continued to take in Joe's every move, while Parker raised a brow.

"And, what job are you doing?" Detective Parker crossed her arms.

She'd used the arms-crossed pose before on him. He wasn't intimidated. Couldn't be intimidated. The truth was too important.

Joe squinted in the sun's late afternoon glare. "Following up on an article I wrote a couple of weeks ago."

"Topic?" Detective McBride continued to scribble on his notepad. His left-hand curled around his pen like Joe's did when he wrote long hand.

"Local women who are community role models."

"When was it printed?" The other man raised a brow at Joe.

"Last Sunday."

Detective Parker stepped forward, her hands propped on her hips. "Why would this article bring you across our path for a second time today?"

"I don't know." He met her gaze.

How could he tell them why he was here when he wasn't sure himself? Would they provide him more details if he offered what he knew? He took a deep breath and opened his mouth. Closed it. His supposition could still be wrong. Mike Griffith could confirm Lacy was alive and well. He didn't want to obstruct justice, but neither did he want to mislead it.

Detective Parker's chin angled upward. "If we find that you know more than you're sharing, you'll see us again in an interrogation room."

"I don't think it will come to that, Detective." His mouth tightened before he turned toward the front door and left the detectives behind.

Her implications that he would break the law brought out the urge to fight for his own honor, but right now he couldn't follow that trail. In spite of the sinking sensation in the pit of his stomach, he had to follow his instincts. He had to know beyond doubt the identity of this morning's victim even if it meant he wound up sitting in that interrogation room.

Chapter Two

Addison fixed an unflinching gaze on her partner's back. McBride's coffee run would give her some time to figure out what was bothering her. They'd spent most of the morning going over facts and evidence, but the open case file spread across their desks deserved unwavering attention.

They weren't even close to solving this crime. She rubbed a hand across the back of her neck and rotated her aching shoulders. She hadn't counted on the cost each senseless murder would demand of her when she'd decided to follow her father into a career in law enforcement. Each closed case always preceded a new one, adding another view of humanity's disregard for life. It never stopped. Yet, every crime scene processed, every victim robbed of life, drove her to balance the scales of good and evil and to see the guilty pay for their crimes. How much of herself was she losing each day?

One piece of evidence could break this case. Just one.

They needed to find it. The throwaway cell phone had been a hopeful find, but the evidence report hadn't come back on it yet. Twenty-four hours had already passed. Another twenty-four and the perpetrator's trail would be corrupted with unreliable witnesses and evidence, making the killer more difficult to trace. She fisted her hands against the desktop. This case would not be filed away as unsolvable.

The police station's cream-colored walls decorated with metal filing cabinets and aging desks faded as she ignored the weeping woman two desks down and the cuffed teen at the opposite end of the room. A hum vibrated down her spine. They were missing something, and she'd bet her last dollar the reporter was part of that missing link. What were his exact words when they'd intercepted him at the fiancé's house?

"Following up on an article I wrote a couple of weeks ago…an article on community role models."

What if Mr. Griffith wasn't the article's subject? What if the reporter talked to him about his fiancé? She turned to her computer. On *The South Fulton Chronicle*'s homepage, she searched for the victim's name, clicking the link that appeared.

LOVE'S HELPING HAND ON THE SOUTHSIDE

An idea struck as the article printed. *What if...* She searched the paper's webpage again? Joseph Vaughn, A.K.A. Golden-boy, had a series of articles that highlighted different women. Women who had turned up murdered after the article was printed.

Well, how about that? He was the link between the two victims. He'd been hiding something after all.

She found the series page listing every article written under those key words and found another article. Could there be another victim? Three articles, two dead bodies. A few keystrokes later, the state database revealed a similar investigation in a neighboring county. Accessing those electronic files, she printed the information.

The reporter linked all three women, making him the common factor.

She grabbed her weapon and badge when McBride returned sipping a mug of coffee sludge. "C'mon. We've got someone to interview."

"Huh? How do you figure that?"

She waved the printed material. "I'll explain on the way."

Her partner set his coffee mug on top of his desk with a long-suffering look before following her to the car. "Un-uh, Parker. I'm driving."

"I know where we're going."

"You can direct me."

She gripped the keys in her hand, then narrowed her glare him. "I'll get us there faster."

He plucked the keys from her grasp. "I'd rather get there alive. You know you can only drive during emergencies."

"Thanks, Big Brother."

He pointed to her, and then pointed to the passenger seat.

She shrugged and climbed in. The twenty-minute drive gave her plenty of time to explain the reporter's connection to both of the murder victims and the probability of a third. She clipped her badge onto a belt loop as McBride stopped the unmarked police car in front of the small brick building. Both detectives stepped from the car into the oppressive ninety-six-degree heat as a high-pitched squeal filled the air followed by a chorus of horns singing their displeasure.

Addison snickered as they started toward the building.

"Ah, the sounds of city life."

"Predictable." McBride shook his head. "You say the same thing once a week."

"Can I help it if I like living outside the big, bad city? I deal with this crime during the day. I don't want to deal with it when I'm off duty." She laughed. "Small-town living is the life for me."

"You're still predictable, and I should've guessed you'd reference 'Green Acres' with your classic TV fetish." He rubbed his hand over his mouth to muffle his laughter.

"How do you want to handle this interview?"

"You've already overwhelmed him, so I'll be friendly while you do you."

She pushed through the glass doors, enjoying the cool blast of air in the newspaper building's lobby. "I'm not as bad as all that."

"Sure, you are. That's what makes you good at your job."

Stopping beside the receptionist's desk, she rested her arm on the tall, waist-high counter and drummed her fingers on the polished veneer as she waited for the young blonde to acknowledge them. The girl turned her shoulder away, continuing to chat into the headset draped across the crown of her spiked hair. "Jimmy, I didn't mean it that way... Of course... I want to go clubbing, but..."

Social Scene Barbie would not put them on hold. Addison cleared her throat. The blonde's eyes widened when the APD badge flashed in the fluorescent lighting. "Uh, I've gotta go, Jimmy... yeah, later." She ripped off the old-model headset, threatening to take a long, dangling earring with the cord.

Addison raised a brow as the girl took several seconds to

untangle them. Yet one more reason to wear minimal jewelry or none at all.

"I'm sorry. Today's my first week...I mean...yes, officers, may I help you?" The small curve of her lips quivered as her hands twisted on the counter.

"That would be Detectives, and yes, you may." Addison spoke in a clipped tone. A rattled receptionist would get them their information that much quicker.

McBride rolled his eyes. "We'd like to speak to Joseph Vaughn." He flipped open his notepad.

"Joseph? Vaughn...Oh, you mean Joe. He's real cute. And sweet. Would you like me to call him down for you?"

"No, we'll meet him at his desk after you give us directions." They moved to the bank of elevators as directed. Stepping through the first set of doors that opened, McBride said, "Do you *always* have to be so hard-nosed?"

"Hey, I worked long and hard to learn how to do that. You saw how compliant she was after I flashed my badge. You know, whatever gets us closer to an answer..." Addison shrugged as they stood shoulder to shoulder while the elevator doors closed.

Several moments later, they found the reporter's cubicle in the huge newsroom. Keyboards clicking, phones ringing, and voices murmuring blended into white noise. Joe Vaughn sat, his back to them, and typed on his computer. His wide shoulders blocked the screen from her view. Very nice, wide shoulders.

Nope. Not going there. His connection to each victim overrode any admiration Addison might have at the reporter's clean-cut appearance. His handsome features would've turned her head at one time, but not now. Not after Jeff. Not after he'd made her a victim. *Focus, Parker, Focus*.

McBride broke their silence. "Mr. Vaughn."

The reporter's attention swung to them. After a moment, Golden-boy took the hand offered. Then, he glanced past McBride. His lips twitched. "Detective, a pleasure to see you again."

Really? She'd have to see about changing that.

"Mr. Vaughn," McBride began again, snagging the reporter's attention. "We have a few questions for you."

"Ah." His grin reappeared. "I'm glad you came. I was working to clear my desk so I could find you."

The corners of McBride's mouth drew down. "Oh?" He glanced around. "Is there somewhere we can speak with you that's…quieter?"

"Sure." Golden-boy scanned the room until he spied an open door across the large room. "We can move to the empty conference room."

McBride caught her gaze, passing along a signal she knew too well. "Lead the way, Vaughn."

Joe turned, pulled a manila envelope out of one of his desk drawers, then led them across the large newsroom, skirting desks, chairs, and people. Conversation and the clatter of keyboards followed them while light filtered through a large wall of windows to highlight dancing dust motes. The reporter's steps were steady, measured, confident.

Interesting. Definitely not the gait of someone hiding a secret.

A crash sounded at the opposite side of the room followed by loud bellowing. Addison jerked a glance in the direction of the commotion. The reporter's voice interrupted her thoughts. "My editor. He's a good guy, but he hasn't had a cigarette in three days. Withdrawal has left him cranky."

They followed the reporter into a mid-size cubicle decorated with framed articles and a lone ficus tree in the corner. The detectives stopped before a conference table that took up most of the space.

She turned as Joe closed the door. Without giving him a chance to sit, she asked, "Are you the reporter who wrote the Southside Heroines series on women helping others in their community?" She kept her gaze trained on him. If he blinked, twitched, or sweated during questioning, she'd notice. One wrong move could indicate he wasn't as innocent as he proclaimed.

"Yes." Golden-boy sat in one of the cushioned roller chairs and swiveled to face them.

McBride plopped his pocket notebook on the table as he sat. "Was Lacy Dalton the last woman featured in your article series?"

"Yes." Another nod.

Calm. No ticks. Steady gaze.

"What can you tell us about Ms. Dalton?" McBride asked.

Joe hesitated before his gaze shifted to her then back to McBride. "I can tell you what I learned shadowing her for the article."

"Shadowing her? That sounds like stalking, Mr. Vaughn." McBride jotted some notes on his pad without watching the reporter while he waited for a response.

She rubbed her jaw to hide her grin. McBride was supposed to be the good cop.

Joe shook his head. "Not at all. That's how I write. True human-interest stories dig deep to give it a personal touch. Lacy knew all about my process and was comfortable with it."

Addison picked up the questioning. "Why did she agree to the article? Did she like the idea of the attention it would bring?"

"No, she was actually a private person. She agreed to the article being written in order to bring publicity to the shelter she volunteered at once a week. That's the kind of person she was. Always thinking about others. She was a great lady." Joe stopped, glanced to the ceiling fan. "A good nurse whose patients were comforted under her care. Engaged to Michael Griffith, and her devotion to him was unmistakable."

"Was Mr. Griffith devoted in return?" Addison asked.

He tilted his head. "Are you a cynic, Detective?"

"We're not talking about me, Mr. Vaughn." She braced her hands against her hips. *Stick to the investigation. Don't let him rile you.*

His mouth curved as silence stretched out. Finally, he answered. "He showed every indication of returning her affection."

McBride paused, his pen hovering over the small notepad. "What type of indications?"

"Holding her chair, rubbing her shoulder as he talked with me, filtering her hair through his fingers." Joe shrugged. "Things like that."

"You're very observant, Mr. Vaughn." She crossed her arms over her chest. "Not everyone would pay attention to those kinds of details."

"My job relies on how observant I am, Detective."

"Did you also feature Rhonda Hewitt and Meredith Banks in your series?" McBride fired back.

Joe's gaze bounced back to her partner. "Yes. Rhonda Hewitt was the first woman featured and Meredith Banks was the second. Since you're here, talking to me, I assumed you discovered that information." He grabbed the envelope and pulled out loose pages as he continued talking. "I pitched the series of articles to my editor as inspirational and uplifting for our readers, spotlighting local women who gave back to their community. I'm often accused of reporting bad news to the exclusion of all else, but that simply isn't true." He handed McBride some of the pages.

McBride shuffled and scanned the papers, his brow furrowed. "Are these copies of your articles?"

"Yes."

No surprise. No vocal inflection. So, he was prepared for their visit.

She shifted her weight. "Did you shadow Ms. Hewitt and Ms. Banks as well?"

"Of course," He tilted his head back as if sending a request for patience. "As I've stated, that's how I write human-interest stories."

"How did you choose the community heroines you wrote about?"

"I received nominations through my email at the paper, and chose each woman based on her job, her actions in the community, and her influence on the lives of those around her."

Her lips tightened to match her hard stare. Time to up the pressure. "Why were you at the crime scene yesterday afternoon, Mr. Vaughn?"

Golden-boy shook his head. Did he find their disbelief unusual when her question was a logical one? "I answered that question this morning, Detective. My answer then is the same as now. My job is reporting events as accurately as possible so that our readers can be informed, can stay safe."

She tilted her head and said, "You could get that information from the press release when it's given out." She waved her hand. "Which, being an experienced reporter, you should've known."

"Yes, I could have, but I wanted to confirm my suspicions about the identity of the victim. If I'd been wrong, I didn't want to bring you information that could hinder your investigation." He scratched his cheek, looking uncertain. "Listen—."

Addison motioned to her partner. "Are you aware, Mr. Vaughn, that all three women you've shadowed have been murdered within days of your articles appearing in print?"

~

"Yes," Joe said. He rubbed the aching tension stretching across his forehead. "I suspected a connection yesterday. That's why I was trying to learn the identity of the victim." Cops. They thought making people repeat themselves over and over would trip them up. That only worked if the person was lying. He wasn't. His jaw clenched until it ached while he inhaled to the count of ten. The detectives were doing their jobs, just as he was trying to do his. He handed McBride the rest of the pages in the envelope. "I found these two articles online Sunday evening. I was shocked at first, but then I realized my third article came out last Wednesday. It was too late to get in touch with Lacy Dalton Sunday night, but I did try to get in touch with her several times Monday morning. Obviously, I was unable to reach her."

Detective McBride folded his hands on the table. "Why didn't you bring us this information yesterday?"

"I didn't want to bring you material that might have nothing to do with your investigation. At that point, all the facts I had were based on supposition. If I'd given you unnecessary information, you could've been sidetracked from finding the real killer. Only two of the murders were connected until Lacy had been identified." He tapped his fingers on his knees. "Look, I showed up yesterday morning to report the news, and to verify that I didn't recognize the murder victim. I couldn't get a clear visual. The make and model of the car seemed familiar, but the license tag was obscured so I couldn't be sure the victim was Lacy Dalton."

"What evidence do you have to back up your reasons for being at the crime scene?" Detective Parker leaned a hip against the edge of the table opposite him. "How do we know you weren't there to enjoy your own handy-work?"

His molars ground. He shouldn't be surprised at the conclusion they'd drawn, but he was. "No, detectives, I had nothing to do with their deaths. Quite the opposite. I was trying to gather facts to stop the person responsible." He pointed to the printed articles under McBride's folded hands. "All I have for you is the sure knowledge that all three women had nothing in common, except being featured in my series."

"By your own admission all three women you wrote about are now dead, Mr. Vaughn. Add to that fact, you show up at the last crime scene as curious as a dog with a scent." She leaned back on the balls of her feet. "Where were you last night between six and ten o'clock?"

"What?"

"Where were you last night between six and ten o'clock?"

"You've got to be kidding me." Both detectives stared at him in silence. Joe took a deep breath and counted to three. "I was covering a charity dinner held at the downtown Marriott. I didn't leave until one a.m. and arrived home forty minutes later after two detours through Atlanta to get back on the interstate. I spoke to several people at the event. Mayor Stallings, the hotel manager, and several guests. Any of those people can confirm my alibi."

Detective McBride slid his notebook into his pocket. "We'll check it out, Mr. Vaughn."

"Right." Joe rose as they headed to the door. "Do I need to consult with an attorney, Detectives?"

She paused and spoke over her shoulder, "Not at this time. I don't have to remind you not to leave town and be available for further questions, right?"

"Understood." His clenched fist tapped against his leg.

As soon as both detectives left the room, he concentrated on his breathing. Leave? He connected three murders. There was no way he would leave town right now. Even if it wouldn't make him look guilty, he wouldn't abandon the three women who'd trusted him with their story. He would make sure he did everything he could to help find their killer.

He walked out of the room and headed for the vending machines. The cacophony of the busy newsroom enhanced his concentration most days, but at the moment the muted noise among the reporters made his head pound with a ferocity he hadn't experienced since his mother's death. He needed somewhere silence reigned to pull his thoughts together, to come up with a plan to help Lady Justice without anyone else getting hurt.

Even with a solid alibi, he couldn't ignore the death of three women when he was the rope that tied the murders together. He strode into the break area and slammed his hand against the drink machine, then cradled his aching hand as he threw himself into a chair. He'd disclosed everything he knew. What more could he do? As of now, the series was finished. He didn't want to be responsible for anyone else's death.

He pushed a hand through his hair and froze. Maybe he could twist this situation to his advantage. Use the facts to expose a killer who was taking lives without mercy. Could he find a way to use his next article to lure the killer out in the open?

Putting himself between the murderer and another victim should be his next step. Better he faced the danger, than expose other innocent women through his articles.

Chapter Three

A shaft of white sunlight speared over Jackdaw's head as he sat at the second-hand table surrounded by the fruits of his labor. His mission had been successful. His genius remained unparalleled.

Of course.

Smiling, he maneuvered the scissors through the small local paper's newsprint, and then laid the sharp tool aside. His latest lovely stared at him from the black and white photo. Such a good girl. A perfect girl. A deceitful girl.

They all hid their treachery, their lies, their sin. And, he'd been charged with exposing and exacting payment for the hidden actions of the traitorous angels. A pure melody floated on the air, rising from his puckered lips, overpowering the profane noise his neighbors always made.

For he's a jolly good fellow,

He tipped his head back as the melody filled the air, closing his eyes against the glare of the descending sunlight lasering through his plain windows.

For he's a jolly good fellow,

The bird rattling the cage beside the table whistled its own melody in response to Jackdaw's light-hearted sounds. He stood and reached a finger between the bars of the metal cage, rubbing down the soft, feathered neck. The bird trilled its happiness.

His grin widened. Yes, this mission overrode society's rules and misconceptions.

For he's a jolly good fellow,

He sat at the table once more and pulled the opened keepsake book to the edge of the table. Taping the trimmed page in place, he rubbed a gentle fingertip over the image of Lacy Dalton. Blunt fingers traced the hair, eyes, and mouth with a soft touch.

Now, everyone knew she wasn't pretty, perfect, pure.

Which nobody can deny.
Which nobody can deny.
Which nobody can deny.

Jackdaw propped the book against the edge of the windowsill and reached for his notepad. New supplies were needed. He must be prepared. His voice rose an octave. A golden tenor underscoring his soul's music.

For he's a jolly good fellow,

New gloves. Rope. Syringe. Needle. Bleach.

For he's a jolly good fellow,

A new jacket. Plain. Black. Unnoticeable. Leather.

He rubbed his left forearm and frowned. The lovely Lacy had ripped his hoodie. He'd disposed of the garment then. He couldn't chance the police tracking him through the small scrap of material. Improbable, but possible. And, unacceptable.

Extremely unacceptable.

For he's a jolly good fellow,

Ah, the next angel would assure his mission would continue. He grinned.

Which nobody can deny.

She would be known soon. Sunday her good works would be told throughout the city, but the truth would be known. Oh, yes, indeed, it would.

Which nobody can deny.

Jackdaw closed the book of memories and returned it to the protective box in his closet. Tomorrow he could hunt again. He rubbed his hands together. For now, he would plan.

His hands swept out with his vocal finale.

Which nobody can deny.

Chapter Four

A shrill summons to work wasn't the way Addison wanted to start her weekend.

She pushed herself out of bed and wandered into the bathroom. Grabbing a clean washcloth, she began her morning ritual. McBride's call waking her meant their current case bothered him as much as it did her.

Finding justice for the innocent always eased her mind, but in this case, justice had yet to supply a name for the crime. Sighing, she laid the washcloth down and rubbed the persistent burn in her stomach.

Every lead had fizzled out. Joe Vaughn's alibi checked out; his innocence supported. Still, the mystery of the murders following each feature story left question marks all over their investigation like the Riddler taunting Batman. Somewhere there must be a piece of information that would lead to this killer.

She stepped into her slip-on sneakers, grabbed her purse and keys on the way to her truck. She turned and glanced at her house. Her chest swelled with a deep breath.

Events from four years flashed through her mind. Coming home from a mandatory training session and seeing the "Dear Addison" letter from her fiancé, Marcus, sitting on her mantle had turned her life upside down. Learning that he'd found another woman left her blood boiling, but when she'd discovered that he'd left her with a mountain of debt as well as the shame of being duped by a con artist, the privacy of her small living space became a blessing, a refuge.

Addison pushed the memories back under mental lockdown. Her life was full, complete. A husband wasn't needed to make her life complete. When the reporter's face swam into memory, she shoved the red-hot poker aside. She would never be taken in by another pretty face again.

Addison drove to the station, refusing to grumble about losing her day off—the one day she devoted to herself. Besides, what other plans did she have? Housecleaning, and, to be honest, there would be plenty of time for that. Constant sound greeted her on the way to her desk. Voices talking, phones ringing, laughter rumbling. Her shoulders relaxed under the sounds of organized chaos.

"Hey, beautiful, you gonna go to dinner with me tonight?"

She glanced over her shoulder at Alan Davidson. The fellow detective sat at his desk with his shirt sleeves rolled up and his dark hair rumpled from constant finger combing. His wide, round face sported a good-natured grin. Returning his grin, she shot back, "Not even in your dreams," without breaking stride.

"You know he's serious." McBride dropped his feet from his desktop as she moved past him to get to her own chair.

"I know." Addison tucked a stray piece of hair behind her ear. "But, I have a rule against dating coworkers." That explanation would have to do. She was not opening the Pandora's box of reasons for her no dating rule. Not even for McBride.

She plopped down in her desk chair and stared at a plate wrapped in aluminum foil in front of her. A plastic utensil packet lay perched on top of the foiled mound. A sigh escaped. Julia McBride was an angel on earth. Unwrapping the plate allowed the heavenly aromas to fill the air. Addison breathed in the scents of sausage, grits, eggs, biscuits. Her stomach rumbled as the enticing scents wafted toward her. Much better than her usual cold bowl of cereal. Possibly worth coming in on her day off. As she silently blessed her food, she added a blessing for McBride's wife, a great cook and an even better friend.

Just as she took a bite, a Diet Coke appeared beside her elbow. Her partner sat down across from her, a satisfied smirk on his face. His khaki pants and loose summer shirt marked his effort to dress better than his preferred fun-in-the-sun wear.

She swallowed. "What are you so happy about?"

"I knew you'd get here sooner or later. Even if you are," McBride looked at his watch, "fifteen minutes late."

"You're lucky I'm here at all." She shrugged and gazed at him across the expanse of their desks. "What's up?" The buttery homemade biscuit practically melted in her mouth as her eyes slid shut.

Silence settled around them as she steadily worked on eating.

He huffed a laugh. "How you can eat so much for such a little thing is beyond me."

Addison shrugged. "Metabolism."

"I did a Google search on our reporter last night."

The swift topic change had her looking at her partner. She swallowed and laid a hand across her heart. "You approached a computer? I'm in awe."

"I can use a computer. I just don't like them. This search found some unexpected results."

"Which were?"

McBride pulled a yellow legal pad over to read his scribbled notes. "He lived in Charlotte, North Carolina before moving here six months ago, and he wrote for *The Charlotte Observer*. Get this; he didn't write human interest stories. He wrote front-page material. Crime scenes, exposés, and the like."

She twirled her fork in the air, her eyebrows pulled down. "Why would he move here to write feature articles in the Lifestyle section?"

McBride leaned back in his chair, drumming his fingers on the desktop. "Don't know. My computer skills don't go that far, but I was thinking with the reporter's prior experience, he could be an asset to us, to our investigation."

"In what way?"

"With his help, there may be a way to trap this killer."

When he volunteered no further information, she stopped a forkful of food mid-air and said, "You're thinking of having the reporter write a story, then keep the subject of the story under surveillance, aren't you?"

McBride sat back in his chair, crossed his arms. "We may be able to work out a deal with him. If he writes the feature story for us, then we can give him the rights to break the full story once the action is over. After all, we both know reporters are always angling for information, and this reporter, in particular, already knows more about the case than any other."

She laid her fork down and shook her head. "I don't know. I don't like the idea of involving a civilian in a murder investigation."

He wagged his finger in a universal *tsk-tsk*. "He's not your average civilian. He's a reporter with investigative experience."

She wiped her mouth with the napkin that came packaged with the fork. McBride must've lost his mind in an ultimate web experience. "Experience that could backfire if he exposes critical parts of our investigation."

"Not if we bargain with him." He leaned back in his seat and clasped his hands across his stomach.

With a reporter? "Bargain how?"

"Offer him an exclusive on the story of a case solved." McBride shrugged. "Besides, he'll be writing the last article for us anyway."

Addison set her fork beside the plate. "That plan may work. It could also give us the means to keep our investigation out of the public eye for a while *if* we can trust Vaughn to sit on the information for the week of surveillance. It's a doable timeline."

"I agree."

She picked her fork up once more. "Who would we get to be the subject?"

He leveled his gaze on her. "It would have to be someone who has a job serving others and who volunteers in her free time."

"I get that. An undercover operation." She speared a sausage link.

"Exactly. I'm thinking we have access to someone in

this building who would be the perfect person for the article."

"Really?" She tilted her head. He couldn't mean another detective. Maybe a patrol officer? "Who?"

"You."

The sausage lodged in her throat. Coughing, she sputtered and reached for her drink, eyes watering.

McBride stared at her.

"What?" She pulled her voice out of the shriek range and leaned forward. "Now I know you've lost your mind."

"Nope. It's perfect. You work protecting the public full time, you help your friends when needed, and you teach children at your church. You're the perfect good girl for the article, and we can have surveillance on you so that if, or should I say *when*, the killer focuses on you," he speared a finger in her direction, "we'll be ready to take him down."

"Yep, you're certifiable." She pushed her plate away as his plan worked its way through her mind. She sipped her drink without taking her gaze off her partner. "There is no way I'm letting that...*that reporter*...write about me. No one invades my personal life, much less an annoying reporter who will air my private business for the entire city to read."

"Now, Addy, we could make sure you get to approve the article before it's printed. The city would not need to know everything."

"No." She forced out the word through clenched teeth.

McBride leaned against the tabletop, his arms clasped. "You want to catch this killer as much as I do. Would you want to slap a target on someone else and risk this killer sliding through our fingers?"

Addison bunched her fists beside the paper plate of cold food. "That's low."

"Maybe, but it's the best idea we have. We both know you are the best female detective this department has. I don't trust anyone else to pull it off without making a mistake."

She shook her head. "No. He'd be a pain in the neck, and I don't even like him."

"The reporter could grow on you." His eyebrows bobbed twice for emphasis.

She gritted her teeth, but remained silent.

McBride leaned toward her, his mouth making a grim line. "Look, this could be the chance we've needed to draw this perpetrator out before he kills again."

"No more articles, no more deaths?" She shook her head. "That doesn't mean he won't kill again, just that he may kill in a different way next time."

"Right. This is the link between the murders. I know you like to remain off grid outside work, but this situation is serious enough to break your rules this one time. Don't you think?"

Addison hummed a mock growl. She knew he was right, but her privacy was paramount. Plus, thinking about spending any time with Golden-boy left her irritated, and she wasn't even in his presence yet. "Find someone else. Besides, the Captain wouldn't agree to this plan."

McBride rubbed the back of his neck. He doodled around the paper edges of the yellow legal pad and said, "You're a trained officer. You know how to protect yourself, plus you know APD procedures. Would you ask another, less qualified woman to do this?" Her partner trained a steady gaze on her. "And you know he'd agree if it was you."

McBride knew her well. She couldn't imagine endangering anyone else. Protecting others defined her, but being forced to speak with the reporter about her private affairs made her skin tighten until she itched to hide.

She'd never hide. Her style was to face her enemy, and she wouldn't change that battle strategy now. Addison stabbed a finger at McBride. "Okay, but if Golden-boy suffers a few injuries in the process, it'll be your fault."

"Golden-boy?"

She trained her gaze on her breakfast plate and mumbled, "Never mind."

~

Joe leaned back in his dining table chair as he looked through his scrawled notes. Preparing for his latest article was doing nothing to distract his thoughts. He stared at the wall in front of him. How could he expose the killer using his articles to take innocent lives? He'd already messed up once, ruined a good man with sloppy investigative work. It hadn't mattered that he'd been overwhelmed with his mother's sickness and death. It hadn't mattered that he'd exposed the true perpetrator and garnered the victim enough publicity to help him be reelected as Mayor of Charlotte. What mattered was that he'd messed up, lost a job he loved, and faced everyday knowing his family had been stolen from him. He'd failed on all fronts.

Joe didn't want to expose another innocent person to hardship, or worse death. Yet, his part in a murderer's plan preyed on his mind and his soul. This situation revolving around his articles needed to be resolved. He blew out a breath. If the need to find the killer's identity wouldn't go away, he might as well act on it. Flipping the page in his notebook, he scrawled across the top of the page. Was the killer targeting him or the girls? Could the killer be drawn out if he made a public appearance to talk about his article series?

As if confirming the idea, his cell phone vibrated across his kitchen counter. Reaching over to pluck the phone up, he said, "Hello."

"Vaughn, boy, where are ya?"

Chuck Burnside's graveled voice boomed. Joe lowered the volume while he replied. "I'm working at home today."

"Why didn't ya say something about it before now?"

"I did. I told Casey yesterday so she could let you know. I believe you were on the phone with a school board council member at the time." He rubbed the tension that stretched across his forehead. Burnside's secretary wrote the memo before he'd left work yesterday.

Rustling papers came through the open phone line before Chuck Burnside grunted, "Huh. Well, how'd'ya like that? She buried it on my desk. No wonder I didn't see it."

"Well, I was getting ready to come into the office anyway."

"Don't see that it makes a difference as long as you get your next piece submitted on time. I want to know why you didn't let me know two police detectives would come to me for an alibi that links you to a murder investigation."

"I spoke with you yesterday about following this particular story. You agreed I could stick with this case. No other reporter has the prior knowledge I have."

"I didn't think I'd find you muddled up in the middle of a murder investigation though."

Joe rested his elbow on the table and gazed at the ocean print painting on the opposite wall. That picture was always so calm, so peaceful. He cleared his throat. "What do you mean?"

"Don't play stupid." Burnside's growl lowered. "If the

police are asking for an alibi, then you're in it up to your neck."

Joe pinched the bridge of his nose. "You know I didn't commit the murder."

"That doesn't mean the paper can't get bad publicity from the implication. Don't make me worry, boy. Worrying makes me cranky."

Pulling the phone from his ear, he stared at it in wonder. Cranky? Worrying? Chuck Burnside must worry all the time. He returned the phone to his ear. "Since I've decided to come in today you can be cranky in person. I've got some ideas to bring the killer out into the open."

"How would this benefit the paper?"

"You don't think helping the police catch a killer would make a great story?"

"You keep in mind that this paper is known for its reporters' integrity."

"I understand." His words were broadcast into silence because Chuck had already ended the call. He unclenched his fingers from around the phone as his shoulders slumped under the invisible weight he carried. Letting down the victim's families, letting down the detectives, letting down his paper. He couldn't seem to find a solution to fix the situation for anyone. Yet again, failing to do the right thing weighed heavily on him.

Joe propped his elbows on the desk edge and laid his head in both palms for a few moments. He plucked a bottle of aspirin from the counter, popped the cap, and tossed two of the nasties back without the benefit of water. The bitter taste did nothing to ease the tap dance of pain beginning behind his eyes.

Noise, activity, people. Silence always made things

worse. He grabbed his car keys from the side table and left. Fifteen minutes later, he entered the newsroom while impatience seethed under his skin. The beautiful detective stood beside his desk. Her average wardrobe of jeans and t-shirt didn't deny her beauty, and her dark brown hair, pulled into a tail, hung down her back added a soft femininity he couldn't ignore. His pulse leaped even though her gaze and stance presented a rigid don't-mess-with-me impression.

Perhaps he should share his ideas of luring the killer into revealing himself. Joe laid his notebook on top of his desk while gazing at her. If he remained cordial, maybe she'd loosen up a bit. "Detective." He inclined his head.

"Mr. Vaughn. A pleasure to see you again." Her flat tone countermanded the friendliness of her words. "Seems we both have jobs that require our attention on the weekend."

What had he expected anyway? A pledge of adoration? She hadn't liked him from the moment they'd met. He took a deep breath and exhaled to a count of five.

"What can I do for you?" He crossed his arms, mirroring her closed stance. "Answer more questions? Provide more alibis?" No more easy-going nice guy. She'd made it clear that she wasn't on his side so why bother?

She propped her hands on her hips. "My partner and I would like to speak with you."

He looked right, left, and then craned his head to look behind her. "I don't see a partner."

"He'll be here in a moment. I'll keep you company until he gets here." Her angelic smile didn't match her narrowed eyes.

Despite the woman's irritable exterior, his good manners surfaced. He cleared his throat. "Can I offer you something to drink?"

She gave a curt nod. "Water would be nice, thank you."

He nodded to his co-workers as he passed through the room. When he returned from the break room, two water bottles swung from his left hand. Good thing he'd gotten two bottles because both detectives stood waiting for him this time. He handed a water bottle to his dark-haired opponent, and then offered the second to her newly arrived partner. His nerves became twitchy at the look on the detectives' faces. Their look made it clear he wouldn't be happy with their visit.

Detective McBride accepted the bottle of water. "Mr. Vaughn, good to see you again. I'm sure you remember us from earlier this week?"

"Yeah, it's kind of hard to forget being considered a murder suspect." Joe looked them both over. They had an agenda. He balled his fists as his nerves tightened like the string on the English Longbow he'd learned to shoot when researching an article. Until he knew what direction the detectives were headed, he'd play their game.

"Is there somewhere the three of us could talk?" Detective Parker asked.

"We can use the conference room again." He invited them with a sweep of his arm, following behind with hands in his pockets.

The small, windowless room remained as lifeless as the solitary silk ficus tree in the corner and hadn't changed since they'd visited two days earlier.

"Mr. Vaughn—" Parker paused, shot a narrow-eyed gaze at her partner, then said, "We think you can help us lure out the killer that struck Wednesday. That's why we're here."

Chapter Five

Lure the killer? Lay a trap?

It sounded so much like his own thoughts that surprise blanked Joe's mind. He cleared his throat. "I have a few ideas along those lines myself."

"What ideas?" Detective Parker's head tilted as she stared at him.

"If I planned a public appearance, advertised that I'd be talking about my series and about the success of the articles—"

"That won't work." She shook her head, punctuating each word.

"Of course, it will." His teeth ground together until his jaw ached.

"If you advertise discussing the 'success' of your article series, other reporters will show to question you about each woman's death. That would hinder our investigation, not help it."

"I have to do something." His fist slammed against the

table.

"You are. You'll help us. Be part of our plan." McBride rubbed a hand across his short hair. "Trust in our experience, our ability to do our job."

Joe snorted.

Detective Parker pulled out a chair. "Look, Vaughn, just listen to our plan. Don't judge until you hear us out."

The ticking on the wall clock sounded in the room, overshadowing the silence. Joe kept his eyes trained on the two detectives. Should he trust them? He wanted to catch this killer as bad as they did. None of those women deserved to die, and he didn't want this killer to focus on anyone else. He would not expose anyone else to danger to further his career.

The detectives shared a look. McBride bobbed his eyebrows, and Parker raised an eyebrow in return. Had the two detectives disagreed over this plan of theirs? Interesting.

When Parker turned back to him, she said, "Let's sit down and talk."

Joe raised his brows. Those sweet, southern manners must've been hard to utter. "Sure. Why not?"

After they were situated around the conference table, Detective McBride turned back to him, stretched his fingers out on the table's surface, and began speaking. "We want you to write one of your articles featuring a woman we choose. We'll keep the woman under surveillance and make sure she remains safe. If the killer decides to strike, then we'll be able to apprehend him."

Put another woman in danger? No way he'd do that. Joe swallowed the knot that rose in his throat and closed his eyes for a moment to ward off the reappearance of the head-pounding ache that vibrated his ears. Every word his mother ever spoke, teaching him to protect and cherish women, flashed through his mind. He opened his eyes to find the Bad News Bearers still seated in front of him.

"We're prepared to offer you an exclusive story to appease your curiosity." Detective Parker's matter of fact words caught his attention even as they tickled the furious fire waiting to flare up.

"How can you offer me an exclusive when other reporters are covering the murders already committed?" He jumped up, paced away from the table. When he turned back, he pushed his words at them in a blast. Joe leaned over the table and tapped on the scarred wood beneath his hand, emphasizing each word. "And how can you make me an offer that strips every shred of decency from my character?"

"Sit down," Parker ordered.

He straightened, stared at her.

She sighed and added, "Please."

He wagged a finger between the two detectives. "You people are crazy." He plopped back into his chair and crossed his arms over his chest, leaning back in case proximity could erase the suggestion.

"You're the reporter that has pieced together the entire story by linking the deaths with your initial articles." The serious look in McBride's eye seared Joe. "As far as your character, your joining with us to catch this killer in no way demeans you. The woman featured will be protected in every way from the time you begin writing your story until the perpetrator is caught."

Curiosity flashed. "Who did you have in mind for the piece?"

The detectives shared another look. Their gazes swung back to him at the same time, and Detective Parker said,

"Me."

His gaze darted between the two. They had to be joking, but the expressions on both faces were anything but lighthearted. His shoulders dropped as he stared at the tabletop. Luck had definitely boycotted him.

He straightened his shoulders and faced them head-on. If there was going to be a collision of wills, then he'd meet them with a backbone as strong as theirs. "There are other ways this killer can be flushed out."

"None that would be as effective as our plan." Addison drummed her fingers on the chair's padded arms. "If we stop the killer now, the murders will stop."

"Is that supposed to make me change my mind?" His shoulders ratcheted tighter with each word. "It is possible that the person committing these crimes will find another way to target his victims."

Detective Parker's back stiffened. Her gaze hardened to match her sour tone. "Possible, but not probable. Serial killers have a specific MO and do not stray from it. Trust us to do our job."

He sat forward in his chair. "Are you sure you could handle being in the spotlight, *Detective*?"

Her back straightened, pulling her shoulders parallel to the ground. "Are you implying I'm not qualified?"

Joe raised his eyebrows. "Not at all. You're just not as open and friendly as my previous subjects."

Parker blew out a breath. "Your previous subjects are dead."

"A point well made." He stood, bracing his hands against the table in front of him, and said, "I refuse to be the trigger leading to anyone else's death. Even yours."

She mirrored his movement. "Sit down, Vaughn. If you

want to catch this killer, then you have to work with us."

He raised his eyebrows. These detectives didn't know him very well if they thought they could push him around. "There are other options. I invite you to find them if you want my help."

The door slammed shut behind him as he crossed the hall, escaping the room before he let loose the maelstrom churning inside him. If only he hadn't written the article series. If only he could have saved those women. If only…

~

McBride rubbed the back of his neck and sighed after the door to the conference room swung shut. "That didn't go very well."

Addison blew out a breath. "Was that your version of 'told you so'?"

McBride was right. She'd messed up by not realizing the reporter wouldn't respond well to orders and taken a different approach. What was it about the man that triggered her defenses? Now, they had to find a way to circumvent one angry reporter. An apology wouldn't work because he was tenaciously hanging onto his convictions. She couldn't blame him for that. Actually, admired him for it.

Still, that didn't change the fact that they needed his help. She refused to step back and wait for another woman to die, hoping to find more evidence. What they needed was someone who could convince Joe Vaughn to work with them. And, she knew the perfect card to play—The Boss Card.

Addison turned to McBride with her tail of hair swinging behind her. "We'll talk to the editor. See if we can get him on board, then he can require the reporter to collaborate with us."

"Sounds like a plan." McBride tilted his head. "How about letting me talk this time?"

"Sure." She motioned him to leave the room, and then followed making sure her steps matched his. Nineteen steps later, McBride rapped on the partially closed door.

"Come in," Burnside shouted, his gravelly voice the timbre of a chain-smoker.

When they stepped into the room, she managed to close her mouth before Burnside saw her. What surfaces not covered with books and papers were bright patches in the room. The mighty oak desk sat tattooed with coffee stains, mug rings, and gouged furrows. Empty nicotine gum blister packs littered the floor around the single trash can. She shuddered. How could anyone work like this?

Chair hinges screeched as the editor shifted in his chair to scowl at them. "What can I do for you?"

McBride presented his badge. "I'm Detective RJ McBride, APD, and this is my partner, Detective Addison Parker."

She stepped toward the editor's desk as the man straightened, centered his full attention on them. "Mr. Burnside, we have an interesting situation we think you can help resolve."

McBride's warning look had her locking her jaw to let him lead the discussion. Addison forced her arm muscles to relax as McBride finished describing the operation they believed would expose the killer.

Burnside scratched his cheek. "Let me make sure I have these facts straight. You want Detective Parker to be the subject of Vaughn's spotlight series in order to draw out the murderer you think is following his articles. And, you've discussed this with my reporter, but he's refusing to work with you."

She nodded once. "That would sum it up."

He stared at them, then rolled his large frame left, reaching for the phone on his desk. "Casey, call Vaughn to my office."

Notepad in hand, Joe Vaughn entered the cluttered room minutes later. Her gaze locked with his and he stopped, as if his entire body froze in time. Standing beside the editor's desk, Addison gave him a tight-lipped smile until her stomach sank in dread at Vaughn's frown. Her fists clenched. She hated pulling rank. It was an unfair move. If he had just agreed to their plan, this wouldn't have been necessary.

Burnside squinted at his new reporter as if Vaughn were an unfamiliar species. "Spoke to the Detectives here." Burnside waved a hand in their direction. "Told me what they want you to do. They think you could help bring a killer down."

"That's *their* plan. Not mine." Golden-boy pushed the words through gritted teeth. His hands fisted before he shoved them into his pockets.

Addison rolled her eyes to the ceiling. Hadn't they already made it clear that their plan was the best option? "You haven't given our plan a chance, Vaughn." She shifted her weight.

"The way you gave me a chance to come up with an alternate plan, Detective?"

McBride touched her shoulder. She nodded her understanding before swallowing her reply. The editor needed to do the talking now.

Burnside's chair squeaked as he leaned back, making a show of getting comfortable. "Not your call, Vaughn. They catch a killer," Burnside pointed his hands toward them, then moved them back to him and Vaughn, "and we get the exclusive. Get busy making it happen."

Golden-boy waved toward the newsroom behind him. "You could pair one of the other reporters with them. Paul Wiesner would be perfect for the job. He doesn't care how his stories affect others."

"They've asked for you." Burnside scratched at the nicotine patch peeking from under his short sleeve. "Your choices are to write the story or find a new job. Show off those fancy skills you assured me in your interview would be an asset to this paper. This is too good an exclusive to pass up."

The reporter turned and squinted through the window. "This psycho is using my work to target innocent women."

Torment laced the reporter's voice. Her heartbeat tripled as she waited. If the situation were different, she might have liked the reporter. Maybe even admired him. His loyalty and compassion to the victims could not be denied.

The sunlight cascaded over framed prints along the wall, refracting again and again to send brilliant colors across the beige carpet. Was the rainbow of colors a message of hope? Did the bright kaleidoscope indicate they were on the right track for catching this killer? Oh, how she hoped so. The volley of words tossed around drew her back into the conversation.

"If that's the case, it seems like you'd *want* to help the detectives."

"I will not be responsible for another woman's death." Golden-boy stared her in the eye as he continued speaking. "Three murders already hang around my neck like the Mariner's albatross. Writing those articles has meant the death of three good women, and you want me to endanger the life of a fourth?" He took a deep breath. "No one deserves to be a killer's target, Detective, not even you. No one can outrun evil."

"We may not be able to outrun evil, Vaughn, but we can face it with courage and faith." Her eyes widened at the words. How long had it been since she'd thought like that? Been that sure of her purpose?

"Harrumph." Burnside took over the conversation. "They're using a trained detective. You've been yammering about covering more hard-hitting news, using your fancy skills. Here's your chance." The editor shifted his weight from one elbow to the other.

Vaughn matched Burnside blunt for blunt. "I can't live with another woman's death."

Burnside leaned forward. "Let me put this another way. I want the feature article outlined by next Wednesday and the finished article on my desk by the following Sunday edition deadline. I'll expect the exclusive on the killer thereafter."

Golden-boy shot both detectives a heated look before he strode from the room, slamming the door as he exited. Addison couldn't prevent the ache that touched her heart nor the grimace that tightened her lips. Knowing they'd manipulated him left her chest hollowed out. It appeared the reporter would be as miserable as she would be during this assignment.

Sometimes you had to count the small victories when you were fighting for justice.

Chapter Six

Joe ground his molars together. The detectives had undermined him, and he wouldn't forget it. He wouldn't be their patsy. He would write the article, but he'd do things his way. He squared his shoulders as he returned to his desk.

Stephanie Foster, one of the secretaries stationed along the main aisle, sent him a flirty wink when he neared her desk. His return nod was quick as he veered away from her. When she called his name, he closed his eyes. Not now. Why couldn't she let him pass without trying to get her claws into him?

He pivoted, staying a short distance away. "Hi, Steph."

"Joe." She used the same well-rehearsed breathless voice employed with every man on the floor. "Have you seen, Mr. Wiesner?"

Well, he couldn't imagine Steph using that voice on the other man, so maybe he was wrong about her intentions this time. "Nope, Wiesner's not around."

"This guy called for him. Sounded like he was in a

hurry, if you know what I mean?" She twirled a strand of hair around her finger.

He tilted his head and waved a hand for her to continue.

"When I told him I couldn't find Mr. Wiesner, he got real irritated, and said he'd speak to another reporter if one was available. Would you be available?" She batted the dark lashes that framed her baby blues.

"Am I available?" His lips quirked. He was a reporter after all.

"UmHm." She pulled her hair forward and leaned toward him.

"Sure."

Her showing of teeth, although seductive in nature, left him feeling cold. "I'll transfer the call to your desk."

"Thanks, Steph." He retreated before she could corner him into another date. Not that he minded being with a pretty woman, but he preferred making his own moves in his own time.

A picture of the detective flashed through his mind. No use thinking of her in those terms. She'd made it clear that tolerating him equaled torture.

The tiny red light next to line three blinked. Who would be calling for Wiesner? Would it even be legitimate or would it be scum trying to wangle fifteen minutes of fame?

He pushed the line button. "This is Joe Vaughn."

"You a reporter?" The male voice, deep enough to be difficult to hear, spoke with the southern dialects of Atlanta's inner-city streets.

"Yes." Joe pulled his ragged notebook onto his desk, flipping to a clean sheet of paper. Jerking a pen out of his drawer, he noted the date and time at the top of the page.

The caller took a deep, audible breath. "I wanted to talk

to Wiesner, but I'm running out of time."

"Well, I'm here. I'll be happy to speak with you."

A pregnant silence filled the phone line before the other man spoke. "I can trust you?"

Joe huffed a laugh. "As much as you can trust Wiesner."

A burst of deep laughter exploded in his ear, and then wound down like a wind-up toy running out of energy. "I like you, man."

He shook his head. It seemed the snitch had low standards for liking someone. "How can I help you?"

"I have… information… you'll want."

"I see. Why don't you come into the offices, Mr.—" The other man spoke over Joe's words, bringing his suggestion to a halt.

"You must be new, Snoop." The caller grunted into the phone. "You can call me JG."

Snoop? He scratched his temple with the tip of the pen. "Okay, JG. I'm listening."

"Centennial Park. Be at the Fountain of Rings two hours from now if you want the information."

He drew a large question mark on his notepad after the scribbled directions. "What kind of information are you sharing? You're not a government spy, are you?"

Another chuckle. "Nah, man. I'm just a concerned citizen who has information that could break a big police case wide open."

"Hm." He added fragments and phrases to his notes as the questions continued. "How will I know who to look for when I get to the park?"

"I'll know."

"What's in this for you?"

"Don't you worry about that none. Trust me, Snoop, you

don't want to miss this gravy train." Silence ended the exchange when the snitch ended the call.

Joe replaced the phone receiver and looked over his scrawled notes. He reviewed what the caller had said, and what he hadn't said.

Male...inner city street lingo...JG...has information to share...two hours...Centennial Park...Fountain of Rings...?...possibly nervous about the information he has...reasons for imparting information suspect...what's in it for him?

He underlined the last notation twice. Even though he tried to avoid using snitches, he'd never known one to give information for free. He had two hours before the scheduled meet, and it would take him at least thirty to get to the park from the paper's offices.

He set the alarm on his cell phone, then got a head start on researching his latest feature subject. A well-researched article would ensure the piece detonated fireworks. Opening the internet, he began researching the good detective.

~

Joe approached Centennial Park on walkways bordered by lush grass, shrubs, and oak trees that provided coverage from the sun's heat. The back of the amphitheater rose in an open square in front of him. The Fountain of Rings sat northeast from where he stood. He hiked his black backpack onto his shoulder and continued along the sidewalk until he reached Centennial Olympic Park Drive. Just another upwardly mobile Millennial. The caller wouldn't look for him to come from the south side of the park. He squinted as the sunlight bounced off a nearby metal sculpture across his face. The sounds of a fountain tinkled and children's squeals of delight echoed.

A group of girls giggled as they passed him heading in the opposite direction. Each wore swimsuit tops with shorts as a concession to the heat and the promise of getting wet in the jets of water shooting from sidewalk spouts. Joe acknowledged them with a nod as he passed the reflecting pool opposite the rings brick design reminiscent of the '96 Summer Olympic Games.

He scanned the area as he began a slow tread. If he could figure out who the informant is before speaking to the man, then he could read his body language and perhaps understand who he was dealing with better. Around the fountain, mothers watched their children romp and play, fathers carried paraphernalia needed for a hot day in the sun, teens gathered in clusters, and single men and women were on the hunt for their next relationship partner. All skin tones, all ages, all sizes. No one who looked like an informant trying to remain unseen, unheard, and unnoticed.

JG wasn't stupid. He'd chosen the meet location well. The park provided a crowd diverse enough to avoid unwanted attention, but crowded enough to allow two people to speak without eavesdroppers interfering. Joe glanced at his own pressed slacks and button-down shirt. With luck, he would blend in as a white-collar worker on his lunch break.

A young male approached. His teeth gleamed white against his mocha skin, and his dreadlocks were anchored away from his angular face with a band of cloth wrapped around the mass. Heavy Jamaican rounded the man's vowels. "Need a new watch, mon? Got some fine timepieces for sale." The man patted a black case he carried. Those watches could be legit, or they could be hotter than a summer day. You never could tell with sellers on the street.

Joe stared for a moment. The caller had spoken with a southern twang, not a Jamaican accent. "No. I'm good." Joe grinned an apology as he pointed at his own Fossil timepiece that had been a graduation gift from his mother.

The man left and stopped to speak to another. "Need a new watch, mon?"

The 1812 Overture blared from concealed speakers as water began jetting from their spouts in choreographed bursts synchronized to the music. As the music captured everyone's attention, someone spoke behind Joe. "You got courage, Snoop. I like that."

Joe stiffened and ran his gaze over the scene in front of him. He spoke over his shoulder. "I'm here as you requested, two o'clock, Fountain of Rings." Water continued to sway and dance across the five intertwined rings. The strong scent of sunscreen and coconut oil saturated the air, and the bright colors of the various swimsuits looked like an exhibit in the Atlanta Art Museum.

A hot gust of wind blew across the area, bringing cooling sprays of water across those gathered closest to the water show. Squeals of delight accompanied the shower and little ones inched closer for a repeat sprinkle.

Steps shuffled at his back, and his shoulder jolted as the man stepped up beside him. The voice spoke low enough to avoid eavesdropping, but higher than a whisper. "See the bench in front of the trees to the left?"

The wrought iron seating sat back from the walkway and fountain, brown and squat.

"Awful lot of secret spy moves, you've got, JG." He eyed the younger man.

"You want the information I got, you go to the bench away from the crowd." At Joe's nod, the man continued,

"Circle the bench to the trees beyond. We'll talk there."

The tree closest to the bench sat in proximity to a group of people standing and talking. Weaving through the crowd, around one person, and then the next, he moved to lean his shoulder against the tree trunk beyond the bench so there would be no possibility of being overheard. The last thing needed would be for a well-meaning citizen reporting misconstrued information.

The snitch followed at a discreet distance, holding up his too large pants and nodding to those he made eye contact with. An Atlanta Falcons cap perched on his head, shielding his eyes from the harshest blaze of sunlight. At one point, the young man paused and leaned in to speak with a fairy-small teen. He let go of his pants long enough to pull out his cell and type in information the girl was giving him. Her phone number? He was trying to pick up a girl while snitching? Joe shook his head and looked away. Unbelievable.

The young man circled the tree and stopped on the opposite side of the tree trunk. The girl's gaze continued to follow the ghetto Lothario until JG made his way to Joe. Her hand tucked a piece of hair behind her ear as she ducked her chin and turned toward the children.

Joe lifted a brow.

The young man shrugged. "Guy's got to get his game on, Snoop. Don't mess up my chances."

"I'm waiting, JG." When the boy didn't correct the name, Joe checked that question of identity off his list.

The snitch scanned the crowd as a police officer would have. "I have information about the women who've been murdered. The ones written about in the paper."

"Really? How do I know I can believe you?"

"You don't, but can you pass up the chance to find out,

Snoop?" Shoulders clothed in a too large jersey jerked up and down.

"Why are you calling me Snoop?"

JG smirked. "You a reporter, ain't you? Snooping for information is what you do, what you are. Out here, we don't use real names. Where you been?"

Joe paused. "Okay, I'll buy that. What do you have?"

"First, you won't tell anyone where you got this information."

He nodded.

The other man's gaze scanned the crowd before turning back to Joe. "The murdered women—I think I know who may be killing them."

His pulse kicked into overdrive. *Don't blow it, Vaughn. He's got to back up the statement.* "How?"

JG shrugged, tucked his hands in his pockets. "Every week, regular-like, this white guy, a real sharp dresser, comes to me for a large purchase of heroin. Enough that should last him a couple of weeks."

"He's buying the same amount every week?" Joe swallowed the ball of anticipation that rose in his throat. If this information turns out to be legit, they might be able to catch this killer without another article appearing in the paper.

"Yep." The snitch met his gaze without a flinch as he continued. "And he's not a druggie. I can spot the druggies a mile away, and he ain't one."

He shook his head at the kid's logic. "He could be buying for a friend."

JG shrugged. "True, true, but he always buys heroin on Tuesday, the women are dead by Thursday morning, and he calls on Friday to put his order in for the next week. When I asked about his use for the drug, the dude got real angry. Told me since I was getting my money, I shouldn't worry 'bout things I had no business knowing."

"So why are you worrying about it?" Joe crossed his arms and stared at the young would-be detective who had just admitted to walking on the wrong side of the law.

The man shrugged. "Those I sell to…they choose drugs. A man's got to make a living, you know? But, if this guy is shooting these women up, killing them, then that's a death they're not making for themselves. That's not what I'm about."

"How do you know the women have died of a heroin overdose?" Joe reached up, rubbed a trickle of sweat rolling down his temple.

"Don't man, but it all adds up. A planned forced overdose would keep this guy on a schedule." The red and black Falcon on his cap danced with the motion of his head. "I don't like being used."

He straightened from his slouch against the tree. "Why not contact the police?"

JG's eyes rounded. "You're crazy, right? No way I'm setting myself up for a bust. I got a good business going, and I ain't stupid enough to throw that away."

He crossed his arms. "Or, you're trying to get rid of a competitor?" At the snitch's wide-eyed look, Joe's lips twisted. "Don't expect me to overlook the obvious, but I will check out the situation. The guy's name?"

"I told you, I don't deal in names, man. In this business, you learn to know as little as possible." The other man waved his arms in front of him as if warding off danger.

"What's he look like?" Joe focused a steady stare on the dealer as he took his phone out to note details.

The Falcon's cap was lifted, repositioned, while the answer was considered. "White guy, like I said. Twenties maybe. Dark hair. Dresses like he has money and spends like it, too."

He lowered his phone. That description could fit half of Atlanta's male population. Perhaps this information wouldn't be so easy to use to solve the case. "Then how can I track this guy?"

JG shrugged. "He'll come by my place on Tuesday night at ten. You keep watch, take his picture or something. However you want to catch him is fine by me. But, no police. Understand?"

Joe dipped his chin.

The snitch pointed his finger at him. "And you don't tie me up in this with the police. I'm just an honest businessman."

Honest? Joe let a grin twist his lips. The kid really thought he could finger a killer and not be implicated in the selling of the drugs being used as the murder weapon? He wiped the expression from his face, and asked, "Where's your apartment?"

"Parkington Estates, building E, on Washington Road. I'm on the ground floor."

Joe tapped the information into his cellphone. "I'll be there."

"I've done my part. Up to you now, Snoop." The young man took several steps away, and then stopped to look at Joe once more. "You double-cross me, Snoop, and I'll come after you. I get even when I'm crossed." With that the snitch sauntered away. One hand holding his baggy pants while the other angled his cap toward the sun.

Joe watched until the red hat disappeared from sight.

What should he do with this information? He couldn't take the unfounded speculation to the police. A drug dealer supplying the area wasn't something he could keep quiet about either.

Obviously, the kid expected Joe to keep quiet about the nature of the business being transacted in his apartment so that meant Wiesner had been trusted with this type of information before. The other reporter's likability factor fell a few more points.

Best course of action would be to identify the guy, at least with a photograph or two, before going to the police. If Joe turned the information over to the police now and the dealer was busted before the killer had been caught, justice lost the advantage. Police did botch investigations. He'd seen an abusive father walk free because of corrupted evidence during his stint as an investigative reporter. A politically, influential father who played golf with the chief of police every week.

He would make sure there were no mistakes to screw up this case. He pushed back the small voice that reminded him he could be hindering the police by hiding evidence, but he had a week to let them know what he'd found out. The article wouldn't appear in the paper until Sunday, so that would give him a couple of days to gather the evidence he needed to nail this killer.

So, he'd show up Tuesday night and wait. Once he had a picture of the buyer, Joe could identify him through the research channels available. After that, he could let the detectives in on the lead. Or, he could turn the picture over to the detectives to let them do the research on the perpetrator's identity. Until then, he'd proceed with the plan the detectives had forced on him.

DANGEROUS EXPOSURE

Chapter Seven

"I need more glue, Miss Parker."

Addison tapped the kindergartner's nose. "Then, we need to get you another one, don't we?"

Across the munchkin table, Mandy held out the orange plastic tube she clutched, her copper tresses pulled into two pigtails.

Addison tried to roll the gummy cylinder out of its casing. She winked at Mandy. "It looks like this one has been used up."

Colorful artwork decorated the walls of the small Kindergarten classroom at Harvest Community Church. The two half-moon tables, one red and one blue, provided just enough space for her, a teenage assistant, and the nine five-year-olds in her class for Sunday morning class.

Addison slid open a supply drawer, chose another glue stick and rolled the white paste up. "Ah, I believe this one works." She strode back to the bright blue table. "Here you go, Mandy."

"Hi, my name is Charles." The cheerful boy's rapid-fire announcement caught her attention.

"Hello, Charles." The smooth tenor that responded made her wince and jerk her head to confirm her suspicions. Joe Vaughn had leaned down to the smiling five-year-old. "Do you know my boss' name is Charles? But we all call him Chuck."

"Really?" The boy's eyes widened. "What's your name?"

"I'm Joe."

Addison turned around as Joe Vaughn extended his hand to the tow-headed child. Charles glanced at her for a nod of approval before clasping the man's hand.

Emboldened by the grown-up handshake, Charles asked, "Why are you here?"

"I needed to make some new friends."

"Okay. I'll be your friend. Tony will, too." Charles pointed to the dark-haired boy beside him. "Hey, Tony, won't you be Mr. Joe's friend?"

Tony's dark hair flopped with his vigorous nod.

Joe's lips quivered. He cleared his throat and shifted the spiral notebook he carried so he could place a hand on Tony's shoulder. "Well, thanks for being my friend boys. I love making new friends."

Addison pushed down the feeling of warmth the exchange brought. She shouldn't be noticing the way his hair glinted under the room's lights or the softening of his voice as if he cared. She couldn't soften towards this man. Softening could open the door to allow him to botch their investigation, and that was not an option.

When both boys returned to their pictures, she closed the distance between them. "You shouldn't be here," she said in an undertone.

"Of course I should."

"We'll talk in the hallway." Addison forced the words through clenched teeth, then spoke to her assistant while shooting him a forced grin that was all teeth. "Tamara, make sure the children finish working on their pictures. I will speak to our visitor outside."

The teen raised her brows. "Sure thing, Ms. Parker."

Once outside, the painted walls lent an unwanted air of levity to her predicament, and jungle animals laughed from the mural that ran the length of the hallway. She pulled the door shut. "Why are you here?"

He leaned over as if letting her in on a secret. "Did you not rope me into writing a feature story on yourself, Detective Parker?"

The second-grade teacher chose that moment to lead several children into the hallway. She waved at them, while she twitched with the urge to send Joe Vaughn packing.

She returned her focus to the man beside her. "Don't call me detective here." Her voice came out in irritated, breathy puffs. "What does the article have to do with your presence here? Why are you *here*?" Both index fingers punched toward the floor.

He stared at her for a moment, then spoke slowly. "I have been tasked with writing an article about your community service. I need to see that firsthand."

She shook her head. No way was she letting this man invade her private life. "I'll be happy to do an interview with you, but my Sunday school students are not going to be used for your journalistic fodder."

"I have already gotten permission from your pastor, who spoke to each parent before today, and I will not mention any of the children by name, but I will need to write from a primary witness' perspective. It lends an intimacy to the reporting and a quality to the writing. My byline always accompanies quality, *Ms.* Parker."

She shoved a finger in Vaughn's direction. "Fine. You stay out of the way." Addison spun on her heel, then shot a glare over her shoulder. "Don't turn my classroom into a circus, *Mr. Vaughn.*"

She'd be sure to thank McBride for this first thing in the morning. He was going to be sorry. She took a deep breath as she re-entered the Sunday school classroom, weaving between the two tables, checking on each child's progress. Every muscle she had tightened each time she focused on Joe. Ignoring him was the best way to handle the situation.

"Great job, Samantha."

The muscles across her shoulders tightened as he settled in a green munchkin chair opposite the story rug.

Ignore him, Addison.

She patted the next child's shoulder. "That's the best crown I've ever seen, Charles."

With the reporter sitting so close, knowing he was watching her every move, the beginnings of a headache crept into her skull.

"Antonio, I know your mother will love that picture."

The little ones started fidgeting several minutes later. Time to move on to the next activity.

"Children, I need you to help clean up and sit on the story rug." She stood as their enthusiasm created a whirlwind of activity.

From across the room, Joe tapped his fingers on his knees. Was he bored? Maybe he would wrap this up sooner.

Ignore him.

Turning her back on her newest nuisance, she knelt next to Michael's chair until she perched eye level with him. She signed as she spoke aloud, "It's story time. We have to clean up and move to the story rug." She allowed her eyes to widen and jerked her head toward the story rug at the end of the table. Michael's smile was a sunrise lighting his face.

Although she'd never had a favorite student, Michael with his chocolate brown eyes held a special place in her heart. Joe shifted in his undersized chair, drawing her gaze. He had relaxed back in his chair as he watched her interchange with Michael.

Sincere interest? Maybe Golden-boy had a heart after all.

Once everyone sat on the circular rug, she made a great show of walking around the group to calm them, murmuring to one, nudging another, then she faced the group and her assistant.

She would enjoy her favorite part of class.

"Okay, does everyone see their listening ears in front of them?" She paused, waited on their nods. "Pick up your listening ears—carefully now—and screw them on."

Around her, their little faces scrunched, and they tilted their heads as little hands made circular motions beside their ears. The movement required in their Sunday story ritual focused their attention span a little longer.

Mandy looked at the class visitor from her seat near his feet. "Did you bring your listening ears, Mr. Joe?"

"I sure did." He grinned at the child as he made the same circular motions beside his ears.

Addison blinked, and tried to ignore the tripping of her heartbeat. She dropped her gaze away from the man who threatened her peace of mind and reached for the manila folder that lay behind the felt board. Slowly she began to reveal the props needed for the story, then signed as she asked, "Who can tell me who Esther is?"

Answers came lightning quick, rolling over one another like rocks in a tumbler.

"A baby."

"Jesus' mom."

"Eve's sister."

"A queen."

A glance revealed Joe bent in the small chair with his elbows resting on his knees and his chin propped on the heel of his hand.

Ignore him. Why couldn't she ignore him?

Addison pointed to the group rotating her arm around the small faces staring at her like a pendulum counting the seconds. "Who said a queen?"

Jenna and Brian Kay shoved their hands up in a synchronized movement.

"You are right. She was a queen. But, our story's not about Esther." Nine small heads gave a negative shake with her. "We're going to learn about Mordecai, her uncle, who helped her become queen." Placing the felt male figure on the blue board, Addison started her story.

Just as she wrapped up the story 15 minutes later, parents began arriving. While Tamara helped the children collect their take-home materials, Addison greeted each parent. Joe had moved to the full-sized seat at the blue table and scribbled in his notebook. He sat, head tilted, and then started writing again, his pen moving across the page with an intense purpose.

Amy Cline stepped into the doorway, last in line. Her honey-colored hair lay limp against her shoulders and dark rings encircled her light blue eyes. The fading bruise high on the young mother's cheekbone caught Addison's attention.

"Hey, Amy," Addison laid a hand on her friend's arm. "Samantha was great today."

"I'm glad. She's doing better at home, too." Amy shifted her weight and gripped her Bible close to her chest. "Um, thanks, Addison, for helping us out like you have. Not many people would have taken the time."

"Amy, we've been friends since middle school. Of course, I'm going to help you. Did you file the restraining order against David?" Addison's gaze flicked right, taking in the light yellowish-blue mark once more. When her friend nodded, Addison said, "Good. If he shows up, you call me. No matter what time it is? Understand?"

Another nod. Samantha gripped her mother's arm. Amy laced her fingers through her daughter's.

Mother and daughter, so much alike—dark blonde hair, pixie features with a bow-shaped mouth, light blue eyes full of heartbreak. Dealing with domestic violence was hard enough, but when someone you cared about was involved it became devastating. A lump formed in Addison's throat.

"I want you and Samantha to have a wonderful Sunday. I know Samantha is dying to share today's story with you."

Both heads bobbed in unison. One with tears standing unshed and the other displaying a solemnness misplaced in a child. As one, the mother-daughter duo turned and left the room.

When she turned, Joe stood an arm's length away. "You're a woman of many talents, Ms. Parker."

She glared and pointed at the door. "If you write one thing about her or Samantha, I will have your career served up to you on a platter. Clear?"

"And you're good at threats." Faint lines crinkled around

his eyes.

Was he not taking her seriously? "I mean it."

"*Detective Helps Mother-Daughter* story is closed. No problem." He bowed his head to hide the curve of his lips.

"What are you grinning at?" Without waiting for an answer, Addison turned her back on him to help Tamara clean the room. The two worked side by side in silence. After watching the routine for a few minutes, Joe began to recap glue sticks, putting the glue in the correct labeled container.

A more natural expression warmed his eyes and replaced the fake, crocodile curve of his lips he'd thrown out earlier. She didn't like it. The unknown was always questionable.

With the clean up finished, she addressed her teenage helper. "Thanks so much for helping me. You're always a blessing."

"I like helping. I'm learning a lot from you. You're great with the kids, and they love you. You should've been a teacher." The fifteen-year-old blew her longish, pink tinged bangs out of her eyes and popped a Dum-Dum sucker in her mouth as she shot an admiring glance at Joe.

Ignoring the teen's look of adoration, Addison answered her. "I do love working with children, but I couldn't do it every day." She winked at Tamara. "I'll see you next week"

A smirk flitted across the young girl's face before she ducked out with a wave and a last longing look at the much-too-old-for-her reporter.

Addison grabbed her purse, dug out her keys, and turned off the classroom light. "Good-bye, Vaughn."

"Wait." Joe grabbed his notebook from the table behind him and crossed the room.

As he moved alongside her, his height caught her off

guard. She didn't like noticing he was almost a head taller than her. Well, she didn't *want* to like it. She took a deep breath and willed her heart rate to slow down.

"Let me take you to lunch."

There was that lazy grin again.

"I already have plans." She tripped out the door, almost losing her balance.

Watch where you're going. The last thing you need is him showcasing you as a klutz.

Joe's longer legs matched her stride. "What about dinner?"

"Call me, and we'll work out an interview time." She flung open the church's back door, nodding at other church members.

"An interview time?" He remained on her heels.

"For the article." She reached into her purse, then dropped her keys from shaking fingers before she could unlock the driver's door.

He reached for them. "Allow me."

"I've got it." She bent to grab the keys, almost knocking her head against his. The intoxicating smell of his cologne invading her senses. Jerking the keys off the pavement, she juggled the hot metal into the lock. The oppressive heat pushing out of the open door stole her breath, but she needed to get away from Joe to clear her head. The man was sapping too much of her attention, and she didn't like the flips her stomach had started doing when he'd watched her with the children. She cranked the ignition and turned her air conditioner on high, making further discussions difficult.

"Good-bye, Vaughn."

"Have a wonderful day, Detective."

She slammed her door shut before saying something that

would cause regret later. To avoid the hot blasts of air in her face the truck heaved out, she faced the window just in time to see him climb into his car two spaces away. She rummaged in her purse and pulled out a scrunchie, yanking her hair into a sloppy knot.

Glancing left again, she spotted him looking both ways before backing out of his parking spot like a Boy Scout following the rules. The face she made at his taillights until they disappeared from her view was juvenile, but it made her feel better. Her head dropped when her hands gripped the wheel.

What was wrong with her? She would not let this man get to her this way. She refused to be drawn to him, to walk down this pathway of oblivion into another relationship only to find heartache at the end of the path. Her temples, her brow, even the base of her skull now pounded thanks to Joe's visit. Dinner with her parents and sisters on Sunday afternoons had become a ritual in their family. Even though she craved quiet time, her family could prove to be the bright spot in her week. One she didn't want to miss. Putting the truck in gear, she turned west toward her parents' home.

Spending at least one afternoon with the reporter on this hare-brained article scheme along with any new cases thrown their way didn't make her week look any better. And, continuing to check on Amy and Samantha was taking a toll. Helping her friend, ensuring safety for one small girl, ranked as high on her personal list as catching a killer preying on innocent women.

She sighed. How did she get herself into these situations?

~

Addison stepped onto her parents' back deck with an

aluminum pan filled with marinating steaks and pulled the door shut. She should leave her Mom and sister Caroline in charge of the kitchen before she messed up the salad or the dessert or something else important. Then her mother would've clucked her tongue and turned the afternoon into a cooking lesson. Talk about kissing a relaxing afternoon good-bye.

The sun rained down on the roof of the house and the country air while the myriad of trees waved in the summer-scented breeze. Barely. "Got the steaks, Dad." She carried the pan toward the grill.

Brandishing his long-handled meat-fork like a sword, Jim Parker looked at her from underneath his John Deere cap. "Good deal. We'll have dinner on the table in no time." He pulled the wooden handled lid open and shifted the foiled wrapped potatoes and corn on the cob to make room for the meat. "Great weather for grilling." He squinted up at the sun, and then winked at her. "No rain."

"Only you could call this great weather. It's almost a hundred degrees not to mention the crazy high humidity level." Pulling the round neck of her shirt away from her shoulders allowed the hot air to soothe her dampened skin.

Her dad closed the lid. "Is that why you look a little pale?"

"Is this you being subtle?" Her eyes narrowed.

He smirked.

"Subtlety I'd expect from Mom, but you?" She shook her head. "Surely not."

"Your Mom's a little worried about you. You haven't been your usual bulldozing self." He leaned against the porch railing and crossed his arms. His interrogation pose. Not good.

"Bulldozing?" She stopped and cleared her throat when her voice rose an octave. If he could settle in for questioning, she could take it.

"Aw, it's your best trait, little girl." He swiped a hand towel across his shining forehead. Guess the heat was getting to him, too.

She propped her hands on her hips. "That's harsh, Dad. Not the compliment a girl wants to hear."

"One of my better qualities you were blessed with." He patted a hand on her shoulder and turned back to the grill.

"So I've heard." A laugh bubbled out, leaving her chest lighter for a moment, but died before she had a chance to enjoy it.

Addison crossed her arms and stared at the old trail that led to the treehouse she'd shared with her sisters. The grass had begun filling in the ruts worn away by rubber-soled sneakers, and wildflowers had grown in to dot the new green line. Funny how nature renewed things worn down by careless actions. If man could repair his actions in the same way, life would be so much simpler.

"Joking aside, what's bothering you?" Her dad speared a steak and flipped it.

A lump formed in her throat.

Oh, get a grip.

She swiped a few escaping strands of hair behind her ear. "I'm just having a few problems at work. No big deal. I'm sure I'll work through them soon."

Her father stared at her in silence while she fidgeted like a child waiting for a reprimand. "What kind of problems?"

"I'd rather not focus on this today." Her father turned to raise a brow at her, holding the grilling fork in the air. He'd never let her get away with avoiding his pointed questions before, and it appeared that wasn't going to change in this moment. "Okay, okay. I'm just…it's just…keeping a positive attitude about work is getting difficult."

"What do you mean 'difficult'?" He speared another steak, flipped, and adjusted its final position on the hot metal.

Addison sank onto a deck chair as her father continued to alternately flip the steaks and rotate the vegetables on the grill. She forced her shoulders to relax, but her thoughts refused to be voiced. She'd never allowed herself to admit weakness. Today was not an exception. Too girly.

"I can't talk about a specific case, but it's getting harder to process the crime scenes, Dad. To maintain objectivity."

He wagged his speared cooking fork at her. "You could always apply for a position in Massey's Sheriff Department."

"You know that if I transfer there, everyone will assume I was given the job because I'm the sheriff's daughter. I want to prove that I'm good at my job without my dad opening doors. Besides, working here in Massey wouldn't help me right now."

He closed the grill lid, then lay the large fork aside before sitting in the chair opposite her. "Do you hate your job?"

"No." A sharp head shake caused her hair to fall from its scrunchie and flopped over her shoulder. Gathering up the heavy mass and corralling it back atop her head gave her something to do while she considered her answer. "I'm having a hard time leaving work at work. And, with Amy and Samantha's situation, I find myself getting angrier at the world every day. At God." Addison stopped, squinted into the sky. "Have you ever felt like that, Dad?"

"Have I been angry at man? Sure. Have I been angry at God? I can't say as I have. But, you have to keep in mind, Addy, I have your mom and you girls to balance out my life. You haven't allowed yourself to have that same balance."

"What do you mean I haven't allowed that for myself?" The words spewed out harsher than she'd intended. Never did she speak to her father in a disrespectful manner. She exhaled and tried to soften her words. "I have friends. I do things outside of work."

It wasn't enough. She knew her reassurances fell short before her father confirmed it.

His gaze softened and he turned from the grill to lay a hand on her shoulder. "No, sweetheart, you haven't. After Marcus treated you so badly and ran off with that other woman, you shut yourself off from everyone that could hurt you. Your life is unbalanced. You need to give God a chance to bring some of those good things your way."

Addison leaned back and fisted her hands on her lap. "I'm happy with my life."

He shook his head the way he always had when she was little, and he had caught her being less than truthful. "Are you?"

"Yes." Her throat tightened around the forced word, and each word that followed became more difficult. "I'm happy."

"Then why are you struggling? Look, witnessing and dealing with criminal actions the way we do means we have to be watchful of developing calluses on our hearts. If you never experience love beyond friendship and having a family of your own beyond us, then you've lost the most important weapon you could ever have to destroy those calluses. Make sense?"

"I don't know, Dad. I'll have to think about it for a

while." She pointed at the smoking grill. "Your steaks are burning."

Addison grinned as her father snatched his grill pitchfork, and grumbled, "What's the world coming to when a man's little girl makes him burn his steaks?"

Her father's scowl darkened when she started laughing.

Chapter Eight

Jackdaw stepped up to the counter in the coffee shop he frequented on Sundays.

"Large Caramel Cappuccino, espresso shot, no whipped cream," the serving girl announced. The visor of her standard issue hat tipped back until the tail of auburn hair pulled through the hat's adjustable tab held it in place. She added a little more tilt to the smile aimed at him.

His dark hair and light eyes set him apart from many others in the small coffee shop. He used it to his advantage. After all, the little wink he'd given the girl, Sandi according to her nametag, had earned him a shot of espresso at no charge, hadn't it?

When you were given little in life, you learned how to get more. By fair means or foul.

"Thanks, *Sandi*." The extra emphasis on her name brought a flush to the girl's cheeks.

As he turned away from the girl's adoring gaze, Jackdaw pulled the Sunday paper he carried out from under his arm.

A vacant table farthest from the counter waited for him with the late morning sunlight streaming through the window on the right.

He settled into the chair, sipped his coffee before setting it on the smooth, dark blue table, and opened the paper to see what the Lifestyle and Community section had for him today. Sunday, the day of the week he anticipated. The day of the week that revealed his next assignment's identity.

The good girl whose sins remained buried from society.

Everyone's eyes but his. No one was perfect. He knew every sin had a price to pay. He knew he was the instrument of justice bringing those sins kept in darkness to the light.

His mother had made sure he knew these things. Every day until her ultimate sin had demanded payment.

The newsprint crackled as he opened the paper. Jackdaw's fist crushed the paper when an article entitled *Hot Summer Fashions* greeted him. He forced himself to exhale and loosen his grip. Higher level thinking separated the human male from the animals, and he refused to be known for his animal instincts. Not when his genius intellect could be much more useful.

Turning pages with the care of beholding something precious, his gaze narrowed as each page withheld the information he needed. He folded the newspaper after long minutes of reading headlines, smoothing out the crinkles. The story wasn't there. His chest moved as if he'd run a 5K race as he smoothed his opened palms across the treasonous news source.

They were trying to abort his mission. The mission he'd been born to complete. He couldn't let them succeed.

"Are you alright, young man?" A matronly woman sitting at a table on his left spoke, her face creased in a frown.

"Yes, of course." His amiable grin reappeared, while hostility beat in his chest. "I'm fine. Missed my favorite news story. That's all."

She glanced at the paper he held. "Ah, you mean the article about women in our community? Yes, I enjoy reading that one, too. Shame an article like that didn't run this week."

"I agree. I'm always encouraged when I see someone who makes a point of being good to others." His feral grin escaped with those words.

"Oh, yes." The woman faltered, and then turned back to the book in her hands. Her cup sat forgotten in her intense concentration.

Jackdaw grabbed his cup and stood, leaving the paper behind. He left the coffee shop and strode to his apartment in the rising heat. He had plans to make and a friend to visit. He would complete his mission.

They wouldn't stop him.

Chapter Nine

Joe sat in his car Monday morning outside the police department and reviewed his observation notes from his shadowing the day before. The low-roofed, brick building standing before him could've belonged to any business on the street, except for the row of marked and unmarked patrol cars that proclaimed the premises a law enforcement location. He'd found himself looking forward to spending time with Detective Parker, Addison, after he'd seen her with the children in her class yesterday.

Needling her was fun, too.

Whether she knew it or not, liked it or not, she'd turned his head at their first meeting. In a good way, of course. She was beautiful and...well... beautiful, and his interest had intensified as he'd learned more about her during his research. Her patience during the children's activities and her handling of her assistant highlighted her beauty within. When they'd nearly collided reaching for her keys, he'd discovered she smelled sweet, too. Now it was time for him to get to know the detective side of her, to find out if the investigator was as honorable as the teacher.

He used the rearview mirror to push his hair back from his face and straighten the collar of his shirt. *Remember to stay on guard, Vaughn. This woman has a way of tying you in knots.*

A sober man stared back at him. Joe knew he should take that warning seriously, but with this woman he couldn't help himself. He had to poke the scorpion to get her attention. Hopefully, he wouldn't get stung in the process.

Joe stepped into the light rain with bag that held his digital camera and notebooks and loped across the parking lot. Through the window of the building's gunmetal gray door, he could see the beehive of activity. He grasped the cool metal knob and pulled, allowing the cacophony of sounds to rush at him. A crying baby reaching for its mother, a man cursing at his captor, a woman shouting her statement.

Nothing like chaos to sharpen the senses and summon his curiosity. His rubber soles didn't contribute to the disorganized music as he moved into the room.

A giant stepped in front of him. "If you're here about the prostitution ring arrests, you can have a seat there by the window."

"Prostitution ring?" Joe considered the row of hard chairs under the window, some occupied, some not. Could be interesting.

The man's round face, at least five inches above Joe's, jerked left. "We'll get to you soon."

No, he had a purpose already. He jerked his gaze back to the officer's round face. "I'm not here for the prostitution ring. I'm looking for Detective Parker."

"You are?"

"Joe Vaughn." He held out his hand.

"Ahhh. That reporter the killer is following." The man squeezed hard enough to make him wince. "Name's Davidson, by the way."

"Nice to meet you, Davidson." *Sort of.* Joe flexed his fingers.

Davidson waved toward the opposite end of the room. "Their desks are over there. Last set before the water cooler." The detective turned away, paused, and turned back. "Tell Parker she can't hog all the goodies."

Davidson smirked, and then sauntered toward a desk on the opposite end of the room.

Goodies? Joe shook his head, then took in the atmosphere surrounding him. The uniformity of the room struck him as being drab, but the constant activity kept everyone from noticing. Men and women stood in pairs or sat at desks. Some wore uniforms and some dressed in street wear. Aromas of coffee, and cinnamon filled the air.

He rubbed his stomach into submission with fingers that twitched. He needed to write down his impressions before he lost them.

RJ McBride sat at the far end of the room with the phone stuck to his ear and crooked his finger over the curled phone cord. Joe took the chair next to the two desks pushed together.

"Everyone loved the cinnamon rolls...uh-huh...Addy ate two of them...yep, she liked them...I've got a visitor, sweetheart...uh...I'll pick some up on the way home tonight...yeah...bye." McBride hung up the phone and swung toward Joe. "The little woman was anxious about everyone liking her baked goods. So, what brings you here today, Mr. Vaughn?"

"Joe, and as you've orchestrated, I'm here to work on the article you've made sure I'd write."

The detective focused an unblinking gaze on Joe as Addison approached them, a platter carrying two fluffy cinnamon rolls in her hands. She fixed a glittering gaze on him. "What are you doing here?"

He sent her his most genial grin. "I'm here to shadow you, detective." He leaned back, dropping his small bag on the floor by his feet. "For the feature story."

Shock raced across her face as her spine straightened and her shoulders tensed. "The devil you are!"

~

Joe's announcement reverberated in Addison's ears. He was trying to make this situation more difficult than it needed to be. He'd already ruined her precious time with the children at church, and now, he was trying to horn in on her work time.

McBride tapped her arm. "What are you doing with the entire platter, Addy?"

The question startled her, and his raised brows let her know she was behaving like an idiot. She glanced at the cinnamon rolls, then back at her partner. "I had to snatch these away from Davidson before he ate them all."

He made a rude noise in the back of his throat.

"He took three, RJ." She gripped the dish tighter.

Another noise.

She shifted the platter farther away as if he were the pastry police taking her pilfered rolls into custody. "Oh, alright. I wanted them."

"Well, give our boy Joe one. His stomach's growling."

Addison's mouth moved into a pout, but she inched the cinnamon buns toward the reporter.

Joe reached for a roll, taking care to pick out the fluffiest one loaded with icing, which aggravated her more. His chosen morsel in hand, he bit into the sticky confection and moaned in delight.

"There's no way you're going to shadow me at work." She plopped the platter down out of his reach and slid into her desk chair.

Joe raised both brows and kept chewing.

"Yesterday was enough. I'll suffer through an interview with you, but no more." There was no way she would spend another day with him. He would not change her mind.

Golden-boy shrugged while he swallowed. "If that's what you want, but I have to tell you, detective, no shadow, no article."

"Are you telling me that you'd compromise this case over a trivial matter? Wasn't yesterday, ruining my Sunday, enough for you?"

"Producing quality work is never trivial to me as I explained to you and Detective McBride, and yesterday highlighted only one part of your life, not the whole of your experience helping others. I need to write from a comprehensive point of view." His reasonable tone rankled more than his words.

She jabbed a finger toward him. "You cannot shadow us throughout our day as police detectives. That requires special permission which you do not have."

"You planned this course of action." He shrugged. "I assumed you had taken care of everything."

"You never mentioned following me around." She grabbed a file from the stack beside her elbow. Maybe if she lost herself in paperwork, she'd be able to forget he was here.

"You never asked. You ordered." Joe crossed his arms, a mirror of her usual intimidating pose.

Addison ground her teeth. *Cocky, irresponsible, miserable cad.* He had a point. Darn it.

"Children, children," McBride stood and picked up the file they had reviewed that morning, "I'll go talk to the Captain while you two learn to play nice."

Both gazes followed McBride's progress down the hall until he entered the last office. As one they locked gazes once more.

Her shoulders straightened.

His head tilted right.

Her gaze raked his posture in the chair.

His legs stretched out in front of him.

Addison took a deep breath. This was getting them nowhere. He would have to change his mind about this shadowing idea. That was all there was to it. "Look, this is not your usual article so it would be fair to say you *do not* have to use the same procedure to write it."

"It might be fair, but I still won't write this type of piece without researching you or your daily routines. If you want the killer to believe you're the next community role model, then you're going to do this my way."

"I never asked to be made a community role model." Her hands fisted against the paperwork she'd pulled out. "I agreed to let you write this story to catch a killer, and an interview should be enough. I'm not a feature like the other women you've written about."

"For your plan to work, I must follow the same protocols as the previous articles. Whatever your reasons, there's just one way I'll agree to write this article, and that's after shadowing you through your day." He pulled his notebook and pen out of his backpack.

She slapped her hand against the desktop. "You aren't asking me to work *with* you. You're asking me to bow down and give in to your demands."

"Not demands. You can refuse, detective." The ringing phone on the desk beside him made him pause until he realized no one was going to answer it, and then turned his attention back to her. "I'm sure you can find another way to bring this killer to justice." He stood and grabbed his jacket from the back of the chair.

"Wait," Addison said, raising her hand in the universal stop sign. "Don't go. Maybe we can work out a . . . compromise."

When he stared at her, she continued, "Finding another way to catch this killer would take too long and endanger more lives. At least, wait to hear what the captain says." Addison tightened her lips. Besides, there was no way her superiors would agree to this hare-brained shadowing scheme.

Joe lowered himself back into the chair. "Okay. I'll wait."

Addison picked up the list of the latest victim's acquaintances, and then picked up the last cinnamon roll on the platter and bit into the melt-in-your-mouth breakfast treat. At least she'd gotten the last bit of sugary goodness even if she hadn't gotten the last word.

A loud bang brought her attention back to Joe as the desk shuddered. She took her hand off her holstered weapon when she took in his flushed face combined with the hand rubbing his right knee. He would have a nice bruise later. A fine example of poetic justice. She coughed the laugh that threatened to escape into her hand.

Addison looked up from her work to check the clock. Thirty minutes had passed, and Joe hadn't interrupted her? He'd been so quiet she'd almost forgotten he was there. A notebook perched on his lap and the pen he held right-handed lay atop a half-filled sheet of paper. He watched the interactions surrounding them with the stillness of a predator.

He shrugged when he noticed her attention. He bent back to his paper and began scribbling. Her gaze swung around the room until it returned to him.

"What are you writing?"

He replied without lifting his head. "Notes, impressions, descriptions." When she continued to stare at him, he said, "Of your work environment."

"But...," Addison glanced around the building again, "nothing's happening."

"Sure there is. The phones are ringing. Your fellow detectives are talking over each other. At least three people have entered the station and two have left." He lifted his head and pierced her with an unflinching gaze. "And, you haven't noticed any of it, which is very telling."

Addison hummed. "Selective hearing. You get used to the noise and tune it out. Kind of like you at your desk."

Joe huffed a short laugh. "Understood."

Da-de-da-da-dum-dum, Dum-de-da-da-da.

"Your ringtone is Hawaii-Five-O?" His question carried the same wonder Edison must have had when the first light bulb lit up a room.

Addison gave Joe a pained look as she reached for the cell phone strapped to her waistband. She checked the ID screen, and then answered the call. "Hey, Mom." She tugged on her right ear as she listened.

"I wanted to remind you about Caroline's baby shower because you've been working such long hours lately. We're having it a week from Tuesday at seven o'clock." Water rushed in the background as silverware clinked. "First Christian Church."

"You know I wouldn't miss this for the world, especially with Robert deployed. I've had it noted on my electronic calendar since you started planning it." Addison made a notation on her desk calendar even though the event was already noted on her electronic calendar in her smartphone. She ignored Joe leaning over to spy. "But I'm writing it down at my desk, too."

Mom paused as the water stopped flowing. "And, don't forget dinner tomorrow night."

"I remember. I'll be there around six." She sighed. Lyn Parker never missed a beat when planning a surprise for one of her girls, even if it wasn't a true surprise. Addison wished she could forget it was her birthday.

"Okay, good. See you then, sweetie."

"Bye." Addison ended the call and reattached it to her belt. She looked over to find Joe staring at her bemused. She raised an inquiring brow.

She opened her mouth to blast him when McBride returned. *Please bring good news. Get rid of the reporter.* "Hey, McBride, what took so long?"

"I had to explain the situation to the Captain, and then wait while he called for approval from the higher ups."

"They turned down the request, right?" Her Cheshire Cat grin bloomed. No way would the Captain allow a wild-card reporter to ride along with two of his detectives.

"Nope. We're good to go with the shadowing, but the Captain was ordered to review anything written before it's

printed to avoid sensitive information being released."
Her grin collapsed as Joe's widened.

Chapter Ten

Addison rolled her shoulders as she filed another report. Paperwork slowed time, and today, one more tedious task slowed her day even more. Ignoring Golden-boy.

Even now, he sat there relaxed in a hard metal chair, right ankle propped on his left knee, writing in his notebook. Who knew what he could be writing about today? She glanced around the room. Nothing out of the ordinary happening today, just a few cops joking around, a few people waiting to see someone who'd been booked. Her lips tilted upward before she could stop them. It would serve him right if every day this week was long, boring, and uneventful.

She straightened and took a deep breath. She was doing it again. Why couldn't she ignore him?

The call came in at ten forty-five.

Gunshots reported at ten. African-American male, age twenty-two. Homicide in College Park. Arriving officers had secured the scene and alerted homicide.

Addison grabbed her jacket and caught the car keys RJ had tossed her way. Maybe if they said nothing to the reporter, he wouldn't realize they were leaving until it was too late.

Joe looked up in surprise before jumping from his chair, one hand on his backpack and the other gripping the notepad and pen.

Dashing to their county vehicle parked in front of the station, Addison checked her holstered weapon. McBride pointed at Joe, and then pointed to the backseat.

Addison slid a glance toward her partner. "What was that address again?"

RJ checked the notepad he kept in his pocket. "Parkington Estates on Washington Road, Apartment E-4."

"Gotcha." She punched the accelerator, and then drove on automatic pilot, her stomach rolling into knots. Ten years on the force and she still found herself shocked at the depths of violence man could commit.

God, give me the strength and wisdom to deal with what I must.

Silence reigned in the confines of the car with intermittent calls from the police scanner filling the void as she zigged, then zagged, through interstate traffic. The apartment complex came into view. Two police vehicles sat with lights flashing, and gathered onlookers stood opposite a roped off apartment.

Addison pulled her badge from her pocket and pinned it to her belt. She tossed a look at Joe. "You stay here. You are *not* to enter the crime scene." She climbed out of the car and strode with her partner into the melee without looking back.

Disarray and the metallic scent of death assailed her as she stepped over the threshold. Pillows scattered across the floor, and a lamp rested on its side amidst scattered drywall. A young male sprawled across a sagging sofa with his head lay at an odd angle while blood pooled on the cushion underneath. His eyes angled toward the doorway, unseeing.

Time to get to work...

Addison pulled on her gloves and approached the two officers who had secured the scene. "Okay, gentlemen, what details do you have so far?"

~

Joe stood by the detective's unmarked sedan amazed they had made it in one piece. Parker drove like a madwoman: aggressive, intense, focused. Exactly what he was coming to expect from her. The NASCAR fan in him was impressed.

He took in the activity around him. Gawkers stood behind him, windows winked across the tan building in the morning sunlight, and uniformed officers questioned neighbors along the sidewalks. Paul Wiesner stood in the middle of the gossiping neighbors and other reporters. Wiesner motioned for Joe to approach him. Yeah, right, like he needed to deal with a Wiesner complication right now.

Turning his attention to the bright yellow strips crisscrossing an apartment doorway, he weighed his options. If he stayed here, he'd miss the chance to see Parker in her element. If he infiltrated the scene, he'd earn her wrath and be in danger of probable arrest and possibly contaminate a crime scene.

His tongue ran across his teeth as he watched the officers move farther away.

There was the opportunity to see a crime scene close-up to consider.

He approached the open doorway.

The police should've closed the door.

Joe leaned his head across the 'do not cross' tape and saw that both detectives were busy analyzing evidence while a camera's intermittent flash lit up the living space turned crime scene.

McBride clapped the young, dark-haired photographer on the shoulder. "Thanks, Darrin."

Joe ducked under the ribbons and strode up to the doorway in time to see the man grin. "Anytime, Detective McBride. Your subjects are easy to work with since they don't ruin the pictures with sudden movements."

Joe raised his brows. Did he hear that right? Was the kid making jokes right now?

Detective McBride shook his head, his mouth set into a grim line as he surveyed the scene. "Addison, do you hear this kid?"

"Yeah, I hear." She tilted her head toward the sofa. "Our guy wouldn't appreciate the joke."

Darrin sobered as he placed his camera into the case. "I'll get these pictures developed by the end of the day."

Joe stepped into the doorway and watched the photographer finish packing his equipment. The iron smell of blood rolled through Joe's nostrils leaving an insidious trail of nausea churning in his gut. Joe's glance slid around the room, then locked with the lifeless body staring at the door. His heartbeat picked up speed until it thundered in his chest.

The black hole on the left of the forehead and a gun dangling from the left hand told the story of a young man who died of suicide, but the state of the room suggested he did not die quite so peacefully. Joe swallowed hard. All thoughts of gathering evidence for a story fled his mind as the dead body of the snitch held him hostage.

JG, who had wanted to protect the girls being forced into the death of a junkie. Was this murder connected to the same serial killer they were trying to catch? Or, had JG crossed the wrong person in his attempt to make money?

"I've got something, McBride." Parker's voice penetrated Joe's motionless, spellbound stare. Joe rubbed his stomach and glanced at her.

Addison. Somehow, she'd become more to him than Detective Parker with her prickly exterior and tender heart. Would she cooperate with him after finding out he'd had contact with the young man that lay dead before them?

Both detectives knelt by the sofa where the silver chain lay. Addison picked up the broken jewelry with the tip of a pen and dropped the evidence into the open bag her partner held. "It looks like a necklace. Silver serpentine from the looks of it."

McBride sealed and labeled it.

Teamwork in action.

She stood up and arched with her hands pressed into her lower back. "Since the crime scene's been documented with photos, we can let the coroner do his job now."

He allowed his gaze to drift back to the snitch's body.

McBride stood next to her. "I'll motion Simpson in to take care of the body so the time of death can be determined." He turned, spotted Joe for the first time, and tightened his mouth. "What are you doing here, Vaughn?"

The sharpness of the man's tone, a voice known for its easygoing affability, dragged his attention from the body once more. "I must see her work to be able to write about it."

"You were told to remain *outside* the crime scene." The detective pointed toward the doorway.

He shook his head. "I understand, but I can't see her work from outside. Besides, I didn't enter the scene. I haven't gone any farther than the doorway."

"Semantics. You've compromised this crime scene." The other man's jaw flexed. "If I see any details in your newspaper before the story is released—"

"I wouldn't do that." He narrowed his eyes, then took a deep breath and straightened his shoulders. "I like to see justice work, too."

"You're no better than any of the other bloodsucking, information stealing rats on the paper's payroll."

He blanched until outrage heated his face. "Are you calling me a liar?"

"Gentlemen, let's calm down." Addison's calm words blanketed the argument as she stared at one man, then the other. "Okay?" She pointed a finger at him. "Vaughn, come with me."

She crossed to the door, expecting him to step aside. He moved his foot to step back, but stopped when the sun refracted off a sliver of metal under the battered coffee table.

A hand against her arm caught her attention. "Wait, Parker. . ."

"You don't want to push your luck right now, Vaughn." She pushed his hand away and angled to go around him.

"There's something under the table next to you." His crossed arms and raised brow must have communicated his unwillingness to move because she stopped, glanced at his face, then dropped her gaze.

When the metal flashed again, she said, "Don't touch anything."

"I know." Joe knelt and pointed at the object, his finger close enough to show the location, but far enough not to touch. "It's here."

Addison hummed and reached into her back pocket for another evidence bag, picking up the object with gloved fingers. Pinched between her fingers, a dirty hypodermic syringe with a bent needle topping the barrel sparkled in the morning's sunlight pouring through the windows.

She dropped the newly discovered evidence into the bag. "McBride, take this."

RJ took the bag Addison held turned until his gaze rested on Joe and flared. "Where'd that come from?"

"Under the table." She jerked her head toward Joe. Her mouth formed and upside-down crescent as she said, "Vaughn spotted it."

Another hostile look. "Did he touch it?"

"Nope. I'm the one who picked it up." She waved a gloved hand, claiming her partner's attention once more. "We can send it in and have forensics do a fingerprint and DNA analysis. This syringe appears to have been used more than once. It could be the victim's, but, somehow, I don't think so. The other rooms in this apartment are neat, which means this guy either kept a clean house or hired someone to do it for him. Not the actions of a junkie."

"I know what we do with evidence found at the scene, Parker." McBride dropped his chin to his chest. Finally looking back up, he accepted the new evidence. "Let me have it and get him out of here."

Addison slanted Joe a look. "Let's go."

Keeping his mouth shut seemed the sensible thing to do. For the moment.

Joe stared at her in amazement when she hooked a hand around his upper arm and pulled him from the doorway. Six inches taller and fifty pounds heavier, but she didn't even blink while trying to force him out the door. He had to admire that.

Beside the police vehicle, she gave him a dark brown stare. "Stay here. If you go in there," she thumbed toward the marked apartment door, "it's hard telling what McBride will do to you. And, next time, I won't stop him." After delivering her ultimatum, she walked away.

Joe stared after her. How could he get himself out of the mess his life had become? In the space of five days he'd gone from the new kid at the paper to unconfirmed murder suspect to unwilling police source. When he disclosed the information he knew about the murdered drug dealer, his status would return to suspect.

To his left Wiesner approached him until an officer covering the scene's perimeter stopped him. Joe turned his attention back to the open doorway.

"Man, you like living on the edge, don't you?"

Joe met the steel gray eyes of the photographer while he breathed in fresh air. "What makes you think so?"

The milling crowd around the apartment building continued to grow, watching with a fascination reserved for violence. The murmuring voices assaulted Joe's ears in waves as his mind spun in circles.

Darrin started ticking points off on his fingers. "Entered the room without permission, going toe to toe with McBride, handling evidence after you'd been told to leave." He stopped, shook his head, then hitched his bag back onto his shoulder. "Living on the edge, my friend. I've seen McBride get mad, and, believe me, you don't want to go there."

"I didn't touch any evidence, and I didn't enter the scene." Joe eyed the camera case slung over the man's shoulder. He couldn't resist. "So, how'd you wind up taking pictures of crime scenes?"

Darrin shrugged, and then grinned. "To get experience. I'm enrolled at SCAD," at Joe's raised brows the photographer explained, "Savannah College of Art and Design. I approached the department for part-time work on my days off from school to get experience and fund the expansion of my portfolio."

"Pay good?"

"Nah, terrible, but I learn something new every day." The young man winked.

Joe tucked his thumb in his front pocket, tapping his fingers on his hip. "Do you work with Detective Parker a lot?"

"Enough." Darrin shrugged, his t-shirt rippling with the effort. "I like working with both McBride and Parker. But I have to tell you, I wouldn't mind spending more time with Detective Parker. You feel me?" He stopped, looked around, then spoke from the side of his mouth. "If you haven't noticed, she's hot, man."

"Yeah, I've noticed." Joe cleared his throat. "Tell me your impression of Detective Parker. Other than she's hot."

"Why you wantin' to know?"

He held his notebook up. "I'm writing an article about her for my paper."

"No kiddin'." The other man eyed Joe speculatively, and then snapped his fingers. "Vaughn. . . you write the Heroines in the Community articles, right?"

Joe dipped his chin. Was that a look of satisfaction that crossed the other man's features? Obviously, he agreed with the choice.

"If you ever need a photographer give me a call." Darrin held out a plain business card, then tugged the equipment bag higher on his shoulder. "Parker would be a perfect fit for your articles. She's great. Smart, funny, helps others, tough as nails when she has to be."

"Does she have any vices?" At the kid's blank stare, Joe clarified. "Any bad habits, things she does that others don't like?"

"Not that I've seen. If she has any bad habits, she keeps them well hidden."

Joe reached out a hand. "Thanks for your input. . . Darrin Gray, wasn't it?"

"Yep." The photographer clasped Joe's hand and pumped it once, then pushed his camera bag in place once more. "Well, I've got to go. I have a big assignment to develop and turn in by tomorrow, plus the crime scene pics. I'll catch you later."

"Sure." Joe watched Darrin leave the apartment complex on foot and decided he'd try to mention Parker's collegiate co-worker in the article.

A bonus to the kid for his service to the community.

Chapter Eleven

With their final sweep of the crime scene completed, Addison strode back to the vehicle while McBride gave final instructions to the remaining officers. Her plan tonight consisted of a long, hot bath, followed by quality time spent with a good book. Escape.

Death had taken its toll on more than the deceased today. McBride had been harping on her to get involved with the CISD team—the Critical Incident Stress Debriefing—to help her cope with what she had to deal with every day, but each time she'd considered meeting with them something had always come up. Perhaps she should try again.

She sighed as she slid into the passenger seat. A glance in the mirror showed Golden-boy writing in his notebook, an intent look shadowing his face. Somehow, when he was concentrating on his work, he seemed younger. "Why use a notebook?" When he paused, she said, "I mean, I would think you'd use a fancy electronic tablet to take notes on."

"Sometimes I do, but I like the feel of handwriting the

words. I seem to think better when I'm writing rather than typing." He shrugged and looked back at his page.

"How old are you?" The question popped out of her mouth before her mind could shut her vocal cords down. Well, if he was going to get nosy about her, she supposed she could nose into his business some.

Her breath caught as he raised his head and met her eyes in the mirror.

"Thirty next month."

Thirty. She pressed her lips together. So, he was younger than her. She couldn't be feeling disappointment over their age difference. It shouldn't matter that he was four years her junior. Why did it matter too much?

A tip-tilted grin flirted with his lips. "My mother always said by the time I reached thirty I would reach my full potential. Don't know what that means, but she was sure about it. Said God told her." He shrugged.

She twisted and faced him. "Your mother's a believer?"

"A believer?"

"A Christian."

He nodded. "Every Sunday she attended church. Prayed every day. Much good it did her." Bitterness laced his words, and he lowered his eyes to his notebook like a hurt little boy.

"What does she think now?" Addison couldn't resist following the line of conversation he'd opened. Especially, after that last comment.

"I don't know. She died last year." His voice faded to a murmur with each word. He glanced back at his notepad.

Her heart ached for him. She couldn't imagine losing either one of her parents. "I'm sorry to hear that. It must've been a hard time for you."

That line seemed so inadequate, but what else could she say? She couldn't say she understood how he felt. She couldn't say he'd get over the loss. Did he believe in God? Only if he released his feelings and gave his life to God could he view his mother's life as eternal, and then hope could be born. Was she meant to cross paths with Joe Vaughn? Addison turned back around, tossing the thought away.

"Why are we both sitting here? Don't you have detective work to do?" Joe placed his notebook and pen into the bag and pulled out his phone. When Addison faced him to answer, he snapped a picture of her.

"You'll have to delete that. No pictures at the crime scene."

"It's not of the crime scene. It's of you."

"Even more of a reason to delete it."

He rested the phone in his lap. "Why are you sitting here? Babysitting me?"

"Maybe. We've done all we can do here. McBride is checking with the coroner, then we'll return to the station to follow up on any leads. Investigating is not always exciting. A lot of it means waiting and following dead end leads. It's not a glamorous job."

"Most necessary jobs aren't."

McBride returned to the car as the coroner's van pulled away. The silence crackled with thick tension on the return drive to the station. She eyed Joe in the rearview mirror. His attention on the cars passing on their left gave the impression he remained lost in thought.

She couldn't allow herself to care about this man. Feelings started as innocent friendship, but she knew where they'd lead. Her fiancé had taught her the value of tender feelings when he had disappeared with thousands of dollars' worth of music equipment and furniture, leaving her responsible for the debt.

No, Father. I can't take that chance.

The prayer became lost in the buzz of their radio. She glanced at him again, a younger man who could have compromised their crime scene and couldn't find the same feelings of animosity she'd had even an hour ago.

I can't risk my heart again, Lord.

All the signs were there. First, coming to protect him from her furious partner. Then, admiring him for his ability to notice details. Allowing her heart to soften further because of his mother's death would lead to her downfall a second time. Soften? Her head must be softening. To start having fuzzy feelings for a reporter with his own agenda must be the beginning of a mental crisis. Her confusion on the subject had to be the forerunner of a breakdown.

McBride parked the vehicle at the precinct. As the trio climbed from the sedan, Addison said, "Who's going to write the report? You or me?" She flipped her glasses down to cover her eyes. "I believe it's your turn."

"Fine. I'll write the report." He ignored Joe and entered the building with fast, clipped steps.

Addison fell into step beside McBride. He stopped, looked at her over his shoulder when he reached the building's front door, and waited until he had her full attention. "You did well today."

She forced her lips to curve. "Gee, thanks." She shook her head and followed him into the station. It wasn't like her partner to give compliments. Did she look that bad?

~

Joe entered the police station and rubbed his hands down

the outside of his pants legs as he trailed behind the detectives. He owed them both an apology. He didn't like it, but he owed it.

They were right. He could've compromised the crime scene, and justice would've been averted. Just as his father's case had gone unsolved. This definitely hadn't been the first time his curiosity had gotten the best of him, but he had allowed his inquisitive nature to overrule common sense at a crime scene. Not something to be proud of. Still, he wouldn't have known the murdered victim was his snitch if he hadn't entered that room. That made it hard to have any regrets.

There was one nagging detail he didn't know how to handle. Should he tell the detectives about his meeting with JG before the young man had turned up dead? Joe admitted to himself that self-preservation answered that question with a no, but the part of him that sought justice said yes. The detectives couldn't find the killer if they didn't have all the details. Plus, could keeping silent get him arrested for withholding evidence? He didn't think so, but jail time didn't hold any appeal if it was a possibility.

Detective McBride's mouth tightened when Joe approached his desk. "What now, Vaughn?" The man clenched his jaw and forced his next words through gritted teeth. "You need to go home."

Advice? Fair enough, but Joe couldn't afford to heed it.

Chapter Twelve

"I want to apologize. I shouldn't have crossed the crime scene barrier today." Joe leaned onto the edge of Addison's desk, pressing his knuckles onto the hard surface until they whitened. "I let my curiosity outweigh my common sense. For that I'm sorry."

Addison sat back, silent.

McBride stood and looked Joe in the eye. "You know, I roped you into this situation in order to trap a killer. And, I played Mr. Nice Guy to keep Parker from flatly refusing to try this plan before calling the GBI for help, but," McBride pointed his finger at Joe's chest, "I don't have to play Mr. Nice Guy anymore. You have enough to write your article." He jammed his finger toward Joe as if forcing his point home. "Just remember, every word of your article must be approved before it's sent to your editor. Understand?"

"I understood that this morning."

"Good." The detective's jaw flexed as if he were grinding his teeth together.

"I want this guy caught as much as you do." Joe stopped and chewed the inside of his jaw.

"Apology accepted." Addison rested her bent arms on her desktop. "Now, go home. Let us finish the paperwork so we can call it a day."

Joe stared at her. Should he continue? Share everything?

"Spit it out, Vaughn." The chair let out a protesting squeak as McBride fixed a glare on him.

The beginning was as good a place to start as any.

Joe stuffed his hands into his pockets. "Two days ago, one of the secretaries at the paper forwarded a call to me. The caller has been a known snitch to one of the other reporters, but that day I was the reporter available. I took the call and agreed to meet the man at Centennial Park."

"What did this snitch want?" McBride folded his hands across his stomach while Addison kept her gaze steady on Joe.

"He'd been selling large quantities of heroin to a single person every Monday. The person was obviously not a user, yet he bought the same amount every week. JG, the name the snitch gave me, said he became suspicious when he started seeing a different woman's death reported in the paper each week after he sold the drugs." Joe cleared his throat before continuing. "He made it clear that he didn't want to be part of anyone using what they purchased for murder." He shrugged. "Obviously, he did have a moral line, even if it was skewed."

Addison's brows formed a V over her eyes. "Doesn't sound like any snitch we've known."

"JG remained adamant about not calling the cops. He was worried about his business being shut down."

"I'm sure he was. And, why are you telling us now?"

She speared her finger onto the desktop.

Joe took a deep breath and jumped in with both feet. "Because the man shot in the apartment this morning was JG. The snitch. Since he's now dead, I think finding his killer trumps Freedom of Speech confidentiality laws. I think JG's killer could be the same person who has killed our article women, and since I know what his plans were to identify this unknown man, I think the appearance of suicide was staged."

Both Addison and McBride stared at him in stony silence.

Was Joe supposed to say something else? Well, he might as well lay everything out for them so they couldn't gripe about it later.

"I had planned to confirm what the dealer told me as truth. I couldn't reveal my source, and I didn't want to bring you false information and send you guys on a ghost chase while the real killer kept prowling for victims. For all I knew the dealer was the killer and was using me to draw the attention away from himself."

"It doesn't matter." McBride stood, a vein pulsing near his temple. "You should've come to us right away."

"Freedom of Speech allows journalists to protect their sources. So, no I couldn't have brought this to you."

McBride rubbed a hand over his face as Addison unhooked her cell phone and pushed a series of buttons. "Hey, Lawson, Addison Parker. We sent some evidence to you today from the College Park homicide. Uh-huh. Listen, we need a rush on anything you can come up with. Yeah, we think there may be a link between this crime scene and the series of women's murders. Okay. We appreciate it. Thanks."

McBride pegged Joe with a gaze so heated steam should've risen from the man's head. "You'd better hope this delay in information doesn't alert the killer."

"I would think you'd thank me for giving you a link between the murders."

Addison spoke in a hard tone for the first time since Joe's crime scene blunder. "No, we would've thanked you if the deceased could've been questioned while he was alive. We might've ended this thing before anyone else died."

Her clenched fists pushed into her desktop as she fought down the desire to go after Joe. She'd focus on McBride right now. If she talked to the reporter, she'd say something inappropriate. The last thing she wanted to do was apologize to the man who'd just copped to withholding information in a serial murder investigation. "Lawson said they'd get any evidence they could processed as soon as possible."

McBride shook his head. "Which could mean a week or more, and we both know it."

"Yeah, but it's better than nothing. In the meantime, we follow our original plan." In unison they turned baleful glares on Joe.

"Go home." Her partner waved his hand, dismissing the other man.

"Why?"

McBride shook his head. "Because you're done for today. If you're lucky, we'll tolerate you tomorrow."

"I'll go, but I am coming back. You wanted me here, detective, so I'll be here." Joe shot Addison a heated look and left without a backward glance.

Addison returned her focus to McBride. "You work on that report. I'll go over the crime scene notes and call Darrin to get prints of the crime scene photos he took ASAP."

"Deal."

~

Joe pulled onto highway running beside the police station. Heading to the newspaper would give the detectives time to cool down, and he could outline the feature story needed by Saturday morning. Hopefully, most would be gone for the day, and he wouldn't have to talk to anyone. He had enough to think about already.

Detective Parker, Addison, had stunned him when she'd started talking to him like a friend. Asking about his mother. Trying to console him after finding out he was alone in the world. What would it have been like to have someone there for him? Someone to care that he'd lost all that was precious to him?

Get over your circumstances. Life is what you make of it. No more, no less.

He turned into a parking slot at *The South Fulton Report* and flipped off the ignition. Grabbing his backpack from the seat beside him, he entered the building, breathing in the cooled air, passed the empty reception area, and headed toward his desk. Pulling out his chair, he sank into the familiar cracked cushion and unlocked the drawer. He grabbed the flash drive containing his previous notes and powered up his computer.

It was time to pull his head together. He had an article to write. Once his computer hummed and his handwritten notes lay beside his keyboard, he closed his eyes.

One deep breath.
Focus.
Another deep breath.
Outline the story.
A third breath.

Plan your steps.

He opened his eyes. Having a plan always helped him achieve his goal so that was where he'd start. His fingers flew across the keys, moving the cursor across the page.

A self-contained person who doesn't share much of herself with others...but makes sure she helps others when possible

Sunday school teacher...competent...good with children...loving...kind...creative...encouraging

Detective...efficient...detail oriented...gets along well with co-workers...compassionate but strong

Friend...caring...sympathetic...ready to help in any way...loyal...honorable

Daughter...

Joe's fingers stilled. Family. He wanted to see her interact with her family. Would she share more of herself with them? Pictures. Maybe he could find some posted pictures of her and her family. He opened his web browser and typed in her name. A personal web page for a Caroline Stafford showed as a link. One click of his mouse button caused Addison Parker's face to fill the screen before him. She stood centered behind a man and woman and between two identical women obviously younger than her. Her parents? Sisters? Had to be her family.

He needed to interview her family. He could ask her to spend tomorrow evening with him. See if she'd humor him, have dinner with him, introduce him to her family, answer his questions. Yeah, right. At least he could be honest with himself. He wanted to spend more time with her. Merging his professional need with his personal want. Perfect solution.

Or impending disaster.

"Vaughn."

Joe's spine snapped into a rigid line as Weisner's voice grated on his ears. His chin dropped. Just what he did not need today.

Great. What he did not need right now.

One deep breath later, he turned to confront his rival with straightened shoulders.

"What's up, Weisner?"

"You and I need to talk." The other man propped his hands on his thickened waist. "I know you saw me at the scene earlier. Why didn't you hook me up with a source? I need information for tomorrow's edition."

"I have my own story to write. If I'm babying you at a crime scene, I'm not researching my story."

"Co-workers should look out for one another. You need to learn to be a team player if you want to succeed at this paper."

"Team player?" Joe shook his head. "Like you telling me to stay away from investigative reporting a couple of days ago? How's that being a team player?"

"That's different. There's no harm in workplace wisecracking."

Joe huffed a dry laugh. "Is that what you've been doing? Look, the police gave me strict instructions. If I want my story, I can't leak details of other cases they investigate. It's how the game is played."

Weisner swiped his arm out as if brushing that reason away. "So. They don't have to know who my source is."

"Oh, come on. Those detectives aren't stupid. They would know exactly where your information came from. Then, I'd lose my story." Joe shook his head and started walking away.

"I'm not done."

Joe suppressed a rude comment and confronted the man once more.

"Stephanie said you took a call from my snitch." Weisner's voice took on the whine of a petulant child.

Joe shook his head. "Yes, I spoke with him."

Weisner pointed a beefy finger at Joe. "You tried to steal my snitch, tried to show me up."

"I wasn't trying to steal your snitch. You weren't available. The snitch had time sensitive information, so I talked to him. That was it. End of story."

"So, what did he want me to know?"

"Nothing you'd find important." Joe ran a hand through his hair. "Look, I thought I was helping you out, but obviously you feel different. I'll make sure to tell Stephanie not to forward any of your future calls to me. That work?"

"You'd better stay out of my business. I won't have you, or anyone else, trying to steal my job," Weisner sneered before stalking down the hallway.

Joe pinched the bridge of his nose. How could such a promising day be reduced to a train wreck of bad choices?

Chapter Thirteen

Jackdaw left the crime scene with practiced nonchalance after he'd waited in the copse of trees west of the apartment complex. He'd had to stay until the police shut down the scene. He knew how they worked, how they planned, and he'd out-smarted them.

Again.

He approached the benchless bus stop and stood waiting for the three-fifteen transit to Union City, a transportation ruse he maintained for appearances, as his mind filtered back through everything, checking for flaws in his plan.

Javarious Glenn, drug dealer turned blackmailer, had earned payment for trifling with him.

Contacting the known drug dealer two months ago had been easy, getting drugs from the man even easier, but unlike other drug dealers, Glenn had a sharp mind clear of toxic drugs. He'd been able to pair his new customer's regular purchases with the recently publicized drug overdoses.

The dealer's subtle probing had turned into an outright blackmail attempt. Blackmail Jackdaw refused to pay. Glenn wouldn't stop him from fulfilling his destiny.

A plan to frame someone else had taken shape in that moment. He'd watched the apartment, but this morning the junkie had left, shot up outside the apartment door, then threw the used needle away. Perfect timing. Evidence nearby with a suspect to frame.

As he'd observed the investigation, the police bagging the used needle as evidence made him smile. He'd left the hidden clue so they could use the evidence to pin the murder on the unsuspecting junkie.

Seeing the reporter snooping around the scene, chattin' it up with the woman detective, had been a bonus. Of course, he'd known who the reporter was. Now, he knew the identity of his next target. She'd know before he was done that her sins could not be hidden. That everyone must pay the price for their unseen acts. Even those on the government's payroll.

Still, a new problem had arisen. Where could he get the necessary supplies to complete his mission? A plan. He needed a plan to find his new supplier, and he had a list of dealers in his treasure book at home. He'd start working on that tomorrow, but for now he had all he needed. He hitched his backpack on his shoulder, making sure the zipper was closed with a mini padlock.

Marta bus 1241 pulled to the curb. An older woman stepped up beside him. Her clear dark skin glowed in the late-afternoon light and her shapeless, flower-print dress swayed in the stifling hot breeze.

Jackdaw stepped backward and motioned the woman onto the bus. He murmured, "Ma'am."

"Thank you, young man." She tilted her chin regally and lifted her foot to the metal steps walking into the gut of the bus. "Gentlemen are hard to find these days."

"Yes, ma'am." He bowed his head in deference, then followed her up the steps, slowing behind her as she slipped into a seat three rows from the front of the bus. He broke eye contact at her friendly smile.

Too much conversation with the locals made him memorable. Memorable led to questions, and questions led to speculation. Best to avoid all that.

When he settled into an empty seat, ignoring the others around him, he pushed out a breath. He'd always been good at chess. Not only would the police never capture him, but he would have the last word.

Checkmate.

Chapter Fourteen

Addison stepped from her truck and locked the door before closing it with a jolt. A new day. A fresh day. A day to find a killer.

Yesterday they'd made some progress going through the evidence—a partial fingerprint they'd processed, a strand of hair sent to the state crime lab—and following up with phone calls. At five o'clock they'd called it a day and went home.

But, today…today could be the day they found that one piece of evidence. Evidence that could expose a killer.

Please, God, let today be that day.

Determination straightened her spine as she jogged through a misting rain to the station doors. Gray clouds hung, forming a heavy blanket across the sky, blotting out the morning sun and obscuring the blue sky beyond.

"Detective Parker?" Joe stood next to the building entrance.

How'd he know when she'd be coming in to work? Or,

did he know? She shook her head. His presence brought too many questions. Hopefully, she'd make it through the article deadline, and they could make progress on this case. "Yes? Haven't you gotten enough 'shadowing' information?"

"No, actually, I haven't. We need to set up a time for your personal interview."

"The shadowing will have to be enough."

"I don't think so." His apologetic tone seemed sincere, but yesterday's events spoke for themselves. He continued speaking when she narrowed her eyes. "Why don't we grab something to eat at the end of your workday? I still need to talk to you about your activities outside work."

A car fishtailed with squealing breaks on the roadway next to the brick building. "I don't think I'll be up to it today."

"Tomorrow then." Not a question, but a statement.

Addison opened the police station door.

He spoke once more, shooting the words out as if he were afraid she would leave before he could finish. "And I need to set up a time to interview your family."

Addison took a deep breath and reached for a polite mask to hide behind when an idea struck. The perfect way to get this man out from under her skin. "I'm having dinner with my family tonight. Why don't you come? Then, we can be done with all of this."

A swift grin crossed his face. "I'd love to. What time?"

"I'll let you know." She turned her back on him once more.

"Directions?"

"We'll square all of that away later. Right now, I've got work to do."

Joe gave her a curt nod. "Of course."

Addison strode through the opened door and began her day with a smile. Tonight would be fun. Wait until her father got a hold of the reporter. The inquisition would begin when her father assumed she was dating the reporter. The dissection process would be fun to watch.

Her smile flipped. Her birthday. She smacked her palm against her forehead. How could she have forgotten that? Tonight's dinner was to celebrate her thirty-fourth birthday. Maybe it wouldn't be as much fun as she thought. She didn't want the reporter involved that deeply in her life. She should retract her invitation, but Joe stood with Davidson deep in conversation.

If she went over and said something, Davidson would react like a bull facing a red cape because he'd been asking her out for almost six months. Talk about complications. Speaking with Joe later would be better.

~

"Vaughn, about dinner tonight—"

Joe watched Addison as she spoke. Her eyes were a little bright, and her gaze continued to skitter away from him. Was she rethinking her invitation? "I'm looking forward to spending time with you and meeting your family. It'll add depth to the article and pull the reader into your life."

Addison shuddered. "I like my privacy."

"Of course you do, but the purpose is to promote your good qualities to draw this maniac into the open. Identify and capture, right?" Joe glanced at McBride as the detective picked up the ringing phone. The man had been ignoring Joe for the last few hours, but he'd been up against tougher adversaries. Besides, Addison was the one he should focus on…for the article.

Addison listened intently to McBride's phone

conversation. He used the time to study her—her long hair tied back, the casual work clothes that remained fashionable, and the glasses she'd shoved on her nose an hour earlier. He rubbed a fist over his breastbone, and then returned to eavesdropping on McBride's conversation.

"Yeah, one of us will be there soon. . . unless you need to see both of us? . . . okay, then. See you in a few." McBride hung up the phone, and then spoke to Addison. "Vonda Foster has found something."

Addison peered over the top rims of her glasses at her partner. "That's great news. All the leads I've been following," she spread her hands, palms up, "have led nowhere. No steady girlfriend. No loud parties. Paid his rent on time. Took care of his mother. If our guy was a drug dealer, he sure didn't live like one."

"How about you visit autopsy and take your shadow," McBride jerked his head toward Joe, then continued, "while I stay here and check the CIC databases."

Joe grinned as he zipped his bag. McBride thought he was talking in coded police speak, but Joe knew and understood the Crime Information Center databases' purpose for researching criminal histories. McBride wanted to look for crimes similar to this killer's pattern.

"Sounds good." Addison laid her glasses on her desktop before she stood, picked up her jacket and badge, then grabbed her keys. "Let's go, Vaughn."

"Absolutely." He tugged his backpack onto his shoulder and sent a mock salute to McBride before following her from the building. The heat and humidity smacked him in the face forcing him to take a deep breath on the way to the car. Man, this kind of weather sucked the breath out of you. "So, you guys think this killer may have struck elsewhere?"

"No, we don't necessarily think he's killed before now. But, if he has, then tracing his pattern and previous locations will help us complete a profile on him."

"You—" Joe stopped, shrugged, "We keep referring to this killer as 'he'. How do you know it's a male?"

"We don't, but patterns found in the psychology behind these types of murders indicate the killer is often a male between the ages of eighteen and forty. It's not an assumption that's one hundred percent accurate, but is often a useful reference to use." Addison opened the driver's door on the unmarked vehicle and hit the unlock button. When Joe slid in the seat beside her, she began speaking once more. "We don't rule out a female killer because there have been women serial killers, but statistically the killer would more likely be a male than a female." She latched her seat belt. Joe squeezed his knees to keep from grabbing the door handle when she made a flying left turn out of the parking lot.

They rode in silence for several minutes. The sun tried peeking out from behind thick clouds multiple times, but the colorless landscape remained unchanged. Hopefully, the weather would be a little more cooperative tonight when he had dinner with Addison. His first date since he'd moved to Atlanta. A business dinner could be considered a date, right? Even if she didn't view it as a date, he did.

Addison rubbed her ear, and then sent a quick glance toward Joe. "Listen, about tonight. What I wanted to say earlier—"

"Where are we going? Is there more information on one of the investigations?" Joe tossed the questions out quickly. Changing the topic seemed the best way to keep her from canceling their plans. He didn't know how he knew her intent, but he did.

She blew out a frustrated breath. "We're going to the medical examiner's office."

Joe gripped his backpack as she zipped through a traffic light. "I see. For which murder has she found evidence?"

"The drug dealer murder we processed Monday."

"Oh." A picture of JG's lifeless eyes staring at Joe had him swallowing. Hard.

He took a deep breath as they pulled into the parking lot of a multilevel brick building. As Addison parked, Joe found himself amazed that he could have been so immersed in her. He'd forgotten to worry about arriving at their destination without injury.

As they approached the building, Joe noted details and surroundings. The landscaped area boasted several large oak and pine trees as well as annual plants adorning the front wall of the building. A large portico oversaw the double sliding glass doors as if to escort visitors into the building in style.

Joe barely suppressed his shiver as he read the bold, black letters mounted on the brick—*Medical Examiner's Office*. He could do this, and he would do this. JG deserved justice and Joe's role was to help set the trap for the killer.

~

Addison made her way toward the front of the building that housed the forensic pathologist and scientist. Vonda Foster and Jeff Lawson made an amazing team even if they didn't agree on much of anything outside of forensics.

Like the reporter and her. She hadn't been able to speak with Joe about the dinner invitation because he kept changing the subject. Maybe she should just suck it up and get it over with. The birthday party would camouflage the real reason for Joe's visit to her family so they wouldn't be worried any more than necessary. She rolled her shoulders as the large weight she'd carried around since issuing the initial invitation dissipated.

As always when she entered the medical examiner's lab, the sharp, pungent odor assaulted her first. The strong scent of formaldehyde stayed with you long after leaving the facility. Luckily, the controlled and cooled environment kept the decomposition at a minimum, but death always made its presence known.

Joe ambled beside her, craning his neck right then left. The man saw everything, and once the questions started, her ears would burn from the nonstop chatter. Annoying, but somehow that was growing on her. His observations often offered a depth she hadn't considered. But, now, this investigation deserved everything she could give it. She sent him a sidelong glance and spoke before they went beyond the doorway. "Don't start asking questions that distract from our investigation."

"No problem, detective." He grinned, and then mimicked locking his lips closed.

She shook her head. If she had to spend much more time with him, he might not make it unscathed. She approached the medical examiner.

Vonda Foster worked over the body of Javarious Glenn, stitching the Y-shaped incision covering the chest closed. The medical examiner had proven to be eerily competent at her job, finding the smallest trace of evidence on the bodies sent to her. Her flame-bright hair secured in a bun shot fire under the fluorescent lights, and her glasses glinted under the plastic shield covering her face when her gaze met Addison's. "Hey, you made good time."

"You call, we come." She hooked her hands on her hips. "Tell me you found something, Vonda."

"Any particular reason for the rush?" The other woman paused after she tied off the heavy stitching twine on JG's chest and clipped it.

"This murder may be linked to our serial killer."

"So that's why this file had a priority tag."

"Ah, I'm sorry, but I have to ask." Joe cleared his throat as both women faced him. "What kind of needle is that?"

Addison closed her eyes. So much for his mouth being locked shut.

Vonda snapped off her latex gloves and pushed her face shield up as she addressed Addison. "Where's McBride? You working this case with a new partner?"

"No, this is Joe Vaughn. He's a reporter getting an inside look at how the department is run." Not the truth, but neither was it a lie.

Joe stared at Vonda, his attention not wavering. He was a patient man, which served his nosiness well.

Holding the curved steel needle so the bright light over the table glinted off the metal, she raised her brows. "This is called a Hagedorn needle. Its primary function is to suture a body back together after an autopsy. A piece of twine is threaded—"

Addison cleared her throat and shot the ME a pointed stare. "You called—"

"Yes. I think I found something." Vonda sauntered to a long table against the back wall. Picking up two round, capped evidence jars, she handed one to Addison. "Mr. Glenn provided a little evidence for us. I found skin cells under the first and middle finger of his left hand." Her tone hardened as her brows slammed down over her eyes when she barked at Joe. "Don't touch my autopsy tools."

Addison glanced back in time to see Joe hold his hands away from the table against the wall, and then moved closer. She narrowed her eyes at him while she spoke to Vonda. "Does this evidence point to a particular suspect?"

"Not yet. I've talked to Lawson, and he said since it's a 'high priority' case," Vonda rolled her eyes, "he'd run a DNA analysis and try to have that to you within a day or two once he gets the samples. He's sending his assistant to pick them up."

"You called to tell us you found evidence that hasn't been tested yet?"

"Of course not. I called to tell you I found evidence of how our friend died." Vonda Pulled on a new set of latex gloves as she moved to the body at the back of the room. "Or, rather, how he didn't die."

Addison snagged a set of gloves and followed. She could feel Joe peering over her shoulder, hear him breathing, but she tuned him out as Vonda shifted the victim's head left, exposing the stitched area behind the left ear from the autopsy as well as a softened patch near the back of the head.

The ME continued to press around the soft spot. "This area is obviously where our victim took a blow to the head." She pulled the skin tight. "Glass shards from the object used left these small puncture wounds in the scalp. My guess would be a ceramic lamp or a vase. Could have been anything that would shatter on impact, but given that the body was found in a living room area, a lamp would make the most sense."

"There was a shattered lamp at the scene." Joe opened his mouth until Addison held her hand up in warning. He closed it and remained silent. She turned back to Vonda in time to see the other woman's eyes taking in both of them with a grin curving her lips.

"I sent the collected shards with the skin cell samples for testing." Returning the head to an upright position, Vonda pointed to the wound behind the temple area. "As soon as I received the body, I swabbed the right temple area and found traces of gunpowder residue, but" she reached for his right hand, "there was no residue found on the corresponding hand."

Addison pulled off her latex gloves. "Then he was unconscious when the gun was used?"

Vonda nodded, paused for a moment, and then looked at Addison. "Mr. Glenn *did not* shoot himself."

Addison raised an eyebrow. "You're sure."

"Oh, yeah. Someone helped our friend to his death."

Chapter Fifteen

"I could've picked *you* up," were Joe's first words as he slid into the passenger seat of Addison's Ranger.

She raised an eyebrow at him. "This is not a date, Vaughn." She looked backwards as she reversed out of the apartment complex parking space. "Besides, I don't want you returning to ask my parents questions."

Joe's glance slid toward her. The dark satin sheet of her hair slid across the shoulders her sundress left bare. He jerked his eyes back to her face. "I'm a journalist, Parker. I can find your parents without your help."

"Then why didn't you?" Her glance slid to him as they stopped at a light.

"Respect for you."

Addison returned her gaze to the mirror. "Okay."

Her tone made it clear she didn't believe his response,

but so what? His explanation was honest, but he forgot about trying to convince her when her dress slid to the top of her knee as she maneuvered the vehicle onto the highway. Joe swallowed several times and contained his runaway thoughts. Thoughts she wouldn't appreciate.

"Vaughn?"

"Hm? Why do you keep looking in the rearview mirror?" He jerked his eyes toward her once more.

"Just being careful, and I asked how that is respect for me?"

Drawing a blank on the thread of conversation, he scrambled to find the memory of how the discussion began. His synapses must have taken a vacation. "Respect?"

"You said not finding my parents without letting me know was showing respect for me."

"Oh." He gazed out the windshield and struggled to keep his voice nonchalant. "Because you deserve to know that I'm talking to your family."

"Hang on. I believe we've picked up company."

That was the only warning he got before she made a sharp turn off the highway without slowing down, and then sped up on a two-lane country road interspersed with wooded areas and narrow driveways. He jerked in a breath and gripped the door handle until he could right himself. His glance searched the passenger side mirror. "What's going on?"

"I thought we had a follower."

"Thought?" Joe swiveled his head to peer out the back window of the truck cab. The road behind them remained empty of other travelers. "I don't see anyone."

"Mm. False alarm. The car continued straight after we turned." She sent him a small smile, almost a reassurance.

Joe's eyes widened as he understood her meaning. "It couldn't be the killer? My article hasn't been printed, or even written, yet." His hands fisted in his lap as possibilities began filtering through his mind.

"Like I said, false alarm."

Joe inhaled a deep breath to give his pulse a chance to slow down. Her abrupt turn combined with her suspicions sent him on an adrenaline rush from which he still needed to recover. Above the tree line a hawk soared, weaving back and forth, back and forth. A predator on the hunt. Like the predator they searched for. A killer with disturbing intent aimed at innocent victims.

Jackdaw.

Joe leaned an elbow on the console between them. "Why Jackdaw?"

Addison glanced his way, and then focused on the road once more. "I don't understand."

"Why would the killer want to be known as a bird? That must be significant."

"Good point." She reached up to push a chunk of hair behind her ear. "What do you know about jackdaws?"

He injected confidence in his answer. "Not much, but I can find out. Anything that would help the investigation." *Help you.*

His unspoken words hung between them as a picture of Addison lying in JG's place caused a shudder to run down his spine. They had to figure this killer out before Addison ran out of time.

The truck rolled to a stop at the single traffic light where an empty two-lane road cut through the town's main street. A sign posted on the corner of the intersection proclaimed, *Massey, Georgia: A beautiful place to raise a family.*

Because he had grown up and had lived around large cities all his life, being in the country, around nature's beauty, should've been a treat, but he couldn't get beyond their current situation to enjoy it.

Joe turned back to face her. "How far do your parents live from here?"

"Not far."

He took a deep breath. Amazing that he could feel fine tremors travelling through his fingers. Why? He'd never had a story affect him like this. What made this one different? Even as his mind shouted "Nothing", his heart continued to pound. He had to get his mind off her and on his purpose in writing the article.

"Are most days at the station like today? Shuffling papers and writing reports?"

"Aside from the visit to the forensics lab, a lot of them get monotonous, but not all." She shrugged in the dusky twilight.

"How do you keep from becoming bored?"

"Tracking down perpetrators and making sure the district attorney has what he needs isn't boring to me. Plus, I'm grateful for those slow days because it means no one else has been injured, arrested, or murdered."

Joe hummed a wordless response as she turned onto a graveled drive.

Wooded areas of oak and pine lined the long pathway until a clearing revealed a two-story plantation style house. Through the dying sunlight, the pale-yellow siding darkened, and the white shutters glowed. Light poured through the downstairs windows while the top level remained dark. The classic elegance fit Addison's personality.

Addison parked between a sky-blue compact car and a

maroon SUV and switched the ignition off with a slowness unnatural for her. Releasing her seatbelt, she rested her arm on the console, her hand fisted "You are *not* to tell my family about this article or the reason behind it. I will not have them worrying about me."

Joe stared at her with his brows beetled. "Why am I here then?"

"We're friends. That's what you're to tell them." She stepped out of the truck.

He faced her across the hood, and then hesitated for a nanosecond. "Are we?"

She rubbed her neck as if wiping away the events of the day. Dusk's light caused auburn fire to dance through the loose, dark strands of her hair. "Are we what?"

"Friends." He tried to force his lips to curve, but her answer was too important.

Addison remained motionless for a moment, looking at him as if she couldn't figure him out, and then shrugged. "Sure." She turned and continued up the walkway to the house's front porch. Her flat sandals crunched on the loose gravel beneath her feet.

He blew out the breath he'd been holding, then jogged to catch up with her. "Okay."

She flipped her hair behind her shoulders absently, and then rang the bell before opening the door.

"Why did you ring the bell if the door was unlocked?"

"To let everyone know I'm here." Her placating tone suggested he wasn't too bright if he couldn't figure that out.

"Ah." Why would she want to announce her arrival? She didn't strike him as a vain person.

When they stepped over the threshold the overwhelming stillness inside the house seemed out of place with the bright rooms. The foyer opened into a living room and a formal dining room facing off across the entryway. Both rooms were decorated with accents of navy blue and brick red so that one appeared to be a continuation of the other. It made a picture that could have graced the pages of a Better Homes & Garden magazine. A comfortable, lived in room.

Addison stood statue-like with her chin dropped to her chest. She squeezed her eyes shut, pressing her fingers against both, before snapping her head back up and speaking to Joe. "Come on, *friend*, let's get this over with."

Get what over with? He opened his mouth to ask, but her closed expression shut it once more. He followed her down the central hallway toward the back of the house. When they entered the darkened kitchen, the lights flickered on as a crowd yelled "surprise" synchronously.

She didn't act surprised, but he almost wet his pants.

His heart thundered in his chest as Addison received hugs and birthday wishes from each person there. She'd invited him to her birthday party? He looked at her forced cheer and clenched fists. Why had she agreed to the dinner when she obviously didn't want to be here?

A woman with silver-salted dark hair released Addison from a long hug. "Happy Birthday, sweetheart." Her gaze rested on him next, brows raised. "Who's this? A new boyfriend?"

The woman carried the same petite form, the same dark coloring, the same unfathomable eyes as Addison. If this is what the detective would look like in twenty years or so, she'd still be a knockout.

He watched in fascination as Addison colored. "No, Mom. We're just friends."

"Ma'am." Joe inclined his head.

"There's my girl," a loud booming baritone echoed from the hallway off the kitchen just before a tall man grabbed Addison.

Addison laughed as her feet left the floor. "Hi, Daddy."

Her father's gray hair had receded until a single ring remained circling his head like a Roman crown of fig leaves, but his pale blue eyes remained sharp as they locked on the stranger in the room. "Who's this you've brought home?"

"Just a friend. Dad, Mom, meet Joe…"

"Joseph Vaughn, sir." He held out his hand and looked up at least two inches to meet the gaze of the man dismantling him with a blue-laser stare.

Mr. Parker lowered Addison to the floor and grasped Joe's hand. Hard. Joe managed to keep the wince from his face as his bones were crushed, and he pumped the man's hand in return, once. Addison smirked at him.

"When's dinner, Lyn?" Parker's baritone addressed his wife, but his eyes remained on Joe.

"In about twenty minutes. You've got time to get to know Mr. Vaughn a little better. We'll hold dinner for the two of you." Lyn Parker shook her head.

"Good, good. Vaughn, walk with me and let me show you my property." Parker clapped Joe on the shoulder then grasped the back of his neck and steered him toward the kitchen's back door.

"But, sir, it's getting dark outside." Joe looked back where Addison stood with her arms crossed and satisfaction glowing from her eyes.

"Scared of the dark?" Parker waited until Joe gave a negative headshake. "Good, good." He shouted to the group behind them. "We'll be back in time for dinner."

All chatter had silenced during the interchange. Joe

straightened the collar of his shirt and cleared his throat. The door closing behind them muted the conversation and laughter that had resumed.

Two hours later Joe sat back in the chair and watched as the family began cleaning up the party remnants and chattering good-naturedly. It had been an interesting night. Being grilled by her father about his and Addison's relationship had been worth getting to spend time with this dynamic family. He stood holding the festive bows he'd collected as Addison opened her gifts before laying them on top of the last gift box opened and spoke to Lyn. "How may I help, Mrs. Parker?"

"You can help keep Justin out of my Peace Lily while this group finishes cleaning my house." She jerked her head to the toddler heading for the large plant beside the corner window.

Everyone had their part in the clean-up process just as everyone had their part in the family, and he could do his. He straightened his shoulders and approached the small boy. His chest ached as he thought of the damage wrought to this family should anything happen to Addison because of his articles.

~

Joe waited in the truck while Addison said good-bye to her family. When she'd almost reached the door, a noise beyond the outdoor lights had her studying the darkness. Shadows condensed until a vague shape hovered behind the trees, but with a blink the shape was gone. Addison suppressed the shiver racing through her as she climbed into the driver's seat and turned the ignition.

"Something wrong?"

Addison jolted at the sudden question. "No. I don't think

so." She exhaled loudly. "I think I'm just jumpy because I've been worried about my family finding out. Thank you for not telling them."

His face in shadow, Joe said, "Your family's great. I enjoyed spending tonight with them. With you."

"Hmm." The evening replayed in Addison's mind like a broken record. Joe walking uncertainly out with her father, Joe's joy in being handed a bow, Joe chasing her nephew down the hallway. Joe, Joe, Joe. . . She should be focusing, planning, preparing to find justice for three women instead of worrying over her personal life.

His voice cut through her thoughts once more. "I didn't know it was your birthday. Happy Birthday."

"Thanks."

"You don't look thirty-four."

Addison could only make out his profile in the darkness of the truck's cab. "What's thirty-four supposed to look like?"

"Well," Joe cleared his throat, "it looks older than you."

The outline of her nodded in the darkness. "A very diplomatic answer."

She accelerated once they were on the highway. When she signaled to pass a slower car, Joe's sharp inhale was audible.

He said, "Do you think you should drive a little slower perhaps?"

She snorted. "Why? I'm a safe driver."

Joe responded with a choking noise. Did he not think she knew how to drive? But he had gotten along with her family, and he had kept the truth behind his visit confidential. Admitting he wasn't such a bad guy after all wasn't easy. Trusting him harder still. Her emotions roiled with unease, her mind rebelling after years of habit, but her heart had begun to beat with an unfamiliar rhythm anytime he was near. Anytime she thought about him. Anytime she heard his name. Just because her family liked him, didn't mean she had to like him as well.

"Your Dad seemed to like me."

"Weird, huh?" Even her father had given his blessings. Could her changing feelings be wrong?

Joe's voice softened until she almost missed his answer. "No, I liked him, too."

As she parked in front of his door and reached out to turn down the radio, Joe took her hand and leaned over to brush his lips across her knuckles.

When he lifted his head, his face scant inches away from hers, he said, "Thanks for tonight."

"You're welcome," came out as a whisper.

When he leaned toward her, Addison found herself unable to move. Eyes opened, staring into his, his lips settled on hers lightly, softly. His hand clenched around hers and his eyes closed as he leaned in to firm the kiss. When he ran his tongue along the seam of her lips, Addison pulled back, shocked at the intimacy and equally shocked at wanting him to continue.

"Dinner tomorrow."

Addison's mind cleared as the surplus of sensations dissipated. "What about dinner tomorrow?"

"I want to take you to dinner tomorrow. In return for tonight."

"Only if you go to church with me too." The hasty statement caused her breath to back up in her throat. After their conversation about his mother, she'd wanted to ask him to church. Through the dim light streaming in through the front window she watched his throat work as he swallowed.

He hesitated, and then his head bobbed in the moonlit darkness. "I'll pick you up. Five-thirty?"

"No time for that. I'll meet you instead." If he picked her up, it would be too much like a date. Better to keep it on a professional level.

"Ok." He sat in the shadows, the streetlights of his apartment complex cutting a swath between them like the Great Divide. Addison watched him get out of the truck and walk to his door. Her truck lights burned against his back until he closed his apartment door.

Every instinct she had shouted that Joseph Vaughn embodied the slippery slope of trouble for her heart. Trouble that may be too late to avoid.

Chapter Sixteen

Addison wrote a final statement on the report covering Monday's homicide. She closed her eyes and rolled her head from side to side.

Lord, please bring us a break in this case soon.

Her gaze rested on her phone. Maybe Lawson would find some new forensic evidence today since Vonda had sent him trace evidence from the body.

Glancing sideways at Joe, she eyed the crop of hair that fell over his brow. He sat in his chair watching the activity around them before scribbling notes on his pad. When her visual survey of the room showed nothing special, she shook her head. The guy was crazy curious, that was for sure.

Addison straightened her spine and jerked her attention back to the paperwork on her desk. Watching him again? She'd lost count of how many times she'd found herself looking at him, wondering, and it wasn't even ten o'clock.

And she'd lost more sleep than she should have because of him. Because of that kiss. The time was at hand to deny him this power over her. In the clear light of morning, it was obvious she'd put too much emphasis on last night. Joe Vaughn was still a reporter, still pushing for an angle, still too immature. Allowing a relationship to form between them would be a mistake.

A big mistake. Colossal.

The thought of trying to survive another bad relationship had her sucking in a fortifying breath. She'd barely made it through the last one.

The phone rang on McBride's desk. "Hey, Lawson." Her partner scrawled across a white notepad with a pencil he'd grabbed. "Yeah. . . I got it. . . so the chain and the syringe have been processed. . . uh-huh, uh-huh."

Addison leaned on her desk.

Finally, McBride hung up. "They determined the chain found at the site to be Javarious Glenn's. Fingerprints on it matched Glenn's according to AFIS. Skin residue in addition to the marks and bruising around the victim's neck indicates he wore the chain during a scuffle, and they likely occurred before his death."

Joe lifted a finger and opened his mouth. Addison glared at him. *If he asked one more question, she would...*

He closed his mouth.

She turned back to her partner. "What about the needle?"

"Lawson said the hypodermic needle did produce a DNA match." McBride stopped, glanced at the paper. "It belongs to Timothy Baxter, a.k.a. Little Tim." He lifted his eyes once more and shook his head. "His rap sheet reads like a druggie's grocery list: armed robbery, vandalism, assault, drug possession."

"Sounds like he may be our man." She finessed her computer keys until she'd accessed the electronic file on Timothy Baxter.

Addison leaned back while she studied the picture on her screen. A gaunt Caucasian male with long, limp brown hair, brown eyes, and a scraggly beard stared at her from the screen. She clicked the print icon, and then switched to view the man's arrest records and personal information. "He's got an Atlanta address. Near the GA State stadium."

"While you're in there," McBride pointed to the computer screen, "request a search warrant based on the evidence we've found at the murder scene, and I'll make some calls to get the warrant processed ASAP. We don't want him bolting."

Thirty-minutes later, McBride stood, grabbed his weapon, and pushed it into his side holster. "I have a go on the warrant so let's pick up Little Tim."

Addison stood and mirrored her partner's actions. She faced Joe before walking out the door. "You can ride along with us since you found the evidence, *but* if you step outside the car, you will be arrested. Do you understand?"

Joe jerked his head once, then moved to follow her.

Once settled, McBride glanced at Joe in the backseat. "Uh-uh, pal, you aren't going." He waggled his thumb toward the brick building. "Get out."

Addison shook her head. True to form, McBride was holding onto his grudge. "I told him he could ride along since he found the evidence, and that I'd arrest him if he got out of the vehicle."

McBride stared at her with his mouth opening and closing like a hooked fish.

Addison crossed her arms and waited.

Her partner took a deep breath. "You've got to be kidding me, Parker. Your now suddenly on his side?"

She laid a hand on McBride's arm. "You know he's essential to pulling off this entire plan. Your bright idea has landed us here so you can't back out now. We've got to stop this guy."

He huffed out a breath and turned to spear Joe with narrowed eyes. "If you get out of this car, you'll have more to worry about than being arrested. Like losing your precious exclusive." He turned back around, reaching for the handset of the radio as Addison started the car. "We'll need back-up to meet us at Trinity Avenue."

During the twenty-minute ride, RJ called out tidbits of information they needed to know while she dodged traffic. The heat seemed to make the pavement undulate before them, but she focused on the task at hand. It would do no good to let frustration cause them to make a mistake. Once parked, she ran her gaze across the area. Their back up sat one block up, visible yet waiting. She parallel parked in front of the run-down complex. The single-story eight-apartment units comprised one of Atlanta's poorest and most crime infested areas.

Addison and McBride climbed out of the car proceeded toward apartment 8C as a unified team. Addison's muscles tightened and she pushed her jacket behind her gun holster as they approached and moved to either side of the door. Addison held the ripped screen door open as McBride knocked.

Before he could identify them, a hoarse female voice called through the warped wooden barrier. "Yeah? Who is it?"

Addison responded. "Police. We're here to speak with Timothy Baxter."

"Ain't no Timothy Baxter here." The woman's rushed words spoken in the octave of panic made a lie of the statement.

Was she hiding something? Or, someone? Addison shouted through the door. "Open up. We have a warrant to search these premises."

McBride signaled Addison with a roll of his eyes just before a window smashed beside Addison. She ducked, one arm covering her head, as glass sprayed over her and the bushes beyond while the other reached for her weapon.

McBride pulled his gun and kicked in the door.

~

Joe watched in fascination as Addison and McBride approached the apartment. Their matched movements seemed almost choreographed like an on-stage production.

His chest tightened at Addison's courage. She wasn't a woman to back down.

When the roar of the window crashed around her, Joe's fists clenched on his mechanical pencil until it snapped in two. One glance proved there was no handle to roll down the window in the backseat. He couldn't yell, couldn't help, couldn't even get out of the car. He slapped a hand against the window before he realized he'd moved.

Addison looked at the door and spoke once more. "Open up. We have a warrant to search these premises."

Joe threw his notebook and broken pencil aside and climbed into the front seat to roll down the car's driver window as two uniformed officers ran past the car.

A shrill scream shot through the chaos. "Timmy, no!" A thin, emaciated man jumped through the jagged opening before scrambling into a run and veering right as the two uniforms headed for him.

Addison ran in pursuit. McBride ran behind her slowing to shout to the two officers, "Secure the house," then focused his attention on Addison and the suspect.

The breathable air around Joe evaporated as Addison closed the distance between her and the suspect. Though the man was a good head taller, she took him down before he crossed the street in front of the apartment. Joe grunted as Addison took an elbow punch on the cheek before her partner could reach them. She was amazing and capable, but protective instincts he didn't know he possessed rose, choking him with the need to keep her safe.

He wiped his sweating brow with his shirt cuff and took a deep breath.

Only a few minutes had passed before the man was subdued and cuffed, but the time had seemed unending. McBride stuffed the man into the black and white vehicle, while Addison interviewed the woman standing in the open doorway.

Finally, Addison limped her way over to him. "You're still in the car, huh?" When he shook his head, she laughed. "Good boy."

"You. . ." Joe stopped, cleared his throat. His gaze ran across her face, stopping on the shallow cuts marring her clear skin. "Are you alright?"

"Yeah. The goon fell on my ankle and a couple of little-bitty cuts." She waved at the slices above her brow. "I'll be fine."

"Your—" Joe motioned to her already swelling cheek.

She pressed the area, winced, then shrugged. "Nothing a little makeup won't cover."

McBride spoke behind her, wiping his bleeding lip on a handkerchief. "Addy, do you need a trip to urgent care?"

She turned sideways. "Nah. I'm fine."

McBride continued. "The search didn't turn up the missing murder weapon. I read Baxter his rights and the officers will take him in for processing."

"Good. Before we get to the paperwork, I believe it's lunch time." Her grin merely bared her teeth. "I'm starving."

When she glanced his way, Joe said, "I could eat."

Her perplexed look at his championing had his face heating and her partner laughing.

~

Five o'clock arrived without fanfare. Addison parked at Waffle House and sat, letting the cool air-conditioning flow across her face and arms.

Had she lost her mind agreeing to go to dinner with Joe? Inviting him to church with her?

When this entire investigation began, she had meant to keep her distance. When had that changed?

When you started seeing him as more than a reporter.

Addison scowled into the visor mirror as she dusted powder foundation over the bruised circle on her cheek. She couldn't lie to herself. She had anticipated this evening's dinner and church meeting. Not exactly a date, but the closest to it she'd gotten in three years. There had been the occasional dinner with a friend, nights out with a blind date, group gatherings where she inevitably found herself paired with someone, but all had been tiresome and annoying.

Then, she'd asked herself, what was the point? She didn't plan on getting involved with anyone, so she began deflecting conversations hinting at evenings out and limiting her outings with her married friends after work to avoid sticky situations.

But, somehow Golden-boy had gotten under her skin. He had wormed his way into her life and into her mind as if she were an apple in the Garden of Eden. She couldn't avoid him because of his role in the murder investigation. She couldn't stop thinking about him, either.

She'd never had trouble controlling her thoughts before. Why was he different?

Except for Marcus. Her ex-fiancé had elicited those same reactions in her. Her excitement to be with him. Her inability to stop thinking about him. Rearranging her schedule to fit his. Never again, she'd sworn, and she meant to stick to that promise. Wasn't the price she'd paid for her belief in Marcus lesson enough?

She pushed into the restaurant's cool, relaxed interior to wait for Joe. He'd left after lunch to begin working on the article. Then, she had been able to concentrate.

Looking around, she found a corner booth presenting a semi-private area for conversation. She wasn't sure what questions he'd ask, but having others covertly listening to her private life wasn't at all appealing. Still, she chose this particular eating establishment because it didn't shout romance, and it would keep them on equal footing.

A waitress, wreathed in smiles, stopped by her table and laid a menu down before Addison. Her name tag read Linda, and her long hair was pulled away from her round face. "Welcome to Waffle House. You ready to order?"

"Not yet. I'm waiting on a friend."

"Um-hm" Linda winked. "Can I getcha something to drink while you wait?"

Addison forced her lips to curve. "Sure. How about a glass of ice water, no lemon?"

"Sure. I'll get that to ya in a minute." The woman walked the short distance behind the counter.

Addison focused on the window beside her. Outside, the traffic passed with soundless speed as a Honda slowed and turned into the restaurant's parking lot. She could see Joe, black shades in place, as he parked in the empty space next to her truck.

The waitress sat a clear glass of water in front of her, and then sat two menus on the table. Addison said, "Thank you," without taking her eyes from the man climbing from his car.

"Anytime, hon." The waitress pulled a straw from her apron pocket. "Let me know when you're ready to order."

"Thanks."

The woman left to check on a family sitting two tables down as Joe sauntered through the double glass doors. He stopped and looked around the small restaurant. When his gaze locked with hers, his lips tilted just short of a grin before walking toward the table.

He sat down across from her and folded his hands. He wore no rings, and an average Fossil watch that could be picked up anywhere rode his wrist. Just the average Joe out for dinner with a friend.

"Hi." His toe began a rat-ta-tat-tat rhythm against the floor. "I see you're sitting facing the door. Looking for me?"

His cheeky grin made her raise a brow even as the tapping sound of his discomfort made her smile. "Habit. I like to know who's entering the building, so I'm not caught off guard. Did you get your article started?"

"Yes." He nodded. "I've gotten the draft finished, and I'll work on adding details from today, revisions, and proofreading tomorrow. The article should be ready by tomorrow evening."

Addison looked at the menu in her hands. If this was the only way the killer could be caught, so be it. She'd deal with the fall out afterward. Before arriving, she'd made a resolution that for every thought she revealed, by golly, he'd reveal one too. She refused to be the only person baring souls. He would have to understand that prying into her life warranted the same invitation for her to pry into his. If she had to be uncomfortable, then he would squirm as well.

Laying the menu down in front of her, she met his gaze. "Okay, let's order. While we're waiting you may question me, but I must warn you: for every question you ask, I will ask one of you in return." She motioned for the waitress.

"And if I don't answer?"

"Neither will I."

He quirked his head and stared at her for a moment. Joe inclined his head and said, "Sounds fair."

"I'm glad you think so. Equality is a high priority for me." She scanned her dinner choices. She loved breakfast foods. Too bad she hated cooking in the mornings.

Both of them ordered and his orange juice arrived before they resumed their conversation. Nothing else could delay the inevitable.

Addison gritted her teeth and bared them at Joe in a grim semblance of a smile. "Let's get this over with."

He shook his head in acknowledgement. "Answering my questions won't be too bad. I mean, what do you think I'm going to ask?"

"Since I don't think like you, I wouldn't know."

"Well, I promise this will be painless." Once more he locked gazes with her. When she gave him a stiff nod, he reached into his jacket pocket and fished out a small notebook and pen. As he laid them on the table, he said, "I have a good memory, but I'll still take some notes."

Joe raised his head and locked gazes with her. A zing bolted through her stomach as his interest became clear, but she took a deep breath and pushed it away. She had to be imagining any kind of feelings for a reporter.

He cleared his throat. "Tell me what your fondest memory from childhood would be."

Addison's mouth opened, closed, and opened again. "When my dad would drive me to school in his patrol car. I loved it. I always pretended that I was solving a crime with him and that we were the dynamic duo of law enforcement." A dreamy look touched her eyes before they cleared to spear him with intensity. "Now, your fondest memory."

Joe paused as he reached for his water glass. He took a long drink, and then cleared his throat. "Okay. It was probably when my father and mother would plan some type of weekend outing for us. We never had much money, but somehow they always came up with something creative for us to do. Once I read *The Three Musketeers*, I came to think of our family as a team like the Musketeers." He paused, glanced over her right shoulder, then trailed his eyes back to her and shrugged. "So, you and your father have both worked in law enforcement. Have any of your sisters or your brothers-in-law followed this career path as well?"

"I am the only one that shares my dad's interest in law enforcement. Both of my sisters are teachers. Like Mom. One of my brothers-in-law is in the military on active duty, and the other is a computer technician for an Atlanta-based company."

"You've never had the desire to teach like your mother and sisters?"

Addison shrugged. "Sure, that's why I teach every week

at church. I love kids, and I love seeing their faces as they learn something new. But I enjoy seeing justice at work on behalf of innocent victims more so that's why I spend most of my time as a detective."

Joe noted her responses on his pad. When he refocused on her, she fired a question back at him. "Where did you grow up?"

"I grew up in Matthews, North Carolina. Outside Charlotte. Mecklenburg County."

"North Carolina, huh? How did you end up in Atlanta?"

"That's two questions."

"You asked me two in a row." She shrugged, and then looked over as the waitress appeared, bringing their plates and placing the fragrant food on the table before them. Taking a deep breath, she closed her eyes to savor the fragrance of bacon, eggs, and waffles. When she opened her eyes, he was staring at her with a small smile on his face. She flushed. "Problem?"

He shook his head. "No."

The other woman broke the moment when she sat the final plate in front of Joe. "Can I get y'all anything else?"

He shook his head. "Not right now. Thanks."

"Okay. Just yell if you need me." With that she returned to the counter and started a conversation with a balding customer seated next to the register.

Joe spoke while Addison poured syrup over her waffle. "How long have you taught children at church?"

She paused and glanced at him, letting him know she saw through his attempt not to answer her question, and then answered anyway. "Since I was in high school. I started out as a teacher's helper, and then by the time I was a senior I was given my own class to teach. I've always loved it, so

I've continued to volunteer in the 5-year-old class."

"The group I saw on Sunday is an active bunch. I bet they keep you busy."

"Yeah, but I can keep up with them for an hour a week. Plus, I have a classroom helper." She gave him the full force of her attention as she repeated her question. "How did you wind up in Atlanta?"

He would answer her this time or she wouldn't play his game of twenty questions.

Chapter Seventeen

One question circled through Joe's thoughts: how deep would she probe?

He chewed as his mind raced through acceptable but vague responses— a response that would satisfy Addison's curiosity without opening past pain. "You could say that I needed to expand my horizons."

"How do you call going from an investigative reporter at *The Charlotte Observer* to a reporter of everything for a small local newspaper expanding your horizons?"

Okay. He should've known that wouldn't work. Her quick mind left him breathless. "I wasn't working as an investigative reporter when I left Charlotte."

Finished with her bacon and eggs, Addison slid the porcelain dish aside and propped her chin on a palm. "Why not?"

"Circumstances dictated a change."

"Oh, no, you are not getting off that easily." She held her hand up, motioning with four fingers for him to keep going. "Give up. What circumstances?"

The crash of a dropped tray and broken dishes faded into white noise as Addison's questions opened the door on facts, events, memories, allowing them to flick through his mind like a silent film showcasing all he'd locked away.

Joe hitched his shoulders once, and then watched the sky darken outside the restaurant window just as his soul had darkened during that time. Maybe he'd never get over what happened...what God had allowed to happen. "When my Mom got sick, I wasn't able to meet my deadlines. By the time everything was over, I didn't have much of a job left. The premier stories I had been covering were given to other, more available, writers." He lifted a shoulder. "I'd do it all over again. My mother was worth more than my job."

Silence stretched between them while Addison studied him.

"My turn." Joe reached for his glass once more. "If you had to explain your belief system to someone else, what would you say?"

"What would I say?" Addison stopped, stared out the window while she flexed her jaw. "I think I would tell the other person that I have never had a friend like Jesus or a father like God. My every need has always been filled. My every hurt, soothed." Addison paused, took a sip of her water. "I'd invite them to church with me so they could meet God through His word and His body of believers. Those who exemplify His love and His caring."

"Like you invited me?" Joe tilted his head as he waited for her response.

"Yes."

"Are you involved with someone in a personal relationship?"

Addison's response was quick and immediate. "No."

"Have you ever been involved with someone?"

"Yes. Once."

"Tell me about it."

"How does this relate to the article you're writing?"

"Your answer will demonstrate how your faith helps you deal with life every day. The article will focus on both your personal and professional life."

"He turned out to be scum. I'm glad to be rid of him. End of story."

"What happened between the two of you?"

"I don't think this is necessary for your story."

Joe's heart raced in his chest. He couldn't let it go. He had to know what had happened. "Your history is more relevant than mine."

She stared at him for a long moment, and then shrugged. "I believed in him as any trusting woman in love would. He was a musician, and he convinced me that he needed certain music equipment for his band and a van to transport the equipment. He had a job, but he hadn't established credit, or so he told me, so everything was purchased in my name."

Addison paused. "Why aren't you taking notes?"

"I'm listening. That's as good as writing everything down." Joe's familiar half-smile appeared.

"He proposed. I accepted. Then we started looking at houses and furniture. The more we purchased for our new life together, the more excited I became." Addison took another sip of water. After a deep breath, she pushed through the hardest part of the story. "About two months before our set wedding date, I was sent out of town for a week of training. When I returned, he was gone."

"Just like that?"

"Yep. He left me a letter, of course, explaining his need to go where his music was appreciated. He left, taking everything we purchased together except the house. So, I was left with an empty house, a huge amount of debt in my name, and a letter." She gave him a grim look. "Asking around where he hung out, I discovered that he and his back-up singer were a hot item, and they had left town together."

Joe's attention refocused on Addison. She picked up her knife and fork before looking at him. "So, after your Mom died, why did you decide to move to Atlanta?"

Joe pushed the eggs around until they resembled abstract art before looking back up. "I found out about this new start up paper in Fulton County online. I submitted a resume, drove down here to interview and look around at living spaces, and two months later, it was a done deal. A fresh start."

Addison tilted her head. "Do you think you'll ever want to move back? To be near where your Mom is buried?"

"I don't know. It's hard to know what the future will bring. She's resting next to my Dad so that gives me comfort that after all the years they were parted, now they're together again." Joe lifted his head.

She lay her hands in her lap as she stared at Joe. "And that gives you comfort?"

He cleared his throat, blinking his eyes several times before speaking. "Yeah, it does."

"Can I ask what caused your mother's death?"

"Breast cancer."

"I'm sorry to hear that." Addison laid a hand over his fist resting beside his plate. "It sounds as if you were close to her."

"I was." The warmth of her hand seeped into his cold fingers and eased the ache deep in his chest.

"I'm sure she was proud of you."

"I hope so." The thought of making his mom proud was what kept him going, but he couldn't tell her that. There were no words that could describe how hurt and lost he'd been once she was gone. And, there were no words to describe how he ached when he thought of everything he wasn't able to share with her.

"She would've been proud of you no matter what. Mothers are like that. Even when they tell you you're wrong, they're still proud of you." Addison pulled her hand back, breaking their contact. She balled her hand into a fist and laid it beside her plate.

The waitress approached, a hot carafe in hand, lips curved in a friendly mask. "Coffee for either of you?"

"No, thank you."

"None, for me either. Thanks." Joe's head cocked left as he glanced at the waitress, details etching into place. She had freshened up, added lipstick and eye make-up. His curiosity spiked. "Big plans after work?"

Her smile widened, became a real smile. A happy smile. "I hope so."

"Well, have a good time."

"Thanks. It'll be a first date, and I haven't had one of those in a while so I'm kind of nervous. He's a little younger than me, but I like him a lot." Linda reached up to tuck a strand of blonde-streaked hair back into a neatened bundle.

"Have you known him long?"

"No, his name is Jack. I just met him." She pulled their receipt from her pocket and laid it on the table's edge.

"Whenever y'all are ready you can pay at the register." With that she turned and bounced back behind the counter.

Joe grabbed the check before Addison could react. "I'll pay since you answered my questions so patiently."

"You answered mine, too."

"Yeah, but dinner last night was on you. Tonight, it's my turn." With that he slid from the booth and strode to the register.

A few moments later, the humid night air surrounded him as he spotted her, leaning against her truck in the parking lot, star gazing. Her hair pulled back from her face in a tail, bounced on her shoulders, and her face was soft and relaxed. He'd thought she was beautiful the first time he saw her, but now, she was stunning. The inner beauty he'd glimpsed this week enhanced the physical that had drawn him in the beginning.

She glanced at him, then back to the darkened sky once he joined her. "I've always loved looking at the stars, trying to find the glorious patterns of nature God provides. Each bright, twinkling dot soothes my soul."

"I've always found astronomy fascinating myself, though I'm far from a scientist."

"You don't have to be a scientist to enjoy beauty."

"True."

"Ready to go?"

"I suppose so."

"Okay." Addison straightened, and then pulled her keys from her purse. She froze and almost suppressed a shiver.

"What's wrong?"

"Nothing, I think." She scanned the parking lot and restaurant windows. "I can't explain why, but I'm uneasy."

Joe glanced around them. "I don't see anything out of

the ordinary." Even as he spoke a shudder raced down his spine.

"Me either." Her keys jangled as she unlocked her truck door. "Follow me, and we'll be at the church in no time."

"Sure."

They drove out of the restaurant parking lot with Joe's fender almost kissing her back bumper. His hands shook, and his mind raced. Was he crazy to go to church with her?

Yeah, he was.

Crazy about her. He'd do just about anything to spend time with her. Should he confess his feelings? Would she even care how he felt? His hands tightened on the steering wheel. Sharing any personal information would have to wait. There could be nothing that might jeopardize their plan to catch the killer hanging onto his words.

Addison turned right into a large parking lot. When he'd first visited to see her Sunday School class, he'd expected steeples and white-washed wooden clapboards and people dressed in finery, but reality mocked his pre-conceived ideas. He saw nothing like the churches in his hometown.

A large, brick building sat mid-way around the circular drive and sported outdoor lights that lined the walkways and highlighted the building's entrance. People of all ages strolled, walked, ran as their excitement dictated. Most everyone's dress remained casual, many wearing jeans. He looked more dressed up in his khaki's and collared shirt than most of the people passing by his car window. His shoulders relaxed, loosening his neck muscles. At least he wouldn't be a weed among roses.

As they entered the church building, Addison mutually greeted those she passed. He followed two steps behind and marveled at her ease in speaking with everyone around her.

At work, she commanded authority and respect, but here she was respected because of the love she demonstrated to others.

Two blond streaks of lightning ran past him, shouting, "Miss Parker, Miss Parker," and wrapped themselves around her legs.

Addison grinned at the little girl and boy Joe recognized from her class on Sunday. "Hey, you two." She leaned over and hugged an arm around each child. "I know you're not supposed to be running around the church alone. Where are your Mom and Dad?"

"Over there," they piped in unison. One pointed left, and one pointed right.

Joe covered his mouth, hiding the snicker that escaped. The scarecrow from Oz had nothing on these two.

"Okay. Let's go find them." She looked over her shoulder as she led the children to find their parents. "C'mon Joe."

He followed at a sedate pace behind the trio, his eyes darting to the different groups they passed. Several people caught his eye and greeted him, so he curved his lips and dipped his chin in return because his larynx wasn't available for speaking. He hadn't entered a church since his mother died and hadn't ever planned to return to the God who had taken everything from him. Why did he think he could do this? He kept his gaze trained on Addison, her fall of dark hair, and her smile. He could be a better man for her. He could definitely do better than her louse of a fiancé.

The children pulled Addison to a tall, slender blonde. The little girl said, "Mommy, look, Miss Parker's here."

"I see that, Rebecca. Both of you know not to walk away from me without permission, even at church."

"I'm sorry, Mommy." The young boy dropped his head.

"I know you are, Brian." The mother sighed, and then turned her attention to him. "Hello, I'm Jenna Kay." She stretched her hand toward him.

"Joe Vaughn." He tilted his head over their joined fingers in a subtle old-fashioned bow.

Jenna raised an eyebrow in his direction before sending Addison a not-so-subtle silent message. "Welcome, Joe. I hope you enjoy class tonight."

"Class?" He glanced at Addison for clarification.

Addison shifted her weight onto her left foot before speaking. "Wednesday nights are for individual classes and prayer. Different subjects are taught so each person can choose which class they want to attend."

"What about preaching?" Joe shook his head. No preaching at a church?

"The pastor delivers a message to the church body on Sunday mornings." Addison's lips curved. "We'll be attending the Living Faith class tonight."

Our class. A tourniquet contracted around his heart and squeezed until the organ sprinted under the extra pressure. Did he want to be part of a church class again?

"Well, I need to get these two to the children's class. It was great meeting you, Joe." Jenna's farewell broke the spell of Addison's words.

"Yes." His murmured words heralded his mind's return. He turned to Addison once more. "Where to?"

"This way." She walked beside him down the left corridor, stopping by the third door. "Joe, if you become uncomfortable or want to leave, I'll understand. Just let me know. Okay?"

"Sure." He swept his hand out, motioning her into the

room. "Ladies first."

Joe followed her into the room with his head held high and his stomach in knots.

Chapter Eighteen

Jackdaw sat, twirling a fluffy, brown feather between his fingers, and waited for his lovely to emerge. Fulfilling his destiny had become routine. Next week his routine would return with the reporter exposing the next good girl to the masses, and his mind would be sharper, keener, edgier for the mission of showing those her hidden sin.

For now, finding his next intended by alternate means would prove he could accomplish his task no matter the circumstance and prove his intelligence. His established timeline could not be compromised.

This morning, while eating breakfast, his middle-aged waitress had alternately flirted with him and tried to mother him. Both had angered him. He didn't need another mother, and he certainly wasn't interested in a woman old enough to be his mother. Still, the napkin she'd handed him with her number and the time her shift ended seemed like the directing hand of fate.

Remembering the birth of his destiny, when his purpose had been realized, always led back to the same person. His mother. She had died a fitting death. Overdosing on drugs and alcohol after she'd finished beating him for existing as her penance for the teenage love affair she'd had with a married man. The last beating of many.

The police had ruled her death an accidental overdose because everyone in their small town knew his mother and her habits. His lips turned up as he rolled down the window, propped his elbow on the window frame, and rubbed his thumb across his eyebrow.

Only he knew the truth about his mother's death. Only he would ever know the truth that began his true destiny. A destiny no one could change, even the police detectives investigating his works of art.

His smile tightened as he picked at a loose thread on the steering wheel cover he used. The detectives wouldn't be able to catch him even though he was right in front of them, had been standing between him and his girl.

His watch dial glowed in the darkness as he tossed the feather onto the dashboard and began tapping the steering wheel. Even though anticipation made his work more enjoyable, that time of faux relaxation before the show started always opened his mind's doorway to doubt his well-laid plans. Even public-school psychologists rated his intelligence with geniuses so why worry about loopholes in his plan?

The door to the restaurant opened as the waitress entered the night. The golden light cast from under the yellow awning circled the small building and cast a halo about her face and arms. A sign he'd made the right choice. She was the chosen one.

He stepped out of his car and approached her, producing the shy demeanor she'd found attractive earlier. Careful to remain in the shadows, out of the line of sight of those seated inside the restaurant, he said, "Hi, Linda."

"Well, hello you. I'm glad to see you again. You had me worried you wouldn't come back tonight." Linda touched a button on his shirt, and then ran her finger along the line of buttons leading to his belt buckle.

Jackdaw's heart rate accelerated. This would definitely be worth his efforts. "No, I wouldn't disappoint you that way. Not after you took such good care of me this morning."

She ran her eyes over him as she purred, "Well, now. That was my pleasure. I usually ride the bus 'cause I don't have another way home. Do you think you could give me a lift? I'll make you the best cup of coffee you've ever had."

"Deal." He led her to his car and opened the door.

"Oh, a gentleman." Linda sent him an air kiss as she ducked into his car.

Jackdaw circled the car's back fender and climbed into the driver's seat. The feather lying on the dashboard fluttered as he shut the door. He picked it up and handed it to his evening entertainment. "For you."

"A feather? How original. Thank you." As the woman stroked her cheek with a feathery brush, the feline smile of a cat cornering its prey spread across her lips. He returned the silent flirtation. If only she knew. . .

He was more predator than she.

Chapter Nineteen

An hour later, Joe exited Harvest Community Church in a daze. Leading the class, the associate pastor had welcomed him like an old friend, and then began a discussion on Ephesians. By the end of the hour, the seventeenth verse 'and He is before all things, and in Him all things consist' danced circles throughout Joe's thoughts. No matter how often he tried to think of something else, every thought led back to that phrase.

He exited the building beside Addison, aware of her, but not with her.

and He is before all things...
in Him all things consist.

"Yo, Joe." Addison snapped her fingers in front of his nose.

He cleared his throat and blinked her into focus.

"Yeah?"

"You okay?"

"Yeah, I am." He balled both hands in his pockets and stepped out of his comfort zone. "How do you know if you're following God's plan?

"Prayer. Through prayer God lights His path for those seeking Him."

"Oh." Joe allowed his gaze to go unfocused once more as he thought through Addison's answer. Pulling himself back to the present, he asked. "Do you still feel uneasy?"

"No. I felt unsettled for a few minutes in the parking lot after eating, and then the feeling passed."

"Do you get these feelings a lot?"

"No. I mean…no. Everything's fine now." She swallowed and watched a couple climb into the car behind them. "Well, I guess I should tell you good-bye since it's late."

"Oh." Joe looked around. "Yeah, good-bye. I'll see you tomorrow."

She turned toward her car before turning back. "You're welcome to come back with me on Sunday if you'd like."

Adrenaline rushed through his system. Did he want to visit this church again? "Do you think that is a good idea? The article would be out on Sunday. Perhaps you should consider skipping church."

"The killer has established a set pattern. Article on Sunday, death on Wednesday. He won't deviate from it. Those that commit these types of crimes are very consistent in their methods, patterns, and practices. It will be safe for me to attend church." She shrugged. "And I refuse to live my life in fear. If I'm scared or hurt or unsure, then church is where I should be."

"I understand even if I don't agree."

"Good. Let me know if you would like to come on Sunday."

"I'll think about it."

Addison nodded and climbed into her car.

Joe watched her taillights fade in the distance while his thoughts circled like a merry-go-round.

and He is before all things. . .

in Him all things consist.

His mother had never wavered in her faith. Through his father's death. Through the years of poverty. Through her battle with breast cancer. She'd always laughed with him, encouraged him, and spoke with him about the Father in Heaven's love for him. To her, God was reality, and everything came through Him. Would his mother be ashamed because Joe had turned away from the God she'd held so dear?

How could he continue to follow a God who'd deserted them both during the hard years?

A deep, resonant baritone startled him. "Are you okay, son?"

Joe faced a man with graying chestnut hair. His coloring blurred in the darkness, but his indistinct features were visible in the light of the streetlamps scattered around the almost emptied parking lot. Silver framed glasses perched on the bridge of his nose intensified the roundness of his lower face.

"I'm fine. Just lost in thought, that's all." Joe turned his lips up.

The other man didn't look reassured. "You've been standing here for more than a few minutes."

Joe laughed a little too loud. "Sorry. You must be ready

to leave."

"Don't worry about that, son. I'm not in a rush." The man held out his hands. "Lawrence James. I'm senior pastor here at Harvest Community Church."

"Joe Vaughn." He grasped the other man's hand and pumped twice.

"You look like a man with a lot on his mind. If you need to talk, I'm available."

The words rolled from his lips before he could stop them. "After listening to the bible discussion tonight, I've been questioning my past choices."

"I see. Want to share?"

Joe rolled his right shoulder, gazed across an empty parking space to the streetlamp beside the main highway. "I visited one of the classes in there," he jerked his head toward the church building, "with a friend, and one topic led to another until I'm standing here wondering if I've made the right decisions."

"Could I ask what decisions you have made or is that question too personal?"

"Yeah, it's personal." He locked stares with the other man, while his tongue continued to ignore the warning signals flashing through him in favor of releasing the chaos inside him. Maybe if he talked about it, he would know what to do. "My dad died when I was twelve. His death pushed my mom into working multiple jobs. Then, when it looked as if everything was looking up for both of us, she was diagnosed with breast cancer. A year later she died. After that, I made the decision to live for myself, not to rely on a crutch of any kind, including God, to take care of me."

"Sounds like circumstances have been rough on your family."

"I guess you could say that."

"Could I offer some advice?"

"Sure."

"Examine your heart. If you don't find peace, it's because God is chasing you, asking to be allowed in your life. You think that God abandoned you when you needed Him most, but He didn't. He held the boy who lost his father. He provided for the mother and son who had nothing. He walked with the man who buried his mother."

"How do you know?" Joe's hands landed on his hips as he looked at the ground, and asked in a low voice, "How can I know?"

The man laid a hand on Joe's shoulder, squeezed. "It's in His word, son. He'll never leave you or forsake you. Through your faith He can work miracles in your life, if you let Him."

"Maybe." Joe faltered for a moment.

"Could I pray for you before you leave tonight?"

Joe stepped backward. "I'd rather you didn't."

"Okay." Pastor James reached into his jacket pocket, pulled out a small index card, and scribbled in the darkness. "If you need to talk anytime, you call me."

Joe stared at the white card that seemed to glow in the darkness before he reached for it. "Thanks."

"Good. Now, go home and pray about your questions. I'm sure you'll find that God will be there to answer you."

Joe dropped his head, and then unlocked his car like a mute. Voiceless. His heart seemed to twist tighter in his chest, and he fought to slow his breathing, until he rubbed a fist over his breastbone.

Pray about his questions? He'd think about it a little more first.

~

The woman leaned across the kitchen table from her seated position as if she'd been allowed a last meal before her death. One arm extended toward a cold cup of coffee while the woman lay in repose. Every appearance of sleeping peacefully.

In this case, appearances were deceiving.

Addison knelt beside the victim sweeping the floor with an intent gaze one last time. As she stood, her eyes landed on the still body again. She had recognized the victim immediately. Linda. The waitress from the Waffle House.

McBride marked a grayish-brown feather found propped in the table's flower vase. The disposable cell phone underneath the chair where Linda sat now lay in the evidence box. The phone and the feather a signature item of Jackdaw's handiwork.

Remembering the woman from the day before, seeing her full of life, made the knot lodged in Addison's throat grow until the need to gag overwhelmed her. She stepped away from the body and took a deep breath. Reminding herself of all the reasons to continue her career as a homicide detective decreased over time, while her questions and complaints about the violence she dealt with daily increased.

McBride stood in the doorway leading to the living area. "C'mon, Parker. We've gotten everything we can. It's time to let Casey do his job." As if on cue, Doug Casey, the county coroner and his assistant, moved into the room with a body bag.

Addison tore her gaze from the lifeless body and followed her partner out of the mobile home. The neighboring units stood in a straight row like angular tin soldiers monitoring the road. Had someone seen or heard anything unusual?

Oh, she hoped so.

As they stood at the edge of the crime scene, Joe stepped out of the unmarked car and watched the crime scene activity. McBride jerked her attention back to him as Joe started making his way toward them. "This is obviously the work of our serial killer, but there was no article in Sunday's paper highlighting a woman. He's acting on his own."

"I know. He's escalating, which means this trap has to work. I've...we've got to stop this man." Addison fisted her hands next to her thighs as she stared into the distance.

"Give up, Parker. What's going on?"

Fluffy shapes drifted across the bright blue sky, festive shapes of cottony joy. Life continued for everyone except Linda. Tearing her gaze from the happy forces of nature, she refocused on her partner.

"I met her yesterday. When I had dinner with Joe at the Waffle House near the station last night."

McBride turned toward her. "The victim?"

"Yes. She was happy, excited, because she had a date after work. Maybe we can check with her coworkers to see who this mysterious date was." She cleared her throat, nudging the hot ball of bile aside so she could speak. "Does it ever get easier?"

"Does what get easier?"

Addison faced her partner and swallowed hard. "Dealing with the senselessness, the violent carnage? I've worked with you for two years now, and I still have a hard time dealing with the scenes we're expected to process and investigate."

McBride rubbed a thumb down his slanting jawbone. "Are you thinking of leaving homicide?"

Addison shook her head. "I love my job. I love finding justice for victims of violence. I love knowing that a killer locked behind bars can't hurt another innocent person. But, how do you reconcile what we have to handle with your faith?"

Joe appeared on the left, remaining behind the yellow flapping tape as instructed.

McBride took a deep breath with his chest falling like a deflating balloon, causing his shoulders to drop. "You have to keep in mind, Parker, God gave man free will. He gave man the ability to make choices and to act on those choices freely. All we can do is arrest the guilty so justice can be met while spreading His word and His plan anytime we have the opportunity."

Unable to stay in one place, Addison paced to the car while she spoke, not caring if the two men followed or not. "Free will? Free to hurt, maim, kill? I know God is all-knowing, and I know He is all-powerful, here," she tapped two fingers on her forehead, then moved those two fingers to tap over her breast, "but here, those facts are a little harder to remember. How can He give free will to those who hurt others?"

McBride stopped in front of her, but stared at the coroner's van. "God can't give free will to you and take it away from others. Free will was not given selectively but equally to all men. It's up to men to choose their path, to choose good, to choose God's path."

"I know you're right." She banged a fist on the car's hood. "I know it. Still, sometimes it's hard to remember when faced with the murder of an innocent woman, a woman who was so full of life yesterday."

"You knew Linda Peters?"

Joe, who had remained quiet in the conversation for once, gave McBride a wide-eyed glance. "Linda? She's the victim?"

Addison gave McBride a run-down of their dinner the night before.

Joe stared at her. "Do you think it had anything to do with your uneasy feelings when we left the restaurant?"

She glared at him. He just couldn't let that go. She had no idea why she'd shared that with him, but she'd know better in the future. "I don't know."

McBride cast a suspicious glance at her. "What do you mean 'uneasy'?"

"I just didn't feel right. I don't know why. I couldn't tell why. I just didn't."

"Okay. Let's talk to her co-workers and any patrons we can track down from last night at that restaurant."

"Wait." Joe spoke. "I asked her if she had plans after work because she'd fixed herself up."

"Fixed herself up how?" McBride pulled out his small notebook.

"You know," Addison waved at her face, "freshened her lipstick, added a touch of eye shadow, straightened her hair. That sort of thing."

Joe joined her description. "She seemed happy, too."

"Her answer?"

Joe blinked several times. "Linda admitted she had a first date after work."

"Did she mention a name?"

Addison glanced back at the clouds dancing across the sky and caught her breath. "She said, 'His name is Jack. I just met him.'"

Jackdaw.

"Why didn't I figure that out last night." Addison rubbed her forehead as a great weight seemed to shift onto her chest.

"You couldn't have known. This is a breakthrough for the case. Now, we have a place to start." McBride patted her shoulder, and then slid behind the steering wheel.

Addison sat in the passenger seat as Joe climbed into the back. They had to catch this guy. She *would* be the last person he would ever target.

The remainder of the day passed with all the haste of a turtle. Watching the clock hands progression didn't improve Addison's mood. Feeding her last quarter into the soda machine seemed normal enough until she returned to her desk.

Until she wrote a report describing the crime scene and the leads found.

Until she informed the victim's family death had stolen their beloved.

Until she faced the reason her chest had hollowed out.

The glaring afternoon sunshine heated Addison's face as she stood at the building's front window fighting get-me-out-of-here thoughts. Half her Coke slid down her throat in a few gulps. The carbonation burned a path to her stomach and made her eyes water. Had she chosen the right career? She could transfer to a different department, but then she wouldn't help find the piece of evidence connecting all the dots, allowing a conviction. She couldn't help remove the guilty perpetrator off the streets so he couldn't hurt anyone else.

She drew a deep breath and returned to her desk. McBride's chair faced her, empty for the last thirty minutes. Across her desktop were stacks of paper, open files, photos side by side. Sinking into her chair, Addison rested her fingers on the keyboard and stared at the open report. Typing a few words, her fingers slowed with each word. She pressed backspace, deleting each word. Why was she still here? Leaning back in her chair, her gaze roamed the room, searching for the answer.

"You okay, Addison?"

When she looked over at Joe, he pushed his notebook into his bag. "Why don't you use something electronic for taking notes?"

Joe's brows formed a straight line over his eyes. "Where did that come from?"

"I was just wondering, that's all."

"I like the process of writing longhand. It gives me a connection with my writing that I can't seem to get when I use my computer. You know, you asked me that question on Tuesday."

"Mm." Addison returned to tapping the keys on her computer, making minute changes on her report.

"Are you okay?" Joe's twice-voiced question snagged her attention.

"Yeah, I am." She sat back in her desk chair. "I think I'm just tired."

He reached out, touched her hand with a gentle caress. "Maybe you should go home and get some rest. Start fresh tomorrow."

Her day felt incomplete, like she had yet to finish all her tasks, but it was time to go home. She gathered her things and grabbed her truck keys.

"Hey, Parker, hold up a minute. You may want to be in on this."

Addison turned toward Davidson with the phone stuck to his ear. As soon as he noticed her watching him from the doorway he went back to scribbling on his notepad. The phone hit its cradle the same moment Davidson lumbered to his feet and jerked his head to motion his partner, Brian Carboni, over to join Addison. "Just got a call in." Davidson looked her in the eye as he said, "Domestic disturbance at the Cline residence."

Air jerked into her lungs so fast she choked. "Amy?"

"Yep." Davidson spoke to his partner. "Let's get a move on. Whatever's happening is going down now." The two men sprinted out the door.

Addison followed at a slower pace though her mind screamed she should run. Davidson and Carboni had to secure the scene before she could enter, and the best way to keep herself in check would be to arrive after them.

"Let me drive you, Addison."

She threw a wide-eyed look at Joe that questioned his sanity. "What?"

"Let me drive you. You're dealing with a lot of stuff right now, and I'd feel better if you'd let me drive you."

"I'm not leaving my car at the station. If you want to tag along that's up to you, but I'm driving myself." Addison climbed into her truck without giving him a chance to refute her decision.

Drive her? Yeah, right, like she wasn't able to take care of herself.

Fifteen minutes later Addison pulled to the curb in front of a run-down ranch home with Joe parking behind her. An ambulance sat in the driveway, blinking red lights catching the neighborhood's attention, while two paramedics focused their attention on the front door, waiting for the all-clear signal so they could care for the injured inside. Addison stood street level, every muscle in her body as rigid as a tightrope.

Joe stood beside her. "Is this the same mother and daughter from your Sunday class?"

"Yes. I've known Amy since the sixth grade. We've been best friends ever since."

"Sounds like a friendship to be envied."

She made a humming response then stood in silence, waiting for permission to enter the house. After an eternity, Davidson stepped out of the house and motioned Addison through the front door. She turned to Joe as she left and said, "You can go ahead and leave." When he shook his head, she rubbed a hand across her forehead. "Fine. Wait here, then."

Addison turned without waiting for his response and ran through the front door.

Chapter Twenty

Addison dropped onto the worn hardwood floor next to her friend, whose battered and swollen face looked nothing like her childhood bestie. "Amy."

Davidson took over wrestling David Cline to the floor so his partner could find the hidden little girl. "You have the right to remain silent, lowlife, anything you say…" While the two continued to grapple on the floor, Carboni motioned the paramedics into the room from the open doorway.

"Amy." Addison knelt beside the small woman and touched her hand.

Amy struggled to open one eye, "Addy?"

"I'm here."

"Take care of Samantha for me."

"I will."

"Take her to my mom's house."

"Absolutely."

"Don't let my baby see me like this."

"I won't." Carboni tapped her shoulder. He motioned her

toward the kitchen with a swing of his head. Addison turned back to Amy, and said, "We'll talk later, okay."

With a wince she murmured, "Yes, later," and sank into unconsciousness.

Addison followed Carboni through the activity in the room until they entered the kitchen. The shabby room glowed in the sunlight as if punctuating the despair of the family.

"What is it?" Addison flexed her hands and forced her shoulders to relax.

Carboni cast a look back at the unconscious mother. "It's the kid."

Sweat broke out across her forehead as her shoulder muscles drew tight once more. *Please, God, let Samantha be okay.* "Her name's Samantha. What about her?"

He laid a hand on Addison's arm. "She's in the room down the hall. I can hear her crying, but she won't come out. I don't want to force the door and scare the little mite anymore than she already is." He rubbed a finger down the scarred side of his face, giving his words visual context. "I thought you could talk her out because she knows you."

She let out the breath trapped in her lungs and watched the paramedics lift Amy onto the gurney through the doorway. Once she'd been taken from the room, Addison continued down the hallway with slow, measured steps and stopped next to the muffled crying.

She tapped on the door. "Samantha, it's Miss Parker. Are you okay?"

"Un-uh. My daddy is mad."

"He's not mad anymore. He's gone, sweetheart. I'm here to take you to visit your grandmother. Can you open the door?"

The crying slowed to sniffles. "Are you sure he's gone?"

"Yes, baby, he's gone. You're safe. Can you open the door?"

"What if he comes back and you don't know?" Fresh tears filtered through the thin wavering voice.

Addison swallowed several times. "No, he won't come back. I brought some friends with me, and we'll protect you and your Mom. Can you open the door?"

"Uh-huh." The lock clicked before a dark blonde head peeked through a small crack. When Samantha saw Addison standing alone in the hallway, the child stumbled into Addison's arms and squeezed her neck in a death grip. "I'm so glad you're here, Miss Parker. My daddy was mad and he scared me and hurt my mommy."

"I know. He won't hurt you or your mommy anymore." Addison hugged the child.

Wet brown eyes held a wealth of experience that grown adults had trouble coping with. Rage swelled Addison's chest at the sight of the red handprint etched on the little girl's right cheek.

Addison rubbed a gentle finger down the marked cheek. "Did your daddy do this?"

"Uh-huh. I was trying to get him to stop hitting Mommy. When he slapped me, Mommy told me to go to my room and stay there. Is Mommy okay?"

"She's hurt, but she'll be better soon. Now, my friends are going to take some pictures of your hurt face, and then we'll get you cleaned up to go to your grandmother's house. Would you like that?"

Samantha's hair swayed with her vigorous nod before her head rested on Addison's breastbone. The child flinched away from the other two detectives, but she suffered through the photos and answered questions that had to be asked.

Fifteen minutes later, Addison's eyes burned as she carried the child into the room that had been a sanctuary moments ago. "Do you have a suitcase, sweetheart?" The child shook her head while Addison rubbed circles over the small back. "That's okay. We'll find something to put your clothes in."

After finding a small toy bag to pack a few clothes in, Samantha said, "I have some clothes at my Gammy's."

"Well, if that's the case, then we have all we need, don't we?" Addison touched her nose to the child's as a small smile graced the little mouth. "Is there anything else you need?"

"Just Molly." Samantha pointed at the cloth doll lying in the corner.

"Okay then, Miz Molly, it's time to go." Addison scooped up the doll and the child. When she reached the family room, Addison turned to look at Davidson and Carboni. "Make sure he's locked up good and tight for a long time, guys."

She exited on Davidson's, "We will, Parker. Trust me, we will."

Joe leaned against his car, eyes trained on the house's front door. As Addison approached her truck carrying the little girl, she stopped when she reached him. "I'm driving Samantha to her grandmother's house. I'll see you later. Tomorrow maybe."

He reached out, ran a finger down the salty tracks crossing Addison's face. "Sure. I'll see you then."

Once she and Samantha were in her truck, Addison scrubbed her hands across her cheeks. Crying? Really? Could she get any more girly?

~

Joe parked his car behind Addison's Ranger in the fading twilight and breathed deep, releasing the breath after a count of five. Surely, she wouldn't be angry at him for coming to her home, but he needed to check on her, to know that she was okay. He'd wrestled with God most of the evening after he left her at the Cline house, his heart pulling one direction and the logic of his mind arguing another. Finally, he'd bowed his head and prayed about the emotional unrest he'd lived with since his mother's death.

When his head lifted, his soul was at peace and his heart joyful for the first time since his father's death. Facing his changing feelings for Addison had become first on his new list of priorities. He'd never loved before. Would he be able to live with not exploring their developing relationship? Could he lock away feelings he'd never experienced before without finding out how deep they went?

He reached for the flat, gaily-wrapped box on the passenger seat, fingering the bow before climbing out. Raking a hand through his hair, he took another deep breath, and approached the front doorstep. The door opened moments later to reveal a pale-faced Addison.

"Hi." Could his greeting have been any lamer? He could kick his own behind for not being more original.

Addison nodded. "Hi, Joe." She opened the door wider. "Come on in."

He should have asked if she was all right. Except, she obviously wasn't so that would have been lame, too. Joe followed her into the family room by the doorway and sat in the chair angled toward the sofa. He cleared his throat. "I know that you've had a rough day, but I wanted to give you a birthday gift." He pulled a wrapped box from under his arm and offered it to her. His lips tilted. "A few days late, I know. Sorry about that."

She accepted the decorated box with a look of bemusement stamped across her face. Addison speechless? A first for him.

Joe cleared his throat. "I hope you like it. I didn't know what to get you."

"I'm sure I will." She picked at the edge of the wrapping paper, then stopped and moved her hand to the bow. She pulled the large white bow from the box and handed it to Joe. "For you, I believe."

That traitorous heart of his swelled as he accepted the bow.

Addison returned to pulling the paper from the box. Balling it into a trash-bound wad, she lifted the lid from the box. Her mouth fell open as she pulled a silk scarf from the box. Patterns of red and purple swirled throughout the silver-gray fabric. "It's lovely, Joe, thank you."

Heat rushed to his cheeks. "I thought those colors would look good with the dress your mother gave you." He pulled at his collar. "At least, that's what the saleslady said."

"Oh, it definitely would. It's perfect." Addison leaned over to give him a kiss on the cheek. "Thank you." She sat back and smiled. "You've brightened my day."

"You're welcome." Was that the best he could do? For a writer, he really lost his way with words when he was around her. He rested his hands on his knees, diving deep to find the strength he needed to give her the rest of his news. "I brought you a copy of the story I finished earlier." He pulled a flash drive out of his pocket and handed it to her. "I haven't submitted it to my editor."

Addison reached for the black unit and took a deep

breath. "Thanks. I'll get it approved tomorrow so you can meet your deadline."

Joe looked through the window behind her. The deeper purple of twilight overshadowed the pink of early evening, darkening the room. Now was the time for honesty, for truth. For confessions. "I won't be meeting my deadline."

Addison's eyebrows v'ed together. "What does that mean?"

He cleared his throat. "I'm not submitting the story for print. I can't do it."

"Why not?"

"Because—" He shrugged his shoulders. "Because I care too much."

"Care too much about what? The women being murdered? This article being printed will stop the murders when we trap the killer."

His negative shake brought his gaze back to hers. "No, I care too much about you." He stood, paced away, then faced the room's front window, his hands stuffed in his pants' pockets. "I want to protect you, and this is the only way I can do that." Turning on his heel, he faced her once more. "I'm not trained in defense like you, but that doesn't mean I can just step aside and let you walk into danger."

"Let me walk into danger? Are you out of your mind? I've been trained to take care of myself. The only reason I agreed to this shadowing thing was to catch this killer, but I don't need a babysitter. I can bring an end to this madness."

His brows raised, and he propped his hands on his hips. "You can? By yourself? A little arrogant don't you think?"

"Arrogant? Of course not, but obviously I'm the major player in this charade. The captain has already put in place increased surveillance at my house as well as someone with me at all times during my workday. All that's needed from you are the words that'll bring the killer out."

Joe scrubbed his hands up and down his face. Tension tightened his neck and straightened his spine. "Look, I don't want to fight. I'm trying to explain how I feel about this. I'm not good with verbal explanations, which is why I write." He crossed the small space between them and took her hands in his. It was now or never to lay his heart out for her. "I didn't mean to fall in love with you, but I did. I wanted to tell you that and explain my reasons for not submitting the article to my editor. I gave you a copy of the draft so my words could show you how I felt."

Addison pulled her hands from his grip. "Love? How do you know what love is? All I've ever seen from you is deception angling for a story. Are you trying to tell me that you're willing to blow your chance for a premier story before your competition and expecting me to believe it?" The redness around Addison's eyes stood out in her pale face, and her mouth tightened in a sneer.

Joe shook his head. Whatever he had expected, it wasn't the suspicion that he was getting. "That's a cheap shot, and you know it. Look, I did a lot of thinking last night, and I prayed for the first time in a long time. I've had to face a lot of things, good and bad, about myself, including how I feel about you."

"Your feelings shouldn't interfere with our investigation."

"This story is not a good idea. I can feel it here," he tapped a fist on his chest, "and I cannot submit to my editor something that will put you in uncontrollable danger."

Addison's lips tightened. "I'm not looking for a relationship, Joe, and if I were, you would not be a candidate."

"Why not?"

She held up a finger. "For starters, I'm not looking for a relationship right now." Ticked off another finger. "You're years younger than I am." Held up a third. "And, you're a reporter. I could never become involved with someone who made their living feeding off others' misery." She crossed her arms over her chest in her best detective stance.

"That's not fair, and you know it. I'm good at my job, and I report a lot of encouraging news." Joe paced away from her and back. What he was hearing was hard to believe after the week they'd spent getting to know each other. "And, why should my age matter? We're both adults, so what if I'm a few years younger. My feelings don't change based on your age."

Addison closed her eyes in denial. "Please, leave now so I can figure out what to do next."

Her words opened a wound in Joe's chest, shooting shards that stole his breath. He rubbed the pain with the palm of his hand. He moved toward her front door when he really wanted to stay. He wanted to be there for her, help her through her difficult times. "I'm sorry. I didn't want this to end in an argument. And, whether you believe it or not, I do love you." He walked from her house with heavy feet.

The ache in his heart swelled until the air around him evaporated, making each breath a battle.

~

Addison stood at the front window and watched Joe climb into his car. Having to deal with another Jackdaw victim and Amy's situation didn't compare to the great black hole that opened in her chest at Joe's words.

Whether you believe it or not, I do love you. . .

She inhaled as the words echoed in her heart. She hadn't asked him to love her. Didn't want him to love her. When her heartbeat accelerated and her breath hitched, she tore her eyes away from his car disappearing in the distance and flopped back onto the sofa. She didn't want him to care about her because she couldn't care in return. Shouldn't care in return.

The jump drive resting on the coffee table drew her attention. She picked the black rectangle up and stared at it as if the small piece of technology were foreign to her. Going over to her laptop, she inserted the USB device. The well-written article held her captivated until the last paragraph. Her breath hitched as she read Joe's final words.

> *Addison Parker, homicide detective and Sunday school teacher, epitomizes the soul of helping others. She sees others, not through the lens of responsibility, but through a window of compassion. She's there to help the wheels of justice, teach her brand of caring, and help a friend whenever needed. I, for one, consider myself privileged to know and love Miss Parker.*

Addison sat staring at the computer screen for many long moments. She hadn't asked for his love so why did her heart seize at the thought of rejecting it?

She closed her eyes and pushed the guilt away. She did

not need this right now. Their plan could not be abandoned. The culmination of the past week's work sat before her, and she could not let this opportunity pass. Not after today.

Joe had said he wouldn't submit the article to his editor. But, he'd given her a copy. After reading the article, she knew there was nothing included that her captain would veto. Except she took exception to the last sentence. Pressing the delete button, she watched as each letter in that sentence disappeared, and then she saved the edited document.

Addison went into the foyer, grabbed her purse, and pulled out Chuck Burnside's business card. The editor's email address jumped out in bold font on the crème-colored card.

If he wouldn't submit the story for publication, she would.

To catch this killer.

~

A hearty laugh echoed across the office. The pecking sound of fingers on a keyboard grated against Joe's nerves as he fought to focus on his computer screen and the fundraiser article he was struggling to complete. He should've stayed home today.

No, he would face his editor today. He had already put the confrontation off until the end of the day. He needed to catch Burnside before he went home. Sooner rather than later would be better. Would he lose his job when he refused to turn in the article?

He regretted not following through on the article, honoring his word, but putting Addison in danger made his palms sweat and his heart race. For the first time in his life, he couldn't keep to his agreement. Handing his heart to Addison had changed everything. An instinct to protect the one he loved, dormant for more than two years, had resurfaced.

He rested his elbows on his desk. There had to be a way to help the detectives without putting Addison in harm's way. There had to be a way.

His desk phone rang a shrill summons. He reached for the handset. "Joe Vaughn."

"I need to see you in my office. ASAP. Understand?" Chuck barked the order with his characteristic bluntness.

"Uh, yeah. Be right there—" a dial tone hummed in his ear, "—Chuck." Joe pulled the phone away and stared at the receiver, lips twisted in amusement. He grabbed his jacket and sauntered toward Chuck Burnside's office.

"Hey, Vaughn, visited any good crime scenes lately?" Paul Wiesner shouted over the chaos of the newsroom, his following chuckle a nasty rumble.

He tightened his lips. *God, show me how to live for you right now, right here.* Joe glanced at the man and nodded like he was an old friend instead of a rival. "Wiesner."

Burnside was going to chew on him for not turning a story in by his deadline, but he could handle it. To protect Addison, he would handle it no matter the outcome. Joe pushed Burnside's door open.

His editor leaned back, sleeves rolled past his elbows, hair standing on the crown of his head in rebellion, and squinted at Joe as if sizing him up. "Vaughn."

Joe cleared his throat. *Begin from a position of power.* "About my article—"

"Read your article. It's good, Vaughn."

"Pardon?"

"Your article." Burnside hooked his thumb toward his computer. "The detective emailed me the piece after her captain gave his approval."

"What? She wasn't supposed to do that. I don't want that article printed."

Burnside sat forward. "Why not? It's a good story. An excellent story. If this," he jabbed his finger toward the computer monitor, "leads to the killer's identification and arrest, a promotion is in your future."

"I don't want a promotion based on putting someone else in danger."

"What're you throwing away an opportunity like this for?" Burnside turned to his keyboard, tapped a few commands, and the printer started humming, spitting out pages one after another. Burnside picked them up and handed them to Joe.

He took the article and glanced at them like he would a ticking grenade.

Burnside pointed to the papers. "That writing is too fine to throw it away like so much trash. I've noted changes you will make. Have the revised piece back to me by five o'clock."

His free hand fisted beside his leg. He regulated his breathing and maintained a normal tone. "This would put Detective Parker in danger. If she's hurt because of this article, I can't live knowing I played a significant role in placing her in danger."

"I'm sure the cops have a plan in place to ensure her safety."

"No plan is one hundred percent foolproof." Joe swallowed. "And if they fail, the blame is mine."

"I see." Burnside leaned back in his chair, folding his hands across his stomach. "Are you letting your personal feelings interfere with your job performance?"

Joe shook his head. "No, sir."

"You don't have a choice here. You will make the revised changes I've asked for."

"And if I choose not to comply?"

"Instead of a promotion, you'll be fired."

"That's a chance I'll take." Joe held his breath.

Burnside stared at him for long moments, then turned and pulled out a list. "It's Friday. There's a charity dinner benefitting the Atlanta mayor's re-election campaign at the Georgia Aquarium. Eight o'clock. Be there and bring back a piece that will elicit tears from the reader."

"What about the feature on the detective?"

"Don't push me, Vaughn. The piece will be in Sunday's edition whether you complete the revisions or not." He called for his secretary on the speakerphone without taking his eyes off Joe. "Janice, have one of the interns come to my office."

The secretary's voice punctured the tension. "Yes, sir."

"Good-bye, Vaughn." Burnside leaned back.

Joe left the room with a heavy tread. Why would Addison do this? He veered to the closest men's room, pushing the door into the wall with a bang. He reached the sinks in a few steps and stood with his hands gripping the counter. The pain of the Formica edge gouging his palms helped him regain some of his composure.

He had trusted her.

Reaching out, he turned on the cold water and leaned down. A deep breath filled his lungs as the icy blast splashed his face. Grabbing a paper towel from the dispenser on the right, he wiped his face and looked at his dripping reflection in the mirror.

He had trusted her, and she'd betrayed him.

Talking to her, making her understand how she'd hurt him should be his next action. He marched out of the room, determination sitting in his heart. He'd make her understand.

Chapter Twenty-One

The smell of roasted coffee assaulted Jackdaw's nose as he entered the small shop. His Sunday morning hang out every week. He nodded to the regulars who recognized him as a kindred spirit and sauntered up to the counter.

Just another cool, struggling college student taking a break.

"Hey, what's up?" He let his gaze rove over the server, Sandi, who flirted in return every week.

"Nothing much until you came in." She tilted her head, causing her auburn ponytail to swing past her shoulder.

He hummed a response and made a production out of giving his usual order, "Light Caramel Cappuccino, espresso shot, no whipped cream," then stepped over to the shelf of newspapers sitting by the counter. He picked up the latest

Sunday morning edition of the *South Fulton Report* while Sandi filled his order.

Several minutes later she stepped to the counter and handed him the large coffee. The cup had her phone number scribbled on the side in blue ink. He took a moment to look at the number, then sent her a wink and enjoyed her blush of pleasure. Even if he were interested, he couldn't enjoy their Sunday interactions more. He should end her flirtations, but the harmless byplay always earned him a large coffee for the price of a medium.

Sitting beside a window as he did every Sunday, he sipped the hot beverage and opened the paper. The front-page bylines didn't hold his interest. He pulled out the Entertainment & Living section. A hum escaped through his teeth. Jackdaw's lips tilted as his gaze devoured the headline.

APD Detective Considered Community Role Model

His good girl. Addison Parker.

The reporter tailing the cops all week had given him a good start on learning about his target. It had been a pleasure to meet the man whose stories inspired him and a bonus of learning about his target ahead of time.

Jackdaw allowed himself to feel a moment's pity because he liked Addison, but she could not be allowed to show the world her good deeds without exposing her hidden sins, too. Everyone had to see that she had hidden secrets, hidden sin.

Laying the paper aside, he removed the lid from his cup and gulped the cooling coffee. Plans had to be finalized because Wednesday was fast approaching. Pretty Addison should enjoy her next few days.

They would be her last.

Chapter Twenty-Two

Addison eased her truck into the flow of traffic as cold air from the AC vents blew loose tendrils of hair across her mouth. She pushed it aside and turned the radio volume up to hear the closing chords of her favorite Third Day song.

Thank God this Monday had been uneventful. No murders. No crime scenes. Just paperwork.

She glanced in her mirror. The tan Ford Taurus she'd spotted behind her that morning had made another appearance, tailing her since she'd left the station parking lot fifteen minutes ago. This car's continued presence was a concern. She tightened her fingers on the steering wheel, her flesh squeaking against plastic. She glanced at the road behind her again. A jingle for a local restaurant provided sufficient reason to switch on the CD player. The bass thumped and a female voice crooned as Addison flicked her signal and turned onto the next road traveling west. The road could lead her home or she could double back to the interstate.

Her knuckles whitened on the wheel as the car turned behind her, maintaining a respectable distance. Too respectable. Sunlight reflecting off the car's windshield wiped away details of the interior, making it impossible to get a look at the driver's face. Goosebumps raced up her arms as her instincts took over. Her fingers flipped the cold air down. If she was in her work vehicle, she could radio in. Should she call McBride?

No, she wouldn't call him yet. It could be a false alarm. After all, how many non-descript sedan vehicles were on the road?

You're being too edgy, girl. It's not time for the killer to strike. Remember he has a pattern.

Her heart rate slowed as she thought about the killer's pattern. Even though the last victim was out of character for this killer, with the article, his profile suggests that he wouldn't strike until Wednesday. The captain had already arranged for her home to be monitored, and McBride was driving her crazy because he'd been stuck to her like glue.

She stopped at a four-way intersection and turned left, opposite her house. Still, the car hugged her back fender. Five o'clock work traffic clogged the interstate. Addison merged, the Taurus never far behind her Ranger. She drummed her fist on the wheel. Her best chances of losing the Taurus would be in the heavy traffic. Seeing an opening on her right, she gassed the truck and moved onto the southbound ramp.

Heart pounding, her eyes darted to her mirror. She

changed lanes. Then again. Her foot stomped the accelerator, forcing her down the far-right lane, passing a long line of traffic and zigzagging through the vehicles like an auto pinball until the sedan remain gridlocked in traffic.

Speeding past two exit ramps, Addison changed lanes twice more before exiting the busy freeway. At the stop light, she raked her hair from her damp brow. She looked right, then left. No Taurus, though she was twenty miles south of her house.

The CD segued into a Barlow Girl worship ballad. She tried to ease her nerves and concentrate on the music.

All of you is more than enough...

Addison turned left, east down Highway 34, and sang along with the song.

For every thirst and every need...

She checked her side mirrors.

You satisfy me with your love...

Her rearview mirror remained clear.

Then, all I have is more than enough...

No tan Ford Taurus. That seemed too easy, but she would alert her partner when she got home. Perhaps her imagination was working in overdrive. Was she so intent on finding this killer that her imagination invented someone tailing her?

A small-town grocery store came up on Addison's left. Safety precautions dictated she break with routine, and she did need groceries. She turned across the opening in traffic and parked her truck between two minivans sitting near the front.

The niggling voice in her head insisted she should call this in, but she could handle herself in dangerous situations. Her training made sure of that. Bothering the captain, or

McBride, would lead to nothing and be a nuisance for them. She paused at the entrance and cast a critical eye over the parking lot. A woman and her three children headed to the blue minivan parked on Addison's right. Various cars had pulled in and parked around the lot. None of them a tan Ford Taurus. Entering the store, Addison took one last look through the store's window as she chose a buggy.

Walking through aisles crammed with cans, boxes and bags of food, Addison rotated her head as her muscles, shoulders, and neck began to ache from the tension ratcheting higher with every step. On top of everything else, it didn't help that no item sat in the logical, expected place. Grocery stores should post warning signs for all those entering. 'Warning: shopping in an unfamiliar store causes frustration.'

The next item on last night's hastily scribbled list: sugar. A quick swallow squelched the groan that arose when she realized the baked goods section was on the opposite side of the store. Addison glanced at the buggy's meager offering and her half-filled list. Hiding from trouble rankled. It really did.

Forty minutes had passed—plenty of time for the tailgater to have lost her scent—so she turned and headed for the check-out line. Time to face whoever waited. She could handle it.

Addison signed the receipt and left with four plastic bags. Never again would she attempt to shop in an unfamiliar store when her nerves were strung tightrope taut. Tossing the plastic bags of food across the console to land on the passenger seat, she slid behind the wheel and flipped the ignition.

Whir, whir, click.

Silence followed her engine's rebellion. She pumped the gas pedal and tried again.

Whir, whir, click.

Her forehead rested on the steering wheel. Could this day get any worse? Addison lifted her head and fished her cell phone from her purse, then froze, phone mid-air. Who should she call? She'd driven out of her way to go home so she wasn't near anyone, and if she called Randy, he would go overboard on the protective partner routine when she knew that had nothing to do with her current predicament. This was her fault for not getting that tune up last month when her father told her it was time. Now, here she was trying to trap a killer, and her car didn't want to work. Stupid.

A tap on the window startled her. Ice gray eyes stared at her through the tinted glass.

Darrin Gray? Did he live near here? She pushed the window control button with no results. *Use your brain, Addy, the car's dead.* She pushed the door open. "Hi, Darrin. I didn't expect to see you here."

He cleared his throat as his gaze shifted across the parking lot. "I was invited to a friend's house for dinner in exchange for taking a few family pictures. They ran out of ice, so I volunteered to pick up a bag." He met her gaze with his trademark grin.

Addison's brows drew together. "I thought you didn't have a car?"

"I don't, but I have a license. Shelley let me borrow hers. That way she didn't have to leave her family during their big get-together."

"Oh." An awkward silence descended.

"Do you need help?" Darrin shrugged. "I may not own a

car, but I know a little about fixing them."

"Yes, I could use some help. Thanks for offering." Addison reached under the steering column and pulled the hood release.

Darrin walked around to the front of the truck. "My uncle had an auto repair shop and I used to go hang out with him after school most days." He stuck his head under the hood, wiggled several wires and metal covers. He turned his head and looked at her. "Can you start it?"

"Oh, yeah, sure." She slid back under the wheel and turned the ignition switch.

Whir, whir, click.

"Okay, you can stop." His muffled voice carried a note of satisfaction.

Addison returned to his side. Darrin withdrew a pocketknife and tightened the battery cable connections. Prickles covered the back of her neck. She reached up to rub them away, and then rolled her shoulders while she glanced around the parking lot. No Taurus in the half-empty lot, but her enemy sat close by. She could feel it.

Darrin glanced at her with a grin. "Your battery cable was loose. That's all."

Addison's unease increased when his fingers danced over the remaining cables to check them, and then he snapped the hood in place. She had never had any problems with her battery before. In fact, she had just replaced it last year.

She hadn't had to unlock her driver door. She had been so preoccupied looking at everyone else, she'd forgotten Security 101: lock your doors. She had never been this distracted before. Had the killer tampered with her truck? Maybe she should've called McBride, but she'd been so sure she was overreacting. Mentally kicking herself, she stepped back from the truck front.

"That should do it. Try to start 'er up again." He rubbed a hank of black hair off his forehead with the back of his grease smudged hand.

She shook off the restlessness racing along her nerves and nodded. The truck started. She closed the door and punched the window control button once more. The glass rolled down with a whispery whir. "Thanks, Darrin. I owe you one."

He shifted his feet and looked off into the horizon. "Detective Parker?"

"Yeah?" She propped her elbow on the window jamb.

"How about going out sometime? I mean—" He swallowed, his Adam's apple bobbing with the effort. "I've been wanting to ask you for a while, and. . . well. . . how about Wednesday? We could catch a movie?" Darrin's eyebrows rose and he became mannequin still waiting for her answer.

Addison's stomach coiled as she saw her co-worker as a man for the first time. Black hair framed an attractive face, and she knew his eyes often experienced the world differently. Taller than her by no more than a few inches with a stocky build indicating lean muscles rather than husky weight, but he wasn't Joe.

Now, where had that thought come from?

She shook her head. "I'm sorry, Darrin. I'm not looking for a relationship with anyone right now." An image of Joe smiling at her family's interaction flashed. Plus, this Wednesday she had other responsibilities to complete. Like catching a killer.

"Oh, okay." He swallowed again. "Well, I need to get

that ice before Shelley starts wondering what's happened to me." His cell phone rang. "That's probably her now." He turned to walk away.

"Darrin?" When he returned his attention to her, she said, "Thanks for your help with my truck. And, for the compliment."

Darrin's face flushed. After a curt nod, he put the phone to his ear and strode toward the store.

She wondered over the unexpected invitation on her way home. Darrin had never shown a personal interest in her. Though she'd never thought him shy, maybe in the field he'd avoided showing another side of himself. She had to admit she was all business at work because each victim deserved her full concentration.

Your concentration wasn't one hundred percent this week.

She shook the small voice from her mind. Of course, she gave her best this past week. She always gave one hundred percent, which is why there was no place for Joe in her life.

There couldn't be.

~

Joe pulled his car onto Addison's driveway, slowing his pace to navigate the dirt surface. He'd rehearsed what he wanted to say to Addison more than once. Still, nothing sounded right. Could he even put how he felt into words? If his written word made no difference, how could his spoken words have any effect?

As he rounded the curve in her driveway, he slowed to a stop. A tan Ford Taurus sat beside her house. Had he seen it before? It seemed familiar in a hazy, half-noticed way. Reversing out of her driveway, he backed in the shallow wooded area by the roadside. He pulled his cell phone out as he navigated back through the foliage to monitor her house.

"This is McBride."

"It's Joe Vaughn."

"Vaughn?" Boys screaming in the background and the slam of a door gave away McBride's movements. "What is it?"

"I'm at Addison's. She's not here, but there's an unidentified car sitting in her driveway."

"It could be someone she's invited." The screaming boys grew louder as if they'd surrounded McBride in an old-fashioned game of Cowboys and Indians.

"I have a bad feeling about this." Joe blew out a breath. "It sounds crazy, I know, but I can't explain it."

"Have you seen the person? It could be one of her family—" A woman's greeting drifted over the phone line followed by a muffled, "Hello, baby."

"It's one person, and I can't see anything other than an outline in the car."

"I'll drive over to make sure. Sit tight. Don't scare the perp away or interact with the person in that car until I get there. Write down the tag number if you can see it."

"Okay. Thanks, McBride."

"See you in a few."

The line disconnected as a hand landed on Joe's shoulder. Addison stood next to him. "What are you doing here? Playing Peeping Tom?"

"Shhh." Joe pointed to the figure climbing out of the sedan silhouetted against the late afternoon sun.

She looked over to see the man rise on his tip-toes to look through her bedroom window. She reached toward her right hip, and then spoke to Joe in a toneless whisper. "Don't let him out of your sight. I've got to get my weapon."

He grabbed her arm as she turned. "I just called McBride."

She pulled away, returning several minutes later with a 9mm in her hands. "I'm going after him."

"No. McBride said to wait until he gets here." Joe started after her.

She arched her eyebrow in the moment's pause before checking the safety on her weapon, and then slid the firearm into her holster. "He told you to wait. Let McBride know where I am when he gets here."

"You're not going after that guy alone. If I've learned one thing over the past week, it's that you should not enter a crime site alone."

"Well, thank you, Officer Vaughn." She blew out a breath. "I'm not letting this man out of my sight, even if that means I act alone. That man will not find a way into my home."

"You are not Wonder Woman. If you refuse to wait for McBride, then I'm going with you."

"You'll hinder me more than help."

"You're not going alone," his voice was firm.

"Fine. Stay out of my way." Crouched low, Addison darted across her front yard, keeping her position away from the intruder's line of sight, as the stocky shadow slipped around the side of her house.

Chapter Twenty-Three

Addison fisted her hands as she scanned for additional intruders. It appeared the man was alone, but caution was always wise. Her shoes crushed the newly mowed grass in silence as she edged closer to her back porch. Breathing slower, she focused on her unwanted guest. About five feet-eleven inches, two hundred-fifty pounds, fortyish, limp brown hair. The late afternoon sunlight glared off the man's balding crown as he tapped on the window above him.

Her heartbeat reverberated in her chest as Joe's form crouched low, keeping a close distance behind her.

God, don't let him get hurt.

Across the yard, the stray dog that had been showing up at her house for the last two weeks emerged from the woods.

Stay in the woods. Please don't spook this guy.

Now was the time or it would be too late. She crept forward. Fifty yards away, she halted, weapon raised. "APD. Stop. Put your hands where I can see them."

The man froze, and then ran toward the front of the house. She sprinted after him. The dog took off in an angling jaunt of happy barks. Joe closed in from the right.

Considerable bulk slowed the man until his rasping breaths grew harsher. His fight or flight response couldn't last much longer. Addison continued to run as the dog stepped into the man's path. He stumbled and went down.

Keeping her weapon trained on the still form, she spoke to Joe. "Hey, check for a pulse."

He dropped to one knee and pushed the dog away. Joe pressed two fingers against the unconscious man's carotid artery. A deep breath of relief blew between her lips when Joe gave her a thumbs up. The man had a steady pulse, he wasn't dead. She pulled her cell phone from her back pocket and put in a call for an ambulance.

She leaned over and spoke to the dog eye to eye. "Thanks for your help, mutt, but couldn't you have waited a few more minutes before trying to play?" The dog sneezed, twice, and then lay down to watch the drama unfold.

She lifted her gaze to Joe. "McBride is going to kill me now." She re-holstered her weapon and swiped her sleeve across her forehead.

"McBride will get us both. That's for sure." Joe looked at the man on the ground. "I can't believe he did this."

"You know him?"

"Yeah. He works with me at the paper. Paul Wiesner." Joe rubbed a hand against the back of his neck. "I wouldn't have ever guessed he could do something like this."

Addison grabbed the man's shoulder and rolled him over

to rest on his back. Blood poured from a gash on his forehead. She glanced at the ground and saw a large rock protruding from the ground. Fresh blood stained the sharp edge of nature's weapon.

Addison winced. "Great."

She glanced at the dog as he whined. The stray's wiry brown hair stuck out every direction as he lay with his chin resting on his front paws. His eyebrows flexed as his gaze moved between her and the stranger. At least one of them had no problems remaining calm, until the shrill call of the ambulance brought the mutt to his fours and sent him in the opposite direction.

"Traitor," Addison mumbled.

McBride's car parked beside the ambulance. He stepped out of the car, a scowl etched across his face. The lights atop the emergency vehicle pulsed red fire across the darkening sky. The perpetrator had been loaded into the back of the ambulance after questioning made it clear lucid and understandable answers weren't possible.

The paramedic shook hands with McBride, then climbed inside the vehicle and closed the back doors. The blinking lights on the vehicle faded into the distance.

"Well, the preliminary guess by the paramedic was a concussion." McBride spoke to Joe as he stepped beside her in the fading twilight. "I'll double check with the emergency room before I go home."

"That could explain some of the answers we received." Joe stuffed his hands in his pockets. He'd remained strangely silent through most of the ordeal. Was he angry at her for not waiting on McBride, too?

McBride shifted his attention to her. Silence fell like a heavy blanket.

"I was listening to his answers as well." Addison blurted.

"Listening? You?" Her partner's eyebrows raised in surprise. "That's a shock."

"Don't be sarcastic. I get you, okay." She shook her head and saw the dog lying near the edge of her yard, away from the humans milling around. "If the dog hadn't shown up and joined in the chase, the guy wouldn't have been injured. I couldn't control what happened." She glanced at Joe. "Neither of us could."

"You could've controlled yourself." McBride folded his arms. "Vaughn said he tried to get you to wait for back-up? You know the rules for taking down a potential perpetrator."

"Watching him look through my windows was more than I could handle." Addison rubbed a hand across her forehead. Her temples were starting to pound, her eyes throbbing from prolonged exposure to the ambulance's flashing lights. The last thing she needed was a headache. "I didn't purposefully put that rock in his path. If he hadn't run, then we wouldn't be having this discussion."

"If you hadn't engaged him without back-up, he wouldn't have run." McBride took a deep breath, let it out and turned to Joe. "I understand you know the perpetrator."

"Yes. The man's name is Paul Wiesner. He's another reporter at the *South Fulton Report* newspaper. He has made himself my rival, but we don't really cover the same type of stories."

"The only lucid thing we could get out of Wiesner was that he received a message from Jackdaw. For Joe Vaughn. Would either of you have any reason to know why he would come to Parker's house looking for you?"

Joe shook his head as Addison replied, "No."

McBride stuffed the notepad in his jacket pocket. "Hopefully, when I speak to the suspect later, he'll be able to remember the message."

"This is another break in routine for Jackdaw. What do you think this change means?" Addison folded her arms over her stomach.

McBride rubbed a hand across his head, then shook it. "Nothing good."

Joe's audible breath betrayed his calmness. "You think he's going to make his move soon?"

"Definitely. We need to increase security around you." McBride gave her a stiff-eyed squinting look. "You go nowhere unless you let me know, and there will be a patrol watching from the road. Do you understand?"

"Yes." Addison expelled the word on a resigned sigh. She barely restrained herself from stomping her foot like a little girl who'd just been grounded.

Her partner faced her. "I'll expect you to follow orders. If you don't, the result could be your death."

She eyed her partner's sagging shoulders as he returned to his vehicle. After the last of the responders cleared out of her yard, tension crept up her back until it took up residence at the base of her skull. She swiveled toward her house and found Joe watching her.

She approached, trying to quell the sudden fluttering in her stomach. "Thanks for being here. I appreciated your help." Though they stood in the dusk, she could see the hardened line of his face.

"Why did you do it?" A steel core of anger laced his words.

"I couldn't let that man break into my house." She glanced up at the orange and magenta rays shooting from the dying sun. "This is my home. I'll not have strangers looking in my windows."

"I'm not talking about tonight."

Her gaze locked with his.

He tilted his head back and closed his eyes. A moment later, he faced her once more. "The article."

Her lips pressed into a grim line as an awkward, prolonged silence surrounded them.

"You knew how I felt, yet you sent it to Burnside anyway."

"Joe—"

"Why, Addy?" His use of her nickname carried a wealth of hurt.

She hesitated, and then closed her ears to his pain. She'd known he would confront her, but somehow, she hadn't been prepared. "We need to catch this killer. This is bigger than you, Joe. It's bigger than either of us. This killer has to be caught, and your story is the link that can lead to a madman."

"We could've found another way to draw him out."

"How?"

"We could've prayed. God answers prayer, right? You said that when I visited your church, so I have to think you believe it."

"I did pray, Joe, and this plan of action came to light."

"I can't believe that, and I can't believe going behind my back to get that article to my editor was in God's plan."

As the arrow struck, pain pierced her chest. "That's not fair. You agreed to this plan."

"I had a change of heart. That was my work, Addison. Mine. You had no right to submit it. It hadn't even been revised."

"Then why did you give it to me?"

"I gave it to you because I thought you would understand how I felt about you through my words. But you proved me wrong, didn't you?"

"I don't know what you mean." *Sure you do. Remember, pride goes before a fall.*

"I guess you were right about us. A relationship isn't possible." Joe cleared his throat. "Good-bye, Addison."

"Good-bye, Joe." Addison blinked several times as he went back to his car. Destroying any feelings he had toward her was for the best, though she hadn't meant to hurt him. Really hadn't considered the possibility of hurting him.

Blast it, she didn't want a relationship. One ride around that merry-go-round had been enough. That one horrifying trip tore her emotions apart and left her with a mountain of debt weighing her down.

He would forget about her in time. He would find someone else to care about.

Why did that thought make her hollowed chest ache?

Chapter Twenty-Four

Jackdaw stood amidst the darkened canopy of trees beside his intended's home. Throughout the shadows lightning bugs flashed intermittent signals, communicating in special patterns to their mates. Moonlight brightened his view, but didn't reach into the forested areas surrounding him.

He chuckled as the ambulance left Addison Parker's residence.

The domino effect of his phone message had provided more entertainment than he'd expected. The detectives still believed they could stop him, but soon they would understand he could kill circles around them.

No one could stop him.

Not even them.

The two detectives had communicated in a silent film

where agitated hand motions faced the frustration. After several minutes, Detective McBride stalked to his vehicle and drove away. Someone was not happy.

Jackdaw smirked. Good thing he was happy enough for them all.

He swatted a mosquito away from his face, and then rubbed his cheek absently where the bloodsucker had landed.

Good girl Parker stood and watched until the reporter's car was out of sight before going into her house. Once the lights came on inside, Jackdaw turned and hiked back to his rented vehicle. Twiggs snapped underfoot as he brushed aside low hanging branches to create his own path.

His and the good detective's destinies had intertwined in a collision of fate on Sunday. A collision that could not, would not, be diverted. Wednesday evening she would go to church services as she had done every week. As every good girl would.

When she returned, he'd be here, waiting, ready to welcome her home. No matter their precautions.

Yes, he knew what they had planned, what trap they had laid.

He'd made sure he knew.

Over the past three days, the police drive-by vehicles lengthened the time between checks on her house after night fell. One passing surveillance vehicle to another timed out at thirty minutes. That left him time enough to fulfill his mission.

He cleared the woods on the opposite side of the property. A hundred meters away sat a black SUV- license plate Georgia EUD 222, rented to Jack Dawes, 211 Parks Estates. His girl had spotted the four-door sedan he'd initially rented, so he'd arranged for another mode of transportation.

Jackdaw pressed the unlock button on the key fob and slid into the smooth leather seat. His new identification lay in the cup holder by the seat, and he grinned at his likeness on the photo. Amazing what having the right contacts can do for you.

Time to rest and reflect and reenergize.

Time to prepare for all that tomorrow would bring.

Taking a deep breath, he started the vehicle and pulled onto the empty roadway.

> *For he's a jolly good fellow,*
> *For he's a jolly good fellow,*
> *For he's a jolly good fellow,*
> *Which nobody can deny.*

Chapter Twenty-Five

Joe rang the doorbell on Paul Wiesner's southern colonial home. The dark golden shutters gleamed against white woodwork, giving the illusion of happiness. It was an illusion Wiesner did not reflect himself.

He continued to wait with his hands fisted by his thighs. Visiting Harvest Christian Church on Sunday, seeing Addison and not speaking to her, made him realize he needed to make clear to Wiesner that she was off limits. That Wiesner had better not harass or harm her.

Joe would not lose his temper even though his heart rate accelerated with an adrenaline rush demanding Wiesner pay for wronging the woman he loved. He pushed the doorbell again. The car parked in the open garage testified to someone's presence in the house. If he had to ring the bell all day...

Several thudding footsteps echoed on the indoor flooring before the front door swung open. "May I help you?" A short, heavyset woman with kind golden eyes smiled at him. Her Hawaiian-print sundress matched her red hair and lipstick.

Joe forced his arms to relax. "Yes, ma'am. I'm looking for Paul Wiesner. Does he live here?"

"Yes." The one-word answer hung in the air, alone, for many seconds.

Joe glanced beyond the woman's shoulder, and then brought his gaze back to hers. "May I speak with him please?"

"What's your name?" Her head tilted as she looked him over. Questions gleamed from her eyes.

"Joe Vaughn. I work with Paul."

"Oh, I see." She swung the door open wider as if Joe's admission were magic words. "Come in. I'm Paul's wife, Mary Anne."

Joe stepped inside, hands clasped in front of him as she preceded him, her sundress swirling around her ankles and bare feet. "Let me make sure Paul's decent. Have a seat, and I'll be right back." She waved her hand toward the small sitting room behind her, then climbed the stairs to the house's second level.

Joe remained in the foyer. A mocha leather sofa and love seat, antique white lace curtains, imitation honey-oak Pergo flooring in the foyer, and cream-colored carpet in the rooms. Definitely not a reflection of Wiesner's sloppy style.

Echoing footsteps from the second floor jerked him from his thoughts as Mary Anne thumped back down to where he stood. She drew a deep breath. "Paul will be down soon." She swept her hand toward the sitting room once more. "Sit,

Mr. Vaughn, and be comfortable." She threw a mega-watt smile at him and followed him, yet her fingers trembled as she motioned him toward the love seat.

"Thank you." Joe sat on the sofa instead. His eyes popped wide and his arms tensed for a moment when he sank deeper than expected into the overstuffed cushions.

"Can I get you something to drink? Tea or water perhaps?" Wiesner's wife fluttered her hands with the question, and then let them hang by her sides.

Joe gave her a slight shake. "No thanks."

A scuffle outside the room had the brightly-colored woman rushing back into the hallway. Her tread on the stairs a fast staccato. "Paul, I told you to stay in bed. You're not ready to walk around yet, and I'm sure Mr. Vaughn would've been happy to see you upstairs."

The returned voice huffed out between deep breaths. "I'm not staying in my bed to talk to that kid, and that's all that will be said on the subject."

Wiesner entered the room's corner and shuffled over to sit opposite the sofa. His pasty-white face was damp with perspiration, and a faded Braves t-shirt topped his grey lounge pants that hung on his frame despite his natural bulk. Comfort over fit must be Wiesner's goal in life.

Wiesner straightened his ever-crooked glasses and grunted at Joe, then laid his head against the seat's padded back. "What do you want, Vaughn?"

"I'm not happy about what happened at Detective Parker's house yesterday."

"You think I am, Rookie? I go out to do a good deed and get a hospital stay for my troubles."

"Good deed?" Joe made a sound of disbelief. "You were peeking through her house windows. How was that a good deed?"

"I was making sure she was there alone—without you—before I let her know I was there."

"There were no cars there, Wiesner, so you knew no one was home." Joe forced his fisted hands to open and relax on his knees where he squeezed the joints until his knuckles whitened. "I'm going to tell you this once so listen well. Stay away from Detective Parker. She deserves better than the likes of you smearing her name and reputation for a sleazy story."

"Sleazy? I'm the best reporter on staff and you know it."

"Were the best reporter, and we both know those good days may well be behind you." Joe blew out a breath and rolled his shoulders. "Look, why did you go out there?"

"When you were out of the office, some guy named Jack left a message for you. I knew you were supposed to be helping the police set a trap for that serial killer, so I went to warn the detective not to trust you."

"What made you think she needed to be protected from me?"

Wiesner's gaze remained steady. "The message was, 'Thanks, Joseph. I appreciate your help.'"

Joe sucked in a breath and stared over Wiesner's shoulder at the white lace curtains dancing in the cool air from the floor vents. Finally, he returned his gaze back to his nemesis. "For the record, I'm not in league with the killer, and if you go near Detective Parker again, you'll have more to worry about than a bump on the head."

Wiesner leaned back and propped his elbow on the loveseat's arm rest. He sat in silence for several moments with a knowing smirk stamped on his face. "Okay, I'll leave this story up to you."

"And you'll leave Detective Parker alone?"

Wiesner inclined his head, wincing with the movement.

Joe narrowed his eyes. "Why are you giving in without a fight?"

Wiesner laughed. "You know, I like you, Rookie, even though I don't want to. It appears this lovely detective has your interest piqued. If there's one thing I don't do, it's come between a man and his woman."

"She's not my woman."

"Yeah, but you'd like her to be." Wiesner folded his hands over the girth of his stomach.

Joe couldn't argue with that statement. He stared at Wiesner as if the man were unrecognizable. After a long moment, Joe stood. "I'll go now, but I meant what I said. Don't push me on this. I won't back down."

He left the room. Mary Anne stood in the doorway wringing her hands, staring at him with wide-eyed panic. He nodded as he passed. "Ma'am."

The woman's persuasive voice fussing over her husband followed Joe as he let himself out. He rolled his shoulders one at a time. Kicking around at home would be torture when his thoughts centered on Addison.

His backpack lay on the seat beside him. With a slight grin, he pulled away from the curb. He knew where to go. An hour later he exited the Electronic Superstore, a blue plastic bag looped around his fingers as he dug in his pocket for his car keys. When he stepped off the curb an Addison look-a-like crossing the parking lot to enter the baby store next door snagged his attention.

Wait. It was Addison. He looked around the parking lot. No patrol car. No unmarked car. No McBride. Joe's mouth tightened into a flat line as he changed directions.

~

Addison entered the Babies Today store. Her sister's baby shower was fast approaching, and Addison hadn't bought a gift yet. Shopping now would take her mind off of…everything.

Joe's brushoff in church and McBride's incessant demands of being notified of her every move had her walking a nervous ledge. She had even been instructed to contact McBride if she planned to leave her house. Unbelievable. All of these security measures were driving her nuts.

When she stopped at one of the store kiosks to print out her sister's wish list, she looked up when someone stepped beside her.

"What are you doing here by yourself, Addy?" Joe's low growl accompanied her heart stuttering in her chest.

"I'm shopping for my sister's baby shower this week." She waved the gift list like a red flag of challenge. "You?"

He held up a blue plastic bag. "Shopping. Just like you."

"Shopping for what?"

"I'm a proud owner of the newest electronic tablet." He opened the bag to show her the thick white box and a new stylus package. "Someone told me that joining the 21st century might be a good idea. I decided she was right so here I am. The question of why she's here without protection still needs to be answered though."

"The article just came out in Sunday's paper. I shouldn't have to account for my every move until tomorrow. So, if you're here to check up on me, you can go ahead and leave."

"You may need my help."

"You're going to protect me?"

He shrugged. "Better I have your back, than you face

this lunatic alone."

"He's not going to do anything today." She shook her head. "Crimes like this always follow the same pattern."

"The last crime scene broke with the pattern. This guy is unpredictable."

She popped her fists on her hips to keep from connecting with his solar plexus. "He'll still follow the pattern with the article coming out in Sunday's paper."

"Of course he will. Just like he followed his pattern with Linda." Joe glanced around the store. "I believe I need to buy a baby gift, too."

"Why?"

"I like your sister, your family. Why wouldn't I?"

"Fine." Addison narrowed her eyes at him. "Just stay out of my way."

"Can't do that."

"What?"

"I've never purchased a baby gift. I think I may need your advice." His grin turned wolfish.

She turned and browsed through the store. Joe stayed on her heels. Her very own watch dog. She huffed. What did he think *he* was going to do if trouble occurred?

She didn't need his help.

She did her best to ignore him. Stopping to finger a red, white, and blue jumper and envisioned a tiny, Uncle Sam look-a-like celebrating the Fourth of July. She dropped the jumper when the longing for her own child surfaced.

To have a child of her own required marriage, but opening herself to another person caused her breath to back-up in her lungs. Thoughts of Joe carrying a small child with dark pigtails and a smile that matched his paraded through her mind's eye. The longing intensified until it turned into an ache in her chest. She jumped when he spoke to her.

"Can I see the list?"

Addison handed the papers to him. She knew it by heart anyway.

Thirty minutes later, carrying a summer short set with matching booties and a case of disposable diapers, she followed Joe through the store, answering his questions, helping him shop. Finally, he decided on a multi-colored play mat.

"Addison?"

"Yeah?"

"How about wrapping this for me?"

She stopped before walking through the automatic doors and shot him a you-have-got-to-be-kidding-me look. "You're asking me to wrap your gift after you've intruded on my afternoon?"

His grin ruined the sheepish look he tried to wear. "Yeah. Is it working?"

"You are unbelievable." She squinted in the sunshine. "Only if you carry it to my truck."

A chuckle rumbled behind her, before he said, "Sure."

As she stepped off the curb into the parking lot, a prickle ran across her scalp and down her neck. Her stride faltered as she craned her neck to survey the area. Joe stood behind her as a mother and her children walked toward the store. No cars moved in the lot. No one waited in parked cars.

Paranoid. They were making her paranoid.

This whole situation, along with McBride and Joe, had her turned inside out. Addison opened the truck door and dumped her boxes on the back-bench seat. Before she could turn to face Joe, she froze.

Twirling a slow dance in the heat of the truck's cab hung

a feather.

Chapter Twenty-Six

Addison had made sure her doors were locked when she left the truck to shop for her sister's baby shower. Yet, fluffy, brown strands filtered the incoming sunlight through a feather's slow twirling dance in the heat. The truck's interior revealed everything as she'd left it, right down to her cup of change resting on the passenger floorboard. Only the feather remained out of place and delivered the killer's message clearly.

Jackdaw was watching, waiting.

She stepped back from the truck, pulled her cell phone out of her pocket, and faced Joe. "Don't touch anything."

His eyes widened as he moved to stand beside her. "Why?"

"He's been here." She flipped the phone's top open and dialed her partner while her eyes continued to dart around the parking lot and the store in front of her. Joe leaned around her to peek into the cab of the truck. His quick inhale let her know he'd seen the feather.

"McBride."

"Hey, I think Jackdaw has been in my truck."

"You at home?"

Addison chewed on her lip before answering. "Um, no. I've been shopping for my sister's baby shower. Joe is with me."

Joe raised his brows at her and mouthed, "Really?"

She waved a dismissive hand at him.

Terse words filtered through the phone lines. "Parker, I told you to notify me if you left your house."

"I'm sorry, but all the surveillance was driving me crazy. And the killer shouldn't strike until tomorrow." Her words sounded defensive even to her.

Joe shook his head, and mouthed, "Told you so."

Her partner's gruff voice snapped his words out. "Where are you?"

She turned her back to Joe so he wouldn't continue to distract her. "Greenview Shopping Center. Babies Today parking lot."

"I'll be there as soon as I can. I'll phone for back-up to meet us there."

"I'll wait inside the store."

"Parker?"

"Yeah?"

"We'll discuss your disobeying a direct order with the Captain when this is over with." McBride had never pulled the superior ranking officer routine with her before. There was a first time for everything.

"Yes, sir." She ended the call, then closed the truck's door, using her key to relock it. Looking at Joe, she motioned for him to join her in retracing their steps back to the store. She took one unhurried, measured step at a time, in case they were watched. They didn't want to alert the killer that they knew of his presence.

Her sense of justice rose, bringing conviction. She was going to nail this nutcase before the week was out.

No matter the cost.

~

Joe wiped his hands down the side of his Docker slacks as he stepped into the burgundy-carpeted room of the Living Faith class at Harvest Community Church Wednesday evening. He had debated the wisdom of returning to this church body knowing Addison would be present, but he'd felt accepted and cared about in this building.

He knew it wasn't the building, but the people inside who had accepted him without hesitation. He'd never had complete strangers treat him with open friendliness until Addison invited him into her life. Her family. Her friends. Her church.

Was it wrong of him to intrude in her life further?

Probably. Yet, he couldn't stay away. An invisible drawstring continued to pull him into an acceptance of all things God. Unbelievable, but true.

Who was he kidding? Tonight, the police were expecting the killer to strike at Addison, and he wanted—needed—to watch over her as much as he could.

He found Addison through the throng of other class members populating the room. Seated against the back wall, her head jerked up as if she'd developed Joe-dar and met his eyes. He gave her a small half-smile. She nodded in acknowledgement before returning to the open Bible lying on her lap, but Joe's gaze lingered. Taking in her hair, clipped back on the sides, he appreciated the way it flowed over her shoulders and glinted in the fluorescent lights. She wore her new red dress with the scarf he'd given her the last time he'd seen her.

His heart stuttered. It was like she wore his colors.

He sucked in a breath. Watching her had a way of making him forget the essentials, and he didn't want to pass out in front of everyone. Exhaling, he rubbed the center of his chest, and then turned at the hand on his arm.

"Hi, I'm Sarah. I haven't met you before, and I wanted to welcome you to our class." The young woman wore a brilliant smile as words continued to tumble out of her mouth, a steady stream of rapid syllables he had to concentrate to understand. "We have a small group that meets for coffee after class. If you'd like, you're welcome to come hang out with us."

Her flowery scent overwhelmed him. He leaned back to find unscented air, then held out his hand. "Joe." When she returned his shake, he continued. "Thanks for the invitation. Maybe another time?"

"Sure." Her megawatt expression dimmed, and then rebounded. "We'd love to have you join us anytime." With that declaration she returned to a small group seated on the left.

The back of his neck prickled. He rubbed a hand across his chin and found Addison watching him from her seat against the wall. Her brow was furrowed, and a frown turned down her lips. Was she upset?

Was she worried about the killer? He hadn't seen her after finding the feather in her truck yesterday, but he had talked to McBride about it. He wouldn't have been able to focus on anything other than Addison until he knew she was protected.

Maybe she didn't like seeing him speak to the woman that approached him? He grinned. Perhaps he'd ask her at the end of class just to watch her sputter.

He looked around the room at the padded chairs filling up fast. Although he didn't consider himself a masochist, Joe took a seat near the middle aisle where Addison remained visible. The night's discussion caught his attention as a woman slid into the empty seat next to his. Her pale face and pinched features made it clear she was uncomfortable.

Joe leaned toward her, held out his hand. "Hi. I'm Joe."

She accepted his handshake. "Grace." Her lips moved to form a tight smile.

"Are you new here, too?"

"Sort of." She pushed the honey blonde hair that fell on her face behind her ear. "I used to be a member years ago. I've recently moved back and need to get reconnected."

"Well, we've just connected." He paused when he saw her face soften into genuine warmth. "It's my second visit, and I need to connect with others too."

She nodded at him, and then turned back to the discussion.

A man stepped to the center chair, carrying his bible and a sheaf of notes. He looked to be fortyish with his salted-brown hair, but his face carried a look younger than those years. "Good evening, everyone. Last week's discussion we ventured into the book of Colossians. This week we'll move into the book of Hebrews. No one can discuss faith without reading Hebrews, chapter 11—The Hall of Faith."

Murmurs of agreement filled the room as everyone opened their bibles with a rustling of pages. Blast it. He'd forgotten he'd need a bible. Last week, Addison had shared hers with him.

He would make the best of it. Listening and taking notes would allow him to go back over the material later. Grace tapped him on the arm and slid her bible onto the seat between them in a silent offer to share.

His whispered, "Thanks," carried to her on a breath of air, and then her gaze returned to the night's teacher.

For the next hour Joe split his time listening to the teacher and trying to watch Addison without her knowing. He had even caught her gaze behind those glinting silver framed glasses, when she snuck a peek at him. He wanted to punch his fist in the air, but he hadn't won her yet. Man, he had to get a grip before he embarrassed himself.

Everyone stood. Some began talking, others leaving, many speaking and introducing themselves. It seemed the harder he tried to reach Addison, the more people herded between them to speak and welcome him. He appreciated the acceptance from everyone, but he had to reach her. She couldn't leave until he at least heard her voice, saw her up close.

A ruddy-faced man stepped up to him and held out his hand. "Good to see you here again this week."

Joe watched as Addison journeyed closer to the room's exit, He'd never be able to reach her in time. He looked back at the man standing before him. "Thanks."

"I'm Kurt Walters." He pumped Joe's hand as if looking for water to flow. "I wanted to let you know that a group of men here at the church are trying to get together a basketball team to play in the recreational league this winter. In case you're interested."

"I'm not much of a basketball player." His eyes

narrowed as Addison wound her way closer to the door while stopping to speak to those she knew.

"Well, you're welcome to join us if you want to give it a try. We're short a few men to make a team."

"I'm more of a tennis player." Joe raked his hair back. "I'll keep my ears open. If I hear of anyone interested in joining, I'll let you know."

"Thanks." Kurt glanced at a small brunette looking their way. "My wife and I will look for you on Sunday. Maybe we can catch lunch together."

Joe grinned while keeping his attention on Addison's progress through the room until he lost sight of her. "I'd enjoy that."

Where had she gone?

Kurt winked. "The wife's motioning for me. Nice meeting you." He grabbed Joe's hand and pumped another couple of times before walking off.

Joe turned away from Kurt's retreating back and scanned the room for a curtain of silky dark hair. A halo of light caught his attention as she passed through the doorway. He weaved around talking groups, nodding as he was greeted. His jog caught her outside the building's foyer. The pansies danced in the artificial outdoor lights lining the walkway, while the scent of freshly cut grass floated on the warm breeze.

"Addison."

She stopped, her shoulders tensing as she faced him. "Joe." She turned. "I'm glad you came this evening."

"Are you?"

"Yes. Of course. Why would you think I wouldn't want to see you here?"

Joe shrugged. Voicing his thoughts would earn her sympathy. He didn't want her pity.

"Have you been careful today?"

"Yes. McBride's making me crazy." She tugged on her ear while she stared at him with a grin. "He's acting like an overprotective mama bear."

"I'm sure he appreciates the analogy."

"Nope. Fumes steamed from his ears when I told him."

Joe chuckled. He sobered a minute later, and then opened the doors to his emotions. "I meant to tell you yesterday that I'm sorry about Wiesner. If I had known he would target you that way, I would have stopped him." He drew in a deep breath.

She looked at him for a long moment. "How?"

He cleared his throat. "I would've thought of something."

Their eyes held. Finally, she smiled. "Well, thank you for that."

A weight lifted from his chest, allowing his lungs to expand with air. He glanced at a group leaving the building. Their bursts of laughter energized him. "Go to dinner with me Friday."

An unfamiliar light touched her eyes, tightened her mouth. A response he'd never seen before. Yearning maybe?

He hurried on, hoping. "I can show you a better evening out than Waffle House. IHOP maybe?" He stepped closer.

She laughed. The whisper of hope vanished with a shake of her head. "I don't think that would be such a good idea. Perhaps we should call ourselves friends and leave it at that." She hugged her Bible to her chest like a shield.

"Are you sure that's all you want? Friendship?" He waited a beat. "What if that's not what I want?"

"That's all I can give." Addison's eyes glazed over with moisture, sadness dulling their brown depths.

"Are you sure?" He fought the desire to place his hand over hers, to take her in his arms. What was wrong? Why was she acting like this? Maybe she wanted to open up to him, to admit she felt more than a tepid friendship.

He touched her chin with his finger so she would look at him. "You found a way into my life that I'd thought was closed to everyone, and now you're telling me you want to be friends?"

She blinked several times, her voice a breathy sound that barely carried to his ears. "Yes."

The aimed arrow hit its mark. His throat worked to swallow. "Okay, Addison. You win."

She turned and began walking at a fast clip toward the parking lot.

"Addy."

She stopped and looked at him, her figure a shadow in the night's darkness.

Evil surrounded her tonight.

Joe shook his head, denying the thought. "Let me watch over you tonight."

She rubbed her hand across her cheek. "McBride is smothering me with overprotective watchdogs. I don't need one more person watching over me."

He swallowed the lump of fear in his throat. "I want you safe."

"Thank you for that." She left him standing there, watching until the darkness swallowed her.

She shouldn't be alone tonight. She said McBride was watching out for her, but he couldn't accept those assurances. He needed to know she was okay. It was

Wednesday, and the killer was out there, had made it clear Addison was his next target.

Instincts to protect the one he loved shouted, urged, prodded. He could guard her himself. His articles had put her in danger. He had to safeguard her, make things right.

Even if it meant sitting in Addison's driveway all night.

Chapter Twenty-Seven

A twig snapped under Jackdaw's foot in the darkened woods. Rays of light streaming through the branches above him created surrealistic shadows and images.

Felt like he walked within his art.

He adjusted his dark jacket and hat when a branch slapped against his shoulder, and his leather-encased fingers flexed around the branch to snap it in two.

His intended waited for him. He would not disappoint.

The perfect plan designed for his success had come easy as most intellectual things did. He sniffed the heavy air that hung around him, smelling of rain. An omen of good fortune since rain would be the perfect disguise. All natural traces of his visit would be washed away.

He broke through the woods into the open space of a well-kept lawn. It was just like her to keep her space neat and tidy. He'd expected nothing less.

A light shone through a window at the farthest part of the house opposite his hidden corner. The perfect waiting place.

Last week he'd learned he was ready to expand his range. This week he planned a more exciting challenge. He'd charmed each of his past victims into allowing him access in public, but last week he'd changed his plan. With perfect results.

And, this week…

This week he'd upped the challenge.

He'd meet his intended on her own turf, and, still, he would win, would accomplish his mission. His record would remain untarnished. Curling his fingers into a fist, he shook it and laughed.

It would be perfect.

Perfect.

Chapter Twenty-Eight

Addison sighed as she entered her house. Dropping her purse on the hall table, she rotated her shoulders on her way to the kitchen. She reached for a glass as the conversation with Joe wound through her mind like a repeating record. His words, his concern, his pain.

Ice clinked into the glass, and tap water submerged the clear cubes before they bounced and floated to the top. Addison lifted the glass to her lips, swallowed. Why did knowing she hurt him affect her so deeply? It wasn't as if they'd known each other for long. She continued to sip the water while looking into the darkness outside, interrupted by quick flashes of light shooting across the sky.

Joe being upset at his co-worker's actions had been apparent. Who was she lying to? Joe, her family, herself? She'd lost her heart to that annoying reporter when a lost little boy peered out from the man's eyes. When he'd shared his pain at the loss of his mother, the death of his father. Only a coward would deny the obvious.

She was no coward. In fact, the word coward wasn't even allowed in her dictionary. She'd cut the word out when she was twelve and faced down a school bully with stubbornness, courage, and inventiveness. Literally opened the home dictionary, took a pair of scissors, and cut the word out. From that point on, cowardice didn't have a place in her life.

Shrugging off the worry, she readied for bed. Routine always calmed her, and she needed to keep up appearances just in case her house was being watched. The killer hadn't made a move tonight as they'd thought he would, but there was always another day. She would be ready when it went down. Walking down the hallway, she entered her bedroom and sat the glass of water on her nightstand.

Her thoughts circled back to Joe. She would tell Joe the truth when this was over. She couldn't hurt him to save herself from pain. Watching him hurt caused her pain. But, how much should she admit?

However much, she owed him the truth, and she would lay everything out in the open. Her love, her pain, her hope. Give the relationship a chance to develop as God intended. Sitting in a class teaching faith every Wednesday wasn't just for appearances. She needed to walk the faith she'd accepted, learned, and talked.

Had she been walking in faith? Faith about Joe, her life, her job?

If she answered honestly, then the answer would be no. Should she have given in to McBride's arguments and allowed a female detective to stay the night at her house?

Everything in her shouted no. She could protect herself. This killer was no different than any other criminal she'd subdued. This situation wouldn't be beyond her ability to protect herself.

Addison pushed her hair behind her ears as she turned down her bedspread, her night shorts and T-shirt the only concession for bedtime she'd make. She'd be ready no matter what came her way.

Joe had accused her of being arrogant. McBride had taken her to task for not following directions. Perhaps she did need to slow down, ask others for help. Sure, she could do things by herself, but wouldn't it be easier to have the help of others?

She grabbed her laptop off her side table and booted it up. Logging in to the department's server, she pulled up the pictures of the Jackdaw victims. Looking through the notes and pictures, had she missed something someone else may have been able to see?

Her heart heavy with regret at how she had handled this case, Addison bowed her head to talk to the only person who could help her fix it.

Father God, please help me slow down and accept help. Help me find justice for the victims in this case without losing my objectivity. Help me admit when I need help and when I need a teamwork mentality. That's hard for me, but I know that You want me in fellowship with others, not only in my personal life, but my professional one as well. It's hard to open up again, but with your help, I can do all things. Amen.

Tap, tap, tap.

Addison straightened and sat her laptop aside. Sitting still she strained to hear the sounds around her. The storm was getting stronger with the thunder right over her house and rattling her windows.

Tap, tap-tap, tap.

She shrugged the uneasy feelings off. The wind must've blown something into the house, or her rosebush was rubbing against the window again. If Davidson and Carboni had noticed anything, they would've alerted her. Still, she pulled her Glock out of her top dresser drawer. Her police issued 9mm remained locked in her vehicle during her off-duty hours, but she had invested in her own personal firearm after she'd moved into her house alone.

Tonight, her unease made her jumpy. She checked the safety, then turned and laid the weapon on her nightstand beside the bed. She remembered the dirty glass on the nightstand as she was sinking into the pillow-top mattress. She groaned. It could stay there until morning. Nothing wrong with that.

Several minutes later, she climbed from the bed and made her way back to the kitchen. The moonlight shining through the kitchen window allowed enough light for Addison to wash the glass without turning on the lights. Attacking the invisible germs, she rinsed and dried the glass, then put it away in the cabinet next to her refrigerator.

A scratching sound echoed as she shut the cabinet door. She reopened the cabinet and reclosed it. No scratching. The sound hadn't come from the cabinet.

Addison stood silent, her head cocked, listening.

Scratch, scratch. She turned and looked at the kitchen doorway leading into her backyard. It sounded like nails raking down her window. Was the stray dog outside trying to get in because of the storm?

She pulled her phone from her pocket and pushed speed

dial six.

"Carboni?" The detective's deep voice reverberated on the line much like the thunder.

"Hey, it's Addison. Anything unusual out there?" She pushed her hair back behind her shoulder.

"No, we haven't noticed anything strange so far. We're still looking out for you though."

She closed her eyes and let her tension ebb. "Thanks, guys. I heard some noises outside, but I think it's a stray dog I've kind of adopted."

"Keep your phone on you. We'll call a warning if anything suspicious is going on." The line went dead with that order. It was so like Carboni to end the conversation abruptly.

Reaching behind her, she picked up the largest roast knife from the block sitting on the counter. Her sock-clad steps remained silent on the kitchen tile as she approached the windowless door. She drew in a deep breath, braced herself, and reached for the deadbolt to calm the upset dog.

As the door opened, Addison pressed herself against the house's exterior wall. The hinges creaked, a piercing screech in the silence she'd never noticed before. The outdoor carport blocked the wash of moonlit rays, leaving darkness free to overwhelm the interior.

Her thigh muscles tightened as a trickle of perspiration licked down her spine. She pivoted to return to the house and call Carboni once more. Another rustling scratch rushed at her from the darkness.

Left.

The noise came from behind her parked truck.

She tightened her fingers against the rubber grip of the knife and brought the weapon closer to her body. If this was the killer they were hunting, she was ready, but how had he made it past the surveillance team outside? Too bad the killer didn't know her. If he knew her, he'd know attacking tonight would be his downfall.

A darkened blur rushed at her, condensing out of the darkness too fast for her eyes to adjust. Her elbow contracted, bringing the knife higher as she leaned toward danger.

The mangy stray dog that had tripped up Joe's co-worker stopped before her and whined. She let out a long breath as her muscles relaxed. "It's just you. Long time no see, huh? Now is not a good time. I don't want you to get hurt. Go away." Addison pushed against the top of his head, then waved her hands, but the animal merely cocked its head and looked at her. She stepped out of the doorway and down two steps to face the dog on even ground. "There'll be no food here tonight. Go ahead. Run." She ruined the directive by rubbing the top of his head. When he plopped into a sitting position, his tail wagging, she flung her hand out toward the wide expanse of the back yard for him to take off. It was her fault. She hadn't been able to resist feeding him, so the mutt had started hanging around. His occasional company had eased her loneliness.

The ringing summons of her phone she'd lain on the counter echoed through the house. Could it be Carboni or Davidson? Had they noticed anything out of the ordinary? She turned, pushing the mutt away when he pressed his head against her leg in a bid for affection. To protect him, he'd have to remain hungry tonight.

She turned on her heel and stepped onto the cool bottom step leading into the house when a vise gripped her throat, cutting off her air supply. She tripped back down the step in her fight to maintain balance. The stray began barking madly, lunging toward the two adults struggling for physical dominance.

The forearm across her throat jerked left as a foot lashed out in a kick aimed at the growling dog. Harsh breathing and pained yelps intruded on the dark silence as the animal raced off, his screams of pain getting fainter. A second arm reached around her until a hand grabbed her wrist and squeezed until her bones rubbed together and the knife clattered to the floor.

Addison kicked backward, her heel connecting with the shin behind her. Pain shot through her bare foot and ankle. Her foot slipped down until she bore all of her weight on the sneaker-shod foot of her attacker while trying to drive her elbow into the face behind her. Even as she fought, she catalogued details. The stocky build, the masculine grunts, the smell of chemicals mixing with aftershave.

The man topped her by a few inches, and the iron grip across her windpipe tightened. Dots flickered in her visual field as her ability to breathe diminished, and her arm changed direction and pulled at the forearm crushing her throat. Her breath rasped out of her in a struggle to find oxygen.

She gathered her strength for one more push at freedom. She drove her elbow into the soft tissues of the stomach behind her while her foot simultaneously kicked back for a second shin attack. The legs behind her blocked the movement.

She punched her head into the face behind her. A crunch sounded when her skull met with a nose and the metallic smell of fresh blood leeched into the air. The arm around her loosened as the attacker cursed and moved to stem the flow of blood so she could push free, escaping back into her house. She slammed the door shut and paused long enough to twist the lock.

The locked door should slow him down, although it wouldn't stop him long. She raced to her bedroom, to her weapon.

The door crashed open behind her as she ran down the darkened hallway. Heavy panting followed, closing in with every step.

She dove across her bed, reaching for the weapon on the nightstand. Her hand fell short as a thick hand shackled her ankle. The heavy weight of the attacker fell on her, but her eyes never wavered from the weapon's outline in the darkened room. An outline her fingers couldn't reach.

Oh, God, help me. I need help.

~

Joe darkened his headlights when he parked under the oak canopy that allowed a full visual of Addison's small house. He killed the engine and cracked his window to let in the fresh summer air. Perfumed scents of nature drifted through his window and filled the interior of his car.

Go check on Addison.

He scratched the tickle on the back of his neck. She had made it clear she didn't want him protecting her.

Oak leaves shuffled in the heavy breeze, providing rhythm for the cricket's song.

Get out of the car.

He tapped his fingers on the steering wheel to nature's tempo.

Fading moonlight punctuated the darkness, until lightning raced across the sky outlining Addison's house.

Go to the house.

He shifted in his seat, and his chest tightened until he couldn't breathe without his ribs screaming. He couldn't run into her house even though his instincts prodded him relentlessly to find her, help her.

Loud yipping pierced the air as a dog ran around the side of the house, racing on three legs as if protecting an injury. It looked like the stray dog from the other day. The dog Addison took care of.

Find Addison.

Joe's breath caught in his throat before he let it out.

A neighborhood dog was no reason to be worried. The animal probably escaped from a canine fight. Addison was safe in her house. There was nothing to worry about.

What if it was the same mutt from Saturday? What if an intruder maimed the dog to get to Addison?

Addison needs your help.

Joe reached for the door handle.

Chapter Twenty-Nine

"You're going to pay for that."

The words spewed out in a guttural voice as Jackdaw pressed his nose onto his left shoulder to stem the flow of blood. His right hand tightened around Addison's ankle and jerked backward, pulling her across the white down comforter. A glow in the darkness that outlined her.

The darkness that swallowed the room kept him in shadow. He didn't want her to recognize him. Yet.

As expected, she aimed a timed kick with her free foot that he deflected with his thigh. He ground his teeth together as he grabbed the free ankle. He knew she could be a tricky one. That's why he'd planned his mission with much more diligence and care. He didn't want her to know who had outsmarted her until he had her bound and unable to flee.

"You won't get away with this." Her legs kept jerking

trying to get free. "My partner will find you." She gasped. "My father will find you." She twisted right, then left, to break free. "Joe will find you."

"You give your trust too easily, Addison." She stilled with his use of her name.

Her response fortified his strength and with renewed power, he flipped her onto her stomach. His mouth moved closer to her ear. "Neither your partner nor your father will be able to piece the puzzle together to discover my identity. I've made sure of that. And your boyfriend? I'll take care of him once I'm through with you. I've proven I no longer need him to finish my work."

He rose and repositioned himself. Seizing the opportunity, her hands sought purchase on the comforter, trying to pull herself away.

He tsked as she inched away. "Now, now. None of that."

Had she whimpered? Only the darkness saw his grin as he straddled her legs, holding them within the vise of his thighs. "Don't cry, sweet."

He reached her, grabbed one arm then the other. She gasped as he jerked them behind her back. He slid the cord out of his pocket and whipped the thin nylon around her wrists. He yanked the cord tighter, the folds of her skin bulging beneath his gloved fingers. One more loop of the cord, then he knotted it.

Tricky in the dark but possible. After all, he had excellent night vision.

"I am prepared as you can see." His voice crooned in the dark, sending shivers of delight through his chest. "Your destiny has come for you." He backed away from her legs as he pulled a second cord from his pocket. She began pushing with her legs.

He watched her for a moment. "Addison, Addison," he said, "why don't you just accept your fate?" He touched his throbbing nose. "Although I knew you wouldn't. That's why I brought an extra cord for your feet."

"I won't be defeated without fighting back." The words shot out between breathy gasps. She rotated her head to look at his outline before pushing all her strength into a spiraling move that pushed her halfway across the mattress.

Jackdaw growled as he lunged across the bed and grabbed her by the knees once more, her nightclothes sliding across her skin. He turned her until she lay on her back once more with her feet within his grasp.

She garnered her strength for one last punch out with her feet, but he controlled the movement and pulled her legs under one arm. He wrapped the second cord around her ankles. He yanked the cord even tighter as punishment for her refusal to accept her destiny. Once her feet were bound, he yanked her up the bed until her head rested on one of the large pillows.

"The others didn't fight this hard, but I can handle it, sweetheart." He leaned over until he was nose-to-nose with her. A finger reached out to brush strands of her hair back from her face. "I always liked you. A lot." His fingers trailed down her cheek to her throat, and then he pulled back. "I was very sad when you were the next chosen one, but you made sure of that, didn't you?"

"You don't have to do this."

He stood and began to pull objects from his pocket, laying them on the nightstand. "Yes, I do. It's my mission."

"I don't understand."

He twirled the syringe around in his fingers as she watched. When she sucked in a breath, he lay it down beside the rubber tie. "It's what I was born for: to punish women who hide their sin. Everyone thinks you're so good, a paragon, but I can see you for who you are."

A boom of thunder shook the windows.

"You're one of the elite, who've been handpicked as an example to those who think they are perfect. Those who think they do no wrong." His finger trailed down her arm until her muscle shuddered beneath his touch. "It wouldn't do for us to conduct our little rendezvous in the dark, now would it?"

The lamp on the nightstand flicked on.

Addison gasped as salty tracks led from her eyes to her temples and wet her hair.

Jackdaw sneered, his face lit with unholy glee. "Surprise."

~

Joe sprinted across the yard as a sprinkling of raindrops fell, keeping his eyes pinned on the front of the house. As he neared a white zig-zag of lightning crossed the sky followed by a loud boom of thunder.

Oh, God, please don't let me be too late.

His breath jerked as his gaze darted along the line of windows tracking two shadowy figures. How had the attacker made it into the house?

He jogged along the perimeter in the direction the injured dog came from, reaching out to jiggle each window. With every locked window, his sweat glands powered into overtime. Turning the corner of the house, he investigated her truck parked for the evening. Undisturbed. The back of the house radiated peace with an undercurrent of evil. He stopped, glanced around the backyard. Nothing was out of place.

A large swell of wind blew across the clearing, rustling leaves and blowing Joe's hair back from his face as another flash of lightning filled the sky. The back door crashed against the wall. He sucked in a breath at the gaping hole yawning into the darkened house.

Joe stepped into the kitchen his gaze scanning left then right and moved to the open space of the hallway. Muffled words floated from beyond the darkness.

He needed a weapon, but what? He didn't know how to use any type of weapon. Hadn't believed in the value of owning one. Until now. A ceramic lamp sat on a corner table. He wasn't an expert on defense, but it was better than nothing.

He paused, picked up the lamp and wrapped the cord around his arm to keep it steady in his sweat-slicked hands. Any fool could bash someone over the head so he should be able to do this without messing it up. She was too important to fail. His heartbeat pounded in his ears. Keeping his breathing steady, he ran through his options. There was only one.

Save Addison.

Please, Lord, show me what to do. Guide my actions.

A calming peace flowed over him. His lungs drew in a deep breath as he stepped forward, moved closer to the muffled sounds. He rounded the doorway and scanned the area. A dresser, a make-up table, a television stand, two nightstands, and a queen-sized bed where Addison lay bound.

His heart thundered as the stocky man sat beside Addison with one arm propped on the bed beside her hip. He didn't know karate or judo. He didn't have a gun, nor would he know how to use it if he did, but he knew what he had to do.

It was just him and the lamp. With God's help they could save her. He stepped up behind the attacker, raised the lamp, and...

Addison continued to struggle against her constraints. When the attacker leaned in as if to kiss her, a raging fire filled Joe's chest. He moved behind the man with noiseless steps and lifted the lamp higher. He brought the lamp down with a whistling crash on the man's head. The attacker froze and turned glazed eyes toward Joe.

Addison had loosened the cords enough to rip her hands free, and then pushed her right fist into the man's jaw and he staggered. The attacker crumpled, falling sideways as Addison pushed the man's inert form away and onto his back.

Joe gaped at the still form of Darrin Gray.

~

Addison allowed herself to lie still and take in deep, gasping breaths. Each exhalation carried the same mantra.

Thank You, God. Thank You, God. Thank You, God.

Joe tugged at the cord on her feet. "Addy, can you hear me? Are you alright?" The binding loosened around her ankles when he said, "Please be all right."

She couldn't fall apart. Not yet.

Pushing herself onto her elbows, she rolled and grabbed her weapon, tripped off the safety, and sat up with the firearm readied while she eyed the unconscious form of her friend and co-worker. Talk about misjudging someone.

When she'd recognized Darrin, she'd allowed him to see her fear. A human response that should have been hidden. Surprise had stripped her of her training. Yet God had her back. He'd sent Joe. She would never refuse the offer of help again.

She reached for her cellphone that usually lay on her bedside table and realized she'd left it in the kitchen. She reached for the cordless handset that was her back up line. No dial tone. Grabbing the base, she pulled until the frayed cord slid from behind the furniture. Darrin Gray had been in her house before she had even gotten home? She squeezed her eyes shut, and then threw the phone across the room, sending her peaceful Thomas Kincaid picture crashing to the floor.

One deep breath later, she rubbed her bruised and burning wrists, and then glanced at Joe. "Do you have a cell phone?" A blast of fire shot down her abused throat with the words.

He lifted his eyes from the prone body, nodded, then reached into his pants pocket and handed her the silver phone. "Wasn't he the photographer at the Dalton's and JG's crime scenes?"

"At all the crime scenes." Addison opened the phone one-handed and laid the cord she'd managed to undo aside. A Boy Scout Darrin was not. He couldn't even tie a knot properly, which had given her an edge. "Tie his hands together with a scarf from the top dresser drawer until I can get my handcuffs from the other room." She dialed the phone while he rolled Darrin onto his stomach and bound his hands with the silken material Joe had given her for her birthday.

"McBride." Addison paused to clear her throat. "It's me, Addison."

"Parker?" Tires squealed. "Thank God. I've been trying to reach you."

"Yeah, well, I've been a little tied up tonight." She

cleared her throat once more, but the croak coming out of her mouth didn't improve. "Look, Jackdaw attacked and with Joe's help, we managed to subdue him, but we need backup."

"The reporter? What's he doing there?"

"I don't know yet, but he was a big help." She motioned to Joe to double check the killer's tied hands. "It's Darrin Gray. Jackdaw is Darrin Gray."

"I know."

"How do you know?"

"He left clues in each of the crime scene photos. Those pictures kept bugging me, and I finally figured out the clues in them about thirty minutes ago. Back up is here. I'm pulling into your driveway now." The crunch of gravel underscored his announcement.

Red and blue lights whirling through the sheer curtains of her bedroom window renewed her confidence in her team. "The kitchen door is broken open. I'll send Joe to open the front door to preserve evidence."

Joe stood, his eyes trained on her, his face pale and his hair disheveled, a frown notched between his brows.

She owed him. Big time.

"Addison? Did you hear me?"

"I'll see you in a few."

Addison lapsed into silence as she ended the call and handed the phone to Joe. She met his gaze over the perpetrator's body. "Thanks." She cleared the gravel from her throat. "Thanks for coming to my rescue. I thought I could handle it, but I don't know if I would've been able to take him down by myself."

Joe raised a brow. "Really? You're admitting you needed help from me?"

Addison tried to smile, but she couldn't force one, so she propped her elbows on her knees and stared at the reporter instead. Courageous and unpredictable. How had he come to mean so much to her?

"Anytime, Addy." A lop-sided grin appeared as he attempted to lighten the moment. "I'm honored to help you." He looked at the flashing lights blinking through the window. "Do you want me to go let them in, or would you rather not be left alone with *him*?" He jerked his head in Darrin's direction.

Addison shook her head. "You go ahead. I'm fine, and I'm not sure I can walk that far yet."

She stood from the bed, her legs wobbling like cooked noodles. Her knees locked into place, steadying her. Pounding came from the front door. She tilted her chin and shot him a commanding look while pointing her weapon at the still form of Darrin Gray. "Go, Joe, before they knock my front door down. One broken doorway is enough for one night."

Once alone, the shakes began coursing through her body, making her hands tremble, her skin crawl, her teeth chatter. She clamped her teeth together and tightened all of her muscles. She couldn't let go yet. Not until the other officers had taken this madman into custody. There would be time enough later to let her emotions take over.

When McBride and the other officers entered the room, Addison backed up and lowered her weapon, clicking on the safety. The officers replaced the scarf around Darrin's hands with handcuffs, and then lifted his still form off her bed. Darrin roused long enough to shout obscenities in her direction when the officers carried him out. McBride stepped up beside her while Joe flanked the opposite side.

More sirens squealed outside as the flickering lights multiplied.

"You okay, Parker?" McBride slid his weapon into his jacket pocket.

"Yes." Man, her voice sounded like a chorus of tween boys. "How did he circumvent our protection detail?"

"I don't know. This wasn't supposed to go down like this."

"You couldn't have known. And, I did have help." Her eyes touched on Joe before returning to her partner. "I'm sorry for making this week hard on everyone."

He laid a hand on her shoulder. "We'll talk about that when you are feeling better."

"It's over. Let's not worry about it anymore."

He shot her a *yeah, right* look then narrowed his eyes. "Go let the paramedics check you out."

"I really don't need to be checked out. My throat is fine, and he didn't hurt any other body part. I just need to decompress."

"You will go with the paramedics to the emergency room. Not only do we need to know you are physically well, but we will need the medical reports and pictures as evidence for the case."

How could she have forgotten that?

Joe spoke for the first time. "I'll make sure she gets there. You go ahead and take care of the police end of things."

McBride pulled his cell phone from its case. "I'll call the hospital to make sure they're expecting you." He reached the room's threshold, then turned, pointed his finger at her. "See a doctor. Tonight."

She snapped off a four-finger salute.

Once alone, Joe looked over. "I'll go check the doors and windows while you get ready. Or do you want to go as you are?"

Addison shook her head. "No. I need to change and bag these clothes as evidence. I'll be out in a few minutes."

She allowed the tension to leave her body once she was alone behind closed doors. Pulling clothes out of her closet, she dressed in a black pair of jeans, top, and black sneakers, leaving her night shorts and t-shirt lying on the bed for those in charge of processing the crime scene. Her house—the scene of a crime. She shuffled to her dresser where her mirrored image stared back. The empty eyes and pale face reflected made her look fragile.

Her feet carried her out of the room, trance-like. She plopped onto the couch and feathered fingers over the bruised lacerations circling her wrists. She knew the procedure, knew photos would be taken as evidence, knew a doctor's examination must be included in the report.

Still, it was her throat, her medical report, her life.

What if Joe hadn't come to help her? What if she hadn't been able to break free of Jackdaw's mad plans? What if? What if?

Tears gathered in her eyes and began to flow down her cheeks in salty tracks.

She buried her face in her hands. Her elbows leaned on her knees as hoarse sounds were torn from her abused throat.

"Addison?"

She never cried, but she couldn't seem to stop herself. The couch shifted with his weight pressing down beside her. His soothing hands rubbing her back brought reassurance. His presence brought security that wrapped around her like a blanket, calming her in ways she thought impossible. Joe pressed a tissue into her hands from the box on the coffee table and remained silent.

Addison uncurled to sit up and with a cleansing breath and dared a look at him.

"Thanks. Again."

"Are you ready now?"

She pushed herself up from the couch. "C'mon. Let's get this over with."

Chapter Thirty

After work, Addison drove by Joe's apartment complex. She had prayed about her plans last night and felt as if God had given her approval when the familiar Honda had been parked in front of his apartment. She knocked after taking several deep breaths.

When Joe opened the door, his mouth opened and closed several times before sound came out. "Hi. What are you doing here?" He winced as soon as he voiced the question.

She slid her sunglasses into her hair until the plastic acted as a headband so she could meet him eye to eye. "I'm sorry if I caught you at a bad time. I can come back later if you like."

"No. Now is fine." He widened the door. "C'mon in. Have a seat. Would you like something to drink?"

"Water would be great. Thanks." Gripping a drink would keep her hands from trembling.

A few moments later, he handed her a rose frosted glass filled with ice water. She took a tentative sip. "That's great.

Thanks."

He sat on the sofa across from the chair she had chosen to use. "How's the hand?"

Of course, he would ask how she was doing. She hadn't expected any less. She flexed the fingers on her sprained wrist not wrapped by a bandage. "Healing. The doctor said it should be okay in a week or two." To move the focus of the conversation from herself, she tapped her nail on the patterned glass. "We processed Darrin Gray's apartment today. We found enough evidence to convict him without your testimony."

Joe sighed. "I'm relieved to hear that. What about your family? Did you talk to them?"

"Yeah. I went to talk to them yesterday." She touched the mottled bruises on her neck and grimaced. "They weren't happy with my decision, but they knew it would have been a distraction for me to know they were worrying. They were happy I was safe and my injuries would heal."

"That's good." He cleared his throat. His foot tapped a silent rhythm on the carpet. "I was hoping you had because your Dad came to see me."

"He did?"

"Yeah."

"Oh, boy." Addison glanced at the ceiling, and then brought her gaze back to him. "What did he want?"

"He'd figured out what was going on, why I was with you at dinner the other night, and wanted to let me know…"

She fisted her hands on her knees when his voice trailed into silence. "Know what?"

"That if anything happened to you, he'd come looking for me." Joe's half-grin appeared. "Seems he was holding me responsible for the entire situation."

"You should have told me. I could have talked to him, let him know the truth."

"He didn't find me until Wednesday morning, and then so many things happened that I didn't have time to think about it." Joe rubbed a finger across his chin. "And, I didn't want you to worry about your family when you needed to be focused on your own safety."

"Fair enough." She had to admit that she had needed his help and support Wednesday evening. She was thankful God had led him to be there. She grinned. "Even though I don't like the protective caveman attitude, I can handle the reasoning."

Joe paused as if hunting for words that had deserted him. He cleared his throat and said, "My exclusive came out in yesterday's edition. The article didn't upset them any more than they already were, did it?"

"No. At least, I don't think so. Thanks for being concerned about my family."

He shrugged the comment away. "I like them."

An awkward silence descended. Ticking from a clock on the wall above her head intensified the dead air, causing her shoulders to tense until they burned.

Just get it over with.

Addison tapped her fingers on the cold glass, streaking the condensation. "Listen, I wanted to invite you to have dinner with my family this Sunday."

He swallowed. "Sure."

She froze at the quickness of his response, and then sat the glass on the coaster next to her. "You can follow me after church? That is, if you're still going to attend Harvest Community Church now that the killer has been caught."

He looked her in the eye, earnestness shining in the light

depths. "Of course. I like the people there. They're real."

"That's a compliment of the highest order."

"It was meant as one."

"So, you can follow me to my parents' house afterwards?" She tilted her head and waited for his response.

"Not a problem." Joe stood as she did.

Addison grabbed her sunglasses from her hair. "Well, I'll get out of your way now."

Joe walked her to the door. "You might like to know Burnside offered me a position as investigative reporter."

"That's great, Joe. It's what you've been wanting."

"Yeah, but, see—" He rubbed the back of his neck. "After Wednesday and seeing him…seeing you . . . well . . . I decided not to return to investigative reporting." Joe dropped his arm. "Burnside was miffed, but he couldn't force me to accept the position."

"Did you get any perks?" Her dismay colored her voice.

"Yeah, I get first pick of new assignments." His smile widened. "And he gave me a raise."

She put her hand on his arm. "Good." She reached for the doorknob, and then turned back as she opened it. "I'll see you Sunday then. Come hungry because my Mom has planned a feast."

~

Joe sat at the Parker family dinner table and wondered if they knew how lucky they were? How rare it was for a family to stick together and stay close throughout the years?

He rubbed his knuckles over his breastbone. The interaction between the members of this family somehow soothed the ache left behind when his mother died.

"Hey, Joe?" Addison's father clapped him on the shoulder.

Joe glanced at the man seated on his left.

"Could you pass over those potatoes? I just can't get enough of my wife's cooking." Jim Parker winked at his wife, then accepted the bowl of mashed potatoes and handled the spoon like an expert. Before returning the bowl to the center of the table, he raised a brow at Joe. "More?"

Joe couldn't suppress his grin. The man didn't have a shy gene in his DNA strand. "No sir." He patted his stomach. "I couldn't eat another bite."

"Well, that's something." The ceramic bowl thumped on the table. "Lyn, you've outdone yourself."

Addison's mother shook her head at her husband from the opposite end of the table. "You say that every week. If I improve every week, shouldn't I reach superior status soon?"

"Then there'd be no room for improvement." He grinned when his wife sent him a narrow look, and he turned back to Joe. "Great article in Thursday's paper. First rate writing." All talk stopped at the table as everyone waited for Joe's answer.

"Thanks. I was relieved everything was over."

"Addy tells me you helped her take down the killer on Wednesday."

"That's how it worked out, but I have to tell you, she did more than I could."

"No matter how it happened, you were there when it mattered. Thank you for helping my little girl."

"I was grateful to be there."

Jim pushed his plate back, empty once more, and looked around the table. "Who else is up for dessert?" The lightning change of topic had Joe glancing around the table.

David agreed with his father-in-law while rubbing Becka's shoulder. "Justin and I are definitely up for dessert, especially since Becka made it. Right, son?"

Two-year-old Justin laughed, and beat his spoon on the highchair tray.

Becka tucked a loose strand of hair back into her bun. "I brought Apple Pie to honor my big sister."

Addison blinked, pushing the moisture aside that gathered in her eyes. She reached up to swipe the renegade tear that escaped to her cheek and squeezed Becka's hand. "My favorite."

Caroline stepped into the awkward silence as Becka and their mother headed for the kitchen. "Joe, do you like apple pie?"

His face heated. This family's inquisitive nature felt like an interrogation. "Um . . . yeah . . . I like it a lot."

Caroline grinned at his discomfort. "How much is a lot?"

"It's my favorite, too. My mom and I use to make one every Saturday to share after church."

"Do you ever make it home to bake pies with her now?"

A bittersweet grimace twisted his lips. "I wish I could, but mom died almost two years ago. Breast cancer."

Addison rubbed Joe's bicep. From his peripheral vision he could see Jim shift in his seat. Even if he made everyone uncomfortable with the topic, he'd keep his vow to God to pursue honesty in all things whenever possible. Even topics that made him vulnerable.

Caroline's eyes glistened. "I'm so sorry. Do you have any brothers and sisters?"

"No. No siblings. Just me."

A hand landed on Joe's shoulder, pushing him with a jolt. "Well, you've got a family now son. You're welcome in this house anytime."

Jim lifted his hand when everyone else chimed in as Lyn

and Becka returned with plates of sliced apple pie and a carton of vanilla ice cream. Joe cleared his throat and blinked twice. He surveyed those around the table, but no one noticed his difficulty. How could he balance the joy of the Parker family's acceptance with the knowledge that his mother would never get to meet them?

Pie circulated around the table followed by the ice cream. Joe allowed his fingers to brush Addison's as he accepted the carton and ice cream scoop from her. His heart buoyed when she didn't flinch away.

After dessert and lots of laughter, the women rose to clean the kitchen. Lyn Parker stopped and shot Addison a look. "Your day off, honey. Spend time with your guest."

"But, I always help clean up."

"Not today. Today you will enjoy yourself, not work." Lyn accompanied her two youngest daughters into the kitchen.

David began wiping his son down, causing the little boy to screw up his face and try to evade the damp cloth. "It's time for champ's nap. I'll lay him on the guest bed, Pops."

Jim grinned at them. "I think I'm going to go get in your mother's way in the kitchen. I might be able to sneak another piece of pie."

"Okay, Daddy." She turned and watched her father leave.

Once alone, Addison glanced around the room as if her eyes didn't know where to settle. Her gaze met Joe's. "Would you like to take a walk?"

His heart thrummed in his chest. "Sure."

He followed her out the door. They remained quiet as she led them to an opening in the backyard fence, crossing into the dense green foliage. A narrow pathway emerged, almost unnoticeable.

"This path used to be so worn down that anyone could follow me and my sisters when we hid out in the woods." She chuckled. A gust of wind rustled the leaves overhead and caused the wildflowers to dance. Her hair blew away from her face, brushing across his shoulder.

He stuck his hands in his pockets to keep from touching the silky strands. "I'm sure it was fun."

She looked at the wooden structure connected to an oak tree and laughed with a huff. Clearing her throat, she motioned toward the rough building before dropping her hands. "This is the playhouse my father built for us when we were small. My sisters always wanted to play house and have tea parties, but I always planned strategic ways to take down the wildlife that had infiltrated our domain."

He raised his brows and stuffed his hands in his pockets. "Well, all three of you seem pretty strong willed. Who won the debates?"

She laughed again. "Debates? That's a nice way of putting it. We compromised. Of course, they outnumbered me two-to-one, so I lost more times than they did." She crossed her arms, and her tone turned dry. "It was much easier to be the big sister when they were little, and I could make all the decisions."

It was his turn to laugh at that statement. "I'll bet."

She slid a sideways look at him. "I'm glad you came today."

"Thanks for inviting me." He cleared his throat, pulled his hands out of his pockets and pushed them back in, while staring into the distance.

She paused, drew a deep breath in. "The last guy I brought home to meet my family. Well, they didn't like him very much."

Joe opened his mouth, and then closed it. What could he say? From her earlier description of the guy, he wouldn't have liked him either.

"He turned out to be slime. So, long story shortened, I know I can trust their judgment." She brushed her loose hair back from her face.

"In that case, I'm grateful they like me."

She glanced at the sky, a pure and perfect blue. "Joe, I'm sorry about the way I treated you—" She faced him and swallowed. "—you know, when you came to my house on Monday with the article for me to read. Marcus dealt me a hard blow, and ever since then I haven't wanted to get involved with anyone else."

"I understand." He stepped closer, lost in her dark gaze. The tension in his muscles increased, and he couldn't look away from her dark chocolate eyes.

"Do you?" Her voice came out a breathy whisper.

The invisible string that had been wrapping around them since their first interaction tightened, pulling them together.

Before he realized his intent, his lips found hers in a soft kiss, his hands gripping her forearms. She pressed her hands against the fabric of his shirt and allowed her eyes to close when he gave her a second, deeper kiss. Fighting to control his breathing, he pulled back and stared at the woman he loved. She lifted her fingers to touch her mouth, and then pressed her lips together as if holding onto the sensation of the kiss a little longer.

She pushed away and began walking back toward the house. "We've got to get back, or Dad may come looking for us."

Joe cleared his throat and followed without comment. As

they returned to the backyard, Addison stopped him with a hand on his arm at the foot of the back patio. She stared at her hand resting on his arm, and then took a deep indrawn breath. "Joe. I am sorry for hurting you."

Joe tilted her chin up with a finger. "It's okay. You don't have to return my feelings."

"No, no, it's not that. I do return your feelings. But, here—" She pushed four-fingers against her chest. "Here, feeling that way is scary."

Joe shifted as he struggled to keep from dancing a jig. Shutting his mouth sounded like a good idea, too. If he opened his mouth, he'd babble through all the words trying to rush out at once.

"I just…I wanted to let you know that I not opposed to exploring a relationship with you. So, anyway," she glanced at the back door, "we should get back inside. They'll wonder what we've been up to and get nosy if we're gone too long." She bounded up the steps.

"Addison."

She stopped and looked back over her shoulder at him. Waiting.

"Wednesday. Maybe I can accompany you to church?" He held his breath.

She faced him with a soft curve of her mouth. "I'd like that."

He couldn't help himself and moved one step up to be closer. He reached out for her hand, holding it with care between both of his. "And Friday. Maybe dinner or a movie?"

She tilted her head. "How about both?"

His breath strangled in his throat, but he managed to push his words out anyway. "That'd be great. Six?"

"Yes." She took a large breath. "And Joe?"
"Hmm?"
"I love you, too."

Emotion choked him as his chest threatened to explode. He raised her hand for a kiss. A smile stretched across his face and his fingers tangled with hers. He'd hit the lottery in love. For the first time since his mother's death he felt complete with a God who loved him, a woman he loved, and a family who accepted him.

He also knew his mother had been right. He had come into his full potential.

As Addison led the man she'd come to love into the melee of her family's living room, a quiet curve touched her lips. Peace in knowing she was following God's plan for her life filled her chest, intertwining with love for the annoying reporter who'd infiltrated her heart.

Acknowledgements:

God graced me with the desire and ability to write, and I thank Him for providing every opportunity for me to follow my dreams, and the encouragement He sent every time disappointment was on the horizon. He sent the right people to foster His pathway for my life, and I will be forever grateful to Him for choosing me.

Even though writing requires a lot of isolation at times, there have been those who were essential to my writing journey. This book would not have come into being without my writing tribe:

Thank you, Rodney, for babysitting, doing laundry, and cooking all the evenings I needed to write and all the weekends I was away bettering my craft. I couldn't have done this without your support.

Thank you, Christy, for reading this story more times than I can count, even when it was in its earliest stages. You reached out to me to become critique partners in the beginning, and I'm proud to say we have learned, written, and faced joys and disappointments together. I look forward to our future pathways and all the writing opportunities we will find.

Thank you, Kim, for pushing me to continue to put my

work out for others to read, even when the results were not positive. Thank you for reading my pages and sharing with me those writing elements that needed to be tweaked, fixed, and polished. You have been a source of encouragement whether you've realized it or not and helped me push forward when I was at my lowest.

Thank you, Cici, for opening your home for writing retreats, and for brainstorming whenever we got together. I love talking about plots and twists and talking through our stories together always helped me clarify what my story needed.

Thank you to my fellow writers at Georgia Romance Writers. Talking writing, learning writing, and sharing writing is always a highlight that pushes me to write better and learn more.

Thank you to everyone who read this story before it was polished and ready to be published. You know who you are. Your feedback helped me improve and make this story the best it could be.

Dianna Shuford writes inspirational contemporary and romantic-suspense fiction. She is a 2017 Golden Heart® Finalist, as well as a past Maggie Award Finalist and a Laurie Award winner. Blessed with an over-active imagination and the obsessive love of reading, Dianna began writing poems and stories in the sixth grade and has never stopped. She enjoys working with other writers in an effort to give back to the organizations that have supported her writing journey. In addition to writing, she is also a mother, grandmother, part business owner, and full-time teacher/learning specialist in the public school system.

Social Media: **Instagram- https://www.instagram.com/diannashuford**

Facebook: **https://www.facebook.com/dianna.shuford**

Twitter: **@DiannaWrites**

Website: **www.diannashuford.com** (It has currently been hacked. I'm working on correcting it.)

Pinterest:
https://www.pinterest.com/diannashuford/boards/

Goodreads:
https://www.goodreads.com/user/show/29809185-dianna-shuford

Made in the USA
Columbia, SC
13 October 2020